The de Vere Papers

The de Vere Papers

by

Michael Langford

Mich. J Lyfd

St Pal's
1944-50

PARAPRESS

Also published by Parapress: *Great Oxford, Essays on the Life and Work of Edward de Vere,* ed. Richard Malim
Also by Michael Langford: *A Liberal Theology for the Twenty-First Century*, Ashgate, Aldershot, 2001

ISBN-13: 978-1-898594-83-3

First published in the UK by
PARAPRESS
The Basement
9 Frant Road
Tunbridge Wells
Kent TN2 5SD UK

British Library Cataloguing in Publication Data
A catalogue record of this book is available from the British Library.

Maps by Harriet Buckley
www.harriart.co.uk

Cover design by Mousemat Design Limited
www.mousematdesign.com

Front cover photograph of Hedingham Castle
by kind permission of Jeremy Crick.

Typeset in Times New Roman by Amanda Helm
amandahelm@helm-information.co.uk

Print management by Sutherland Eve Production
guyeve@theeves.fsnet.co.uk

Printed and bound in Great Britain
by Cromwell Press, Trowbridge, Wiltshire
www.cromwellpress.co.uk

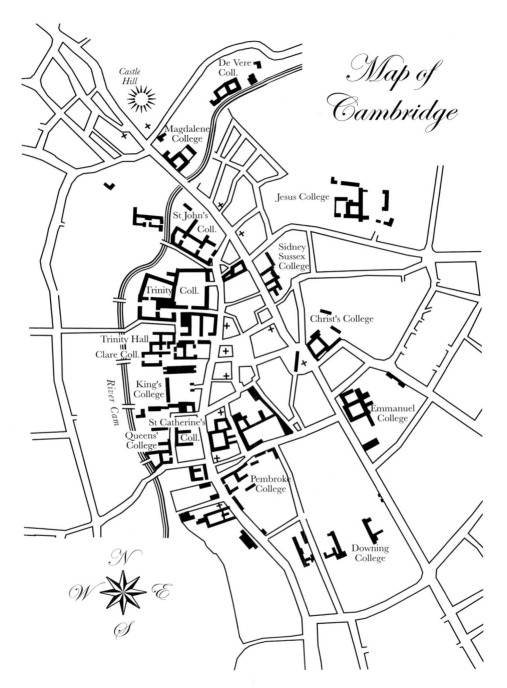

Castle
Hill

De Vere
Coll.

Magdalene
College

Map of
Cambridge

Jesus College

St John's
Coll.

Sidney
Sussex
College

Trinity   Coll.

Christ's College

Trinity Hall
Clare Coll.

River Cam

King's
College

St Catherine's
Coll.

Emmanuel
College

Queens'
College

Pembroke
College

Downing
College

N
W *E*
S

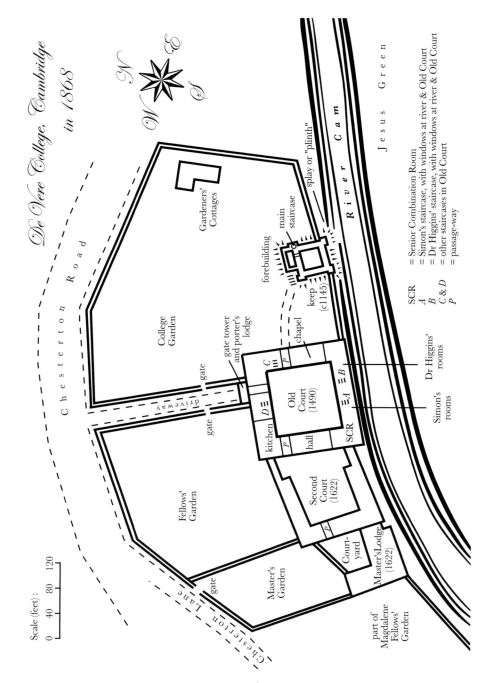

De Vere College, Cambridge in 1868

Scale (feet):
0 40 80 120

Chesterton Road

Gardeners' Cottages

College Garden

forebuilding

main staircase

gate tower and porter's lodge

gate

gate

driveway

chapel

keep (c1145)

splay or "plinth"

River Cam

Jesus Green

kitchen

hall

Old Court (1490)

SCR

C

D

P

P

P

A

B

Dr Higgins' rooms

Simon's rooms

Second Court (1622)

Court-yard

Fellows' Garden

Master's Garden

Master's Lodge (1622)

gate

Chesterton Lane

part of Magdalene Fellows' Garden

SCR = Senior Combination Room
A = Simon's staircase, with windows at river & Old Court
B = Dr Higgins' staircase, with windows at river & Old Court
C & D = other staircases in Old Court
P = passage-way

vi

Chapter 1

Simon Weatherspoon knocked loudly. There was no answer. He knocked again, and then – with a sudden catching of breath – he noticed the dark-red stain that was oozing from under the door. It extended about four inches onto the floorboards of the landing and was very slowly expanding.

In normal circumstances he wouldn't bother a fellow of his college when the outer door was shut or, as the Cambridge community would say, when the 'oak was sported', knowing this was a signal that the occupier did not want to be disturbed. However, on this occasion Simon's worry took precedence over the normal rules of college etiquette. Last night, during the general conversation after formal dinner in hall, Dr Higgins had welcomed Simon's request to look at the collection of documents he had found in the library, and had asked him to come to his rooms immediately after Sunday morning chapel. But Higgins had not been at Morning Prayer, which on a Sunday was unusual; neither had he been at the informal fellows' lunch in the Senior Combination Room that followed it. In these circumstances it seemed probable that he was ill, so Simon felt he ought to check on him, even though it was Higgins who was the college's physician.

Five minutes later he had returned with the porter, a much-flustered Mr Alcock, who carried the spare keys kept in a locked cupboard in the gatehouse tower. As Simon unlocked the oak and pulled it open he was gripped with an awful sense of foreboding.

It was fortunate the door opened outwards, for otherwise it would have been jammed by the body that lay right behind it. Lionel Higgins, the college's librarian and tutor in Medicine, lay in a crumpled heap, the back of his head smashed open by some heavy implement.

Alcock uttered a startled cry and bent down to examine the body. Simon knelt next to him and put one hand to the side of Higgins's neck. There was no pulse, and the flesh was cold: he must have been dead for several hours. While Alcock, in a kind of daze, stayed by the body, Simon – remembering the librarian's discovery of valuable documents – passed through the open, inner door, placed about three feet from the oak, and entered the principal room.

The likely sequence of events flashed through his mind. Either last night after dinner in hall, or early this morning, Higgins must have heard a knock, which would probably have been on the outer door, or 'oak'. He had opened the door, probably to someone he knew. He asked the person to come in and then, just as he turned to lead the visitor in, he was hit from behind. Almost certainly the murderer must have been after something in the room and this had led Simon to think of the revelation only a few days ago when Higgins had told the assembled fellows about his discovery of old papers, and his hint about the momentous importance they might have.

He went quickly to the long, Cromwellian table, placed in front of the window that looked out over the river. Higgins always kept things in orderly piles, but the papers on the table were scattered around, with some fallen to the floor. On one paper were two spots of blood. It seemed likely the weapon had still been in the murderer's hand when he went over to the papers.

At the far end of the table there were three cardboard boxes, labelled 'Letters from Henry Courcey', 'Letters from Edward de Vere' and 'Courcey – general', in a handwriting that Simon recognized as that of Higgins. All three were empty.

"Alcock," said Simon, "Go straight to the Master and tell him what we have found – but don't speak to anyone else about this. I think Dr James will almost certainly be in the Lodge – but if he's not you had better come back here and tell me. If the Master is there, after you've spoken to him, please go straight to the police station and bring a constable."

Alcock departed and Simon was left alone in the room. The place had been fairly well known to him since his election to a college fellowship five years ago. He had been Higgins's friend, although not one of the librarian's small circle of really close friends, all of whom, so far as he knew, were fellow librarians. On two occasions he had been asked to small dinner parties in these rooms, and had been here at least a dozen other times for sherry, when the two of them had talked about many things, including theology, and in particular the current controversy over the writings of Charles Darwin.

As if by instinct, he sat exactly where he always had for those conversations, opposite Higgins's favourite armchair. He was upset, not only saddened by the death of a friend and colleague, but feeling positively ill at the shock of seeing the body, and wondering if he were going to be sick. Through the window that faced onto the courtyard he could hear the voices of a group of students arguing about something to do with the training for the boat races on the river. Otherwise it seemed strangely quiet, although he became acutely aware of the ticking of Higgins's antique grandfather clock, made in the middle of the previous century by a London clock-maker.

He recalled the old myth that when someone dies their clock stops. This had not happened now. Like the supposed ghost in his own set of rooms it was a matter of superstition. Perhaps, he thought, although he was a clerk in holy orders in the Church of England, it was all –

3

that is all his religious beliefs – a matter of superstition, or at the best, of myth. Higgins, despite Cambridge University's requirement that all college fellows have at least a nominal acceptance of Church of England teaching, had been sceptical about many traditional Christian doctrines, but – he knew from the private conversation in these rooms – he had really believed in God. At present, Simon wasn't always sure that he did, so perhaps Higgins had been more of a believer than him.

The sober reflections seemed to have cured his stomach. He got up and went back to the long table, keeping his back to the body that protruded into the room, a sight that unnerved him. Although it looked as if the old papers had been taken, he decided to see what else was on the table, remembering that it was here that Higgins nearly always kept the things he was in the process of working on.

In addition to a draft of the new library catalogue there were a couple of business letters, a personal letter – probably from his only close relative, a married sister who lived in the north of England – and some notes about new books that needed to be bought for the library. Then, underneath the business letters Simon found a small notebook, on the cover of which Higgins had written 'Summary of the Courcey and de Vere documents'.

He heard footsteps on the stairs leading up to the rooms. Quickly – under some impulse that later he found hard to defend – he slipped the notebook into his pocket and walked across the room to meet Dr James, Master of De Vere College.

The Master was in his late fifties, but looked younger. He was tall and well-built, the good food and wine of college living apparently offset by regular exercise, including long walks in the fens. The walks were always solitary, for he seemed to have no close friends of either sex. His election to the Mastership of De Vere College six years ago had come as a surprise to almost everyone in Cambridge. One reason for surprise was that he was a bachelor, and although this was quite common in some colleges, ever since the Reformation De Vere College had been one of those that almost always chose married Masters – whose wives could help to entertain in the large Lodges provided for college heads. Another reason for surprise was that even before his election Dr James had a reputation for being 'difficult'. However, in his few last years the previous Master had been so frail that the business of the college had fallen into chaos, and it was said to be on account of his reputation for hard work and efficiency that Dr James had been elected. Simon did not particularly like him, but respected him: among other things for his scholarly work in ancient history.

They met by Higgins's body and, after a quick look at the crumpled figure, the Master started to drag the body right into the room and stretch it out. Simon protested that they ought not to move or touch anything until the constable arrived, but he replied, "Nonsense. We can't leave the poor fellow like this."

Reluctantly, Simon lent a hand. When the body was fully inside the room, the Master added, "Anyway the police aren't that clever – we're probably better able to make out what happened than they."

Dr James examined the body carefully, and Simon remembered he had begun his studies at Cambridge with the intention of becoming a physician, before changing to Greek and Roman history two years into the medical course – a move that Simon had always found puzzling. This must explain the surprising calmness of his behaviour. The Master's next words confirmed his medical knowledge. "Rigor mortis is just beginning to affect the jaw and neck muscles, and this, combined with the way he's dressed tells us the attack must have happened this morning, shortly before the chapel service he was already dressed for. Did he take breakfast in the Combination Room?"

"No, but he seldom did. In the mornings he preferred to take a small meal in his own rooms."

The two men passed through the main room and into a passage that led to a bedroom, a bathroom and a small kitchen – a pattern that represented one of the variations on the sets of rooms occupied by fellows of De Vere. On a small table by the bed lay a fine gold Hunter watch and a copy of *Essays and Reviews* that looked as if it had been well used. Instinctively, in part because of his general delight in books, and in part because of his particular interest in this volume, Simon picked it up and thumbed through the heavily annotated pages. This was the book which, ever since its first edition in 1860, had caused consternation in more conservative circles because of its modern approach to Biblical scholarship – including the use of the same kinds of literary and textual criticism that were applied by scholars to all other ancient texts. For the second time since entering Higgins's rooms he felt an almost overpowering sense of sadness. The volume intimated a common interest, and another link with the friend he had lost.

Simon sensed an irritation in the Master at this unnecessary examination of the book, and they passed through to the kitchen, where they found the remains of a light breakfast. Next, they went back to the oak to examine where the crime had taken place, and here the Master uttered an exclamation – suddenly seeming more startled than at any time since entering the room. "Look at this," he said, holding up an open wooden box, some twelve inches long, full of tools and keys. They put the box on the long table and the Master examined the contents carefully. Simon held back, still shocked at the cavalier way in which the evidence was being handled, although recalling that his own activities had not exactly been beyond question.

"Skeleton keys," said the Master. "I've seen the odd one before, but never a set like this. We're dealing with someone who is a master of his craft. But why the violence?"

Suddenly the shock of the situation seemed to take hold and the Master sat down. Simon went to the kitchen, where he had noticed a decanter of brandy, and poured some for the Master and some for himself. They both drank in silence.

Eventually Simon said, "While I was waiting for you I looked round a bit. On the table there are three boxes that look as if they contained the papers Higgins told us about, but they're all empty. It seems the murderer was also a thief, which would help to explain the skeleton keys, but it's odd that only the papers should have been taken. Nothing else looks as if it has been disturbed, and you probably noticed the fine gold watch still lying in the bedroom. There are a lot of puzzles here. First, where is the weapon that was used to kill poor old Higgins? I can't see the thief carrying that away from here as well as a large

The Master, Dr James.

pile of papers, all hidden under a gown or outer coat. Second, why leave these valuable tools and keys? If the thief were intelligent enough to go straight to the one thing he wanted and then walk away with it, it's very odd he should forget the keys – especially as he had to walk right past them on his way out! Third, what possible value could the papers have – except to someone who knew of the conversation we had last Monday night, the one about the de Vere letters and the Lolworth treasure? But that would point to someone in the college, or just possibly to one of the guests, and that's – well, unbelievable."

The Master stared at Simon, and then, in a quiet, extremely serious tone said, "Dr Weatherspoon, I think it would be wise not to say anything about the de Vere papers and the other documents to the police. I don't think they will know anything about the history of the college, and I certainly don't want to awaken public interest in the possibility of treasure – or, of course, in the de Vere hypothesis we were also discussing last Monday. You and I know the papers might have something to do with either of these things, but I strongly suggest we show puzzlement about why nothing valuable seems to have been taken, while admitting to the police that some papers may be missing.

Later, I think you and I had better do some of our own detective work inside the college. As you say, there are several puzzling things about this case, but I don't think the police are as likely to sort them out as we are. Meanwhile we have got the reputation of the college to think about. It's much better if we let everyone assume the murderer is someone from outside: which, after all, is most probably the case."

Simon was pondering his response to this suggestion when heavy boots could be heard on the staircase and three policemen arrived. Two were in the regular uniform of the Cambridge constabulary, while the third, who introduced himself as Mr Stanley, was in civilian clothes, evidently being one of the new brand of 'detectives' that were now employed in a number of boroughs. Mr Stanley took statements from both of them and indicated, although politely – given the Master's status – that it would have been better not to have touched or moved anything. Then they were asked to leave. One uniformed constable was posted outside the door, while the other two men began their own examination of Higgins's set of rooms. Although unsure of its wisdom, Simon followed the Master's suggestion and volunteered as little information as possible. His last memory of the murder scene was of the police carefully going through the box of skeleton keys, with an interest that suggested they had never before seen such a large variety of instruments for burglary.

When Simon reached the courtyard, he found that half a dozen students had already gathered near the entrance to the staircase. Langhorne, a second year classics student came up to him.

"Dr Weatherspoon, is it true there has been a murder?" he asked.

Simon frowned. It looked as if Alcock had not been able to restrain his eagerness to spread the news. "There has been an incident," he replied, "but I cannot say anything more at present."

Unfortunately, there was going to be a sensation in the whole Cambridge community. Simon walked past the students without answering any more of their questions. He needed to think.

Chapter 2

Simon had intended to spend the afternoon working on the volume he was currently writing – a critical edition and translation of the apocryphal book known as *Second Maccabees*. This was part of a wider project, dealing with all the Maccabean literature, which he had decided to undertake some years before, partly because such a project would be good for his academic career, and in part because of an intrinsic interest he had in the writings and in the historical period they represented – centring on the Jewish revolt against Greek invaders. Unfortunately, the current volume was already behind schedule, given his promise to the publishers of his earlier *First Maccabees*, and because of this he had planned to continue to work on it until Sunday Evensong and sermon in the college chapel at 6.00, which was followed by dinner in hall at 7.30. However, after a brief attempt to get down to his translation he realized that he was far too unsettled to study, or to read anything requiring close attention. He shuffled a few papers around on his desk and then decided to re-read an article in the *Lambeth Literary Gazette*. It was of interest on several counts, including a reference to the de Veres, the ancient family of the earls of Oxford, one of whom had given his name to the college. The monthly journal was dated February 24th, and in it an un-named assistant editor had written as follows:

> The reading public of England awaits Friday, 28th February, with eager anticipation. Amelia Buzzard's fourth and, it is strongly rumoured, most outrageous novel, is to be published that morning. Outside a few people

in the know, all of whom are connected with the publishing house of Fisher-White, only the title of the new book is known. This title, *The de Vere Papers*, has caused some puzzlement because it seems so different from the provocative titles of the three forerunners. As most readers will know, the first of these, *The Male Courtesan* caused a scandal within a week of its appearance in June 1864. In graphic detail that only just keeps within the limits of the law (and that too when the law is interpreted as liberally as possible), it describes one year in the life of a gentleman who has a series of affairs with rich and beautiful married ladies, all from high-born English families. What made matters worse was that while the names of the characters are obviously fictitious, several of the escapades described in the book have clear similarities with recent scandals. Although explicit sexual language had been avoided, within a fortnight of publication the outcry and calls for censorship reached Parliament, where the Archbishop of York called for the Lord Chamberlain to take immediate action. This fuelled a new controversy as the gutter press (as the establishment likes to call it) took up the cudgels on behalf of Amelia Buzzard. While being careful not actually to approve the sexual nature of the book, it defended the rights of freeborn English people to write in new and challenging ways. More support, along with still more controversy, came from within the growing women's movement. "Too often," wrote Theresa Brown, the most influential literary critic working for the *Old Chelsea Review*, "from Fielding to the present day, we find male novelists parading the lives of fallen women whose inner feelings and struggles they cannot comprehend. Here, as a welcome change, we have the authentic voice of a liberated woman with her special insights into the depravity of fallen men."

Amidst all this controversy two things are certain. First, the furious debate has helped to sell the book. Thirty thousand copies went into circulation within a year (easily outstripping the 16,000 achieved by George Eliot's *Adam Bede* in 1859), and within two years an official translation was circulating in French, together with illegal, under-ground translations in German, Spanish and Italian. Indeed, it was a realization of the interconnection between outrage and circulation that eventually stilled the call for legal sanctions. It was rumoured that at a private dinner party the Archbishop of York let slip how he now regretted his public condemnation of the evil book because it had so boosted its sales. (It has also been claimed with, it might seem, an element of glee, that the worthy bishop had been shocked to find a copy of the offending item under his wife's pillow!) Second, Amelia Buzzard (obviously a pen name for some well-educated woman, who for very good reasons wants to remain anonymous) is now very rich.

The second book confirmed both the alleged wickedness and the popularity of the new literary star. *The Errant Archdeacon* (1865), set in the close of a Gothic cathedral in the west of England, includes acute descriptions of the inner workings of cathedral life that suggests familiarity with the real thing. It documents the life and loves of an archdeacon who has much more than an eye for the ladies. The storm, if possible, outmatched that caused by *The Male Courtesan*. Among the results was the launching of yet another lady novelist, writing under the name of Emily Dove. Her first novel, *The Upright Canon* (1866), while making no direct reference to the works of Amelia Buzzard, was clearly meant as an antidote to her mischievous productions. Not only did the new book describe a series of clergymen who were totally chaste: there were frequent parodies of situations described in the offending novels, but all given a new and edifying twist. According to the more severe critics, the general effect would have been to reduce the book to triviality and utter boredom were it not for the fact that the lack of prurient excitement is compensated by action of a very different kind. In the opening pages, the Dean of Rockingham Cathedral is murdered when a gargoyle on the west front is deliberately dislodged as he passes beneath. During the course of many adventures the heroic Canon not only solves the murder but shows outstanding courage in a series of exciting incidents (as well as displaying a commendable orthodoxy of belief). The establishment, although somewhat uneasy about the explicit violence, has taken the book to heart and encouraged young people to read it. Here, it is said, is a rival novelist who writes 'wholesome' literature that can be recommended to tender minds. For example, when the Canon rescues the beautiful heroine from drowning, he is most careful to see that a female attendant is called in to effect the revival on the shore. In the last chapter, after a most proper courtship, the canon, now appointed as the new Dean, is married by the bishop to the damsel from the river, with due solemnity and general rejoicing.

In her third novel, Amelia Buzzard, in her turn, made an obvious response to *The Upright Canon*. In *The Coachman and the Countess* (1867), not only has she continued her catalogue of obscene relationships, in this case (as an added outrage) between a countess and someone of a much lower social class, but also the setting for many of the seductions is a castle garden in which stands an old cannon, which, by a combination of its great weight and the softness of the ground, has gradually begun to point almost vertically upwards. In one chapter the piece of ordnance is actually referred to as 'the upright cannon'. The clearly phallic nature of the image made any re-reading of the novel by Emily Dove take on a totally new, and (so one presumes) totally unintended set of meanings. Most outrageous of all was a passage in which the heroine, during a lonely and anguished walk in the middle of a storm, holds on to the cannon's barrel, "which, by the greatness of the wind, seemed to vibrate under her clasp".

The popular press, needless to say, has had much amusement with the names of the rival authoresses. One recent article is headed 'Buzzard devours Dove', and there have been many others in a similar vein. Fuel is being added to the fire by leaked reports from the house of Fisher-White (who publish the books of both novelists) which indicate that 'rage' is an inadequate word to describe the feelings of the author of *The Upright Canon*, and that another novel by Emily Dove, due out in the autumn of this year, is going to respond in an appropriate way. Meanwhile the book sales of both authors continue to soar and the scene is truly set for the first printing of *The de Vere Papers*.

Simon felt himself smiling for the first time since the terrible discovery of the early afternoon. He liked the journal's style, with its mixture of accurate description and slight mockery – so that one could never be sure exactly where the editors stood – thus, to some extent, insulating them from more conservative critics. The next edition of the *Lambeth Literary Gazette* would certainly contain a review of *The de Vere Papers* and it would be interesting to see what it said, as well as whether his own college – given its name – was in any way drawn into the affair. The Master's friend, Lord FitzSimmons, certainly held the college to be denigrated by some sort of indirect association; but then Lord FitzSimmons was hardly a neutral figure. His own interests in the proposed new theatre and guest houses at Stratford-upon-Avon gave him good grounds for disliking not only the title of the new novel but, much more, the story it told. Financial interest was certainly a powerful persuader of opinions.

Simon picked up his own copy of *The de Vere Papers*, received in the post two days after publication. He wondered how many other college fellows or students, probably fascinated by the title, had brought copies into the college. They would be unlikely to admit their ownership, given the conservative views of the vast majority of the Cambridge elite.

Chapter 3

The Great Hall and the Senior Combination Room,
De Vere College, the same day, 8. 15 p.m.

Formal dinner that night was a sombre affair. The Master sat at his usual place at the end of the table near the oriel window while nine of the fellows, all properly gowned, sat along the sides. Until that night there had been twelve fellows, and normally all of them would have attended formal hall on a Sunday night, but one was now dead and two had excused themselves, as had the three guests who had been planning to come before the news of the murder broke. A few inches lower than the high table were ranged the tables for the undergraduates, almost all of whom – some hundred and twenty – were dining in an eerie quiet.

Simon, sitting at the side of the high table that faced the hall, emptied his glass of claret and looked round. The hall was handsome as well as historic, and must, he reflected, have been the scene of

many other poignant occasions. Finished in 1489, it had remained almost unchanged, unlike many medieval halls in both Oxford and Cambridge where a combination of changing fashions, and sometimes of too much money, had wrought havoc with the original beauty and simplicity of the buildings. The hall contained a number of portraits and Simon had a particular reason for being interested in some of these. Notable among the portraits were those of former masters, distinguished fellows and fellow-commoners, all but one of which were later than the hall. The exception was a small portrait of the founder (or more accurately re-founder) of the college in 1488, John de Vere: thirteenth Earl of Oxford, which, it was believed, had hung in the hall from the foundation of the college. However, Simon was sure it was not this portrait, which bore the date 1487, but one of the others, that held the essential clue to the fabled college treasure. The possibility of finding this clue had set his heart throbbing with excitement when he stumbled upon a reference to it only ten days ago, while working in the old library.

The reference, which must have been written before 1606 when its author died, probably pertained to a portrait, and almost certainly a portrait that was in the college at that time. It gave the impression that the painting in question had been deliberately planned, or possibly altered, so as to include a certain detail. Therefore, it had to be a painting that was made between 1539, when (as he now knew) the monastic treasure had been hidden, and 1606. Since the college did not appear to have any portraits from the first years of James I, this, Simon reckoned, narrowed the search to the nine Tudor portraits the college possessed – not counting the one of the founder, which was too early.

It was possible, of course, that the portrait referred to was no longer in the college, but given the way in which the paintings had always been valued this was unlikely. Moreover, he had examined the college inventory of 1652 and at that time there were catalogued the same number of Tudor portraits that the college still possessed, all but one of which, he had established, were in the Great Hall, while the exception was in the Master's Lodge. Ever since his discovery he had been anxiously waiting for a chance to examine the ones in the hall while he was alone (in case his careful scrutiny aroused questions), and while the light was good. If none of them seemed to correspond to the indications given in the clue, then he'd have to find some way of looking at the one in the Master's Lodge. Either way he faced a problem, since the hall – in daylight hours – was in regular use, and the Master was anything but hospitable.

One of the Tudor portraits that hung in the hall was on his left, next to the door that led into the Combination Room. It was quite small, about eighteen inches square without its frame, and showed the head and shoulders of 'Dr Samuel Timpson'. Unfortunately it was undated, but his research in the college archives had told him that this fellow died in 1597, so the painting was clearly one of the nine candidates. However, in this light and at this distance he could not see anything in the details that made sense of the information he had found.

Simon's thoughts were interrupted by the Master banging the gavel: the signal for the Senior Scholar to say the Latin grace that ended the formal part of the meal. This said, all those at the high table moved into the Senior Common Room – or more strictly, in the arcane language of the university – the Senior Combination Room, where fruit was served, along with port, Madeira, and on some occasions, a sweet Sauterne.

The Master took his seat at one end of the semicircle of

Chippendale armchairs that faced the fifteenth-century fireplace. To his left sat the Senior Fellow, a somewhat decrepit latinist, Professor Townend, who had been a fellow of the college since 1817, then the other fellows who were present, in order of seniority, until one reached the Junior Fellow at the far end of the line, opposite the Master at the other side of the fire.

Simon sat on the right-hand side of the Junior Fellow, Mr Hubert Talworthy, a twenty-three-year-old mathematician and recent Senior Wrangler, who had been elected to a fellowship only last Michaelmas. Although twenty-nine, Simon had been Junior Fellow for five years, prior to Talworthy's election, and he had been only too happy to give up the responsibilities that went with that position, especially those that occurred after dinner. The ritual varied slightly from college to

 college. In the case of De Vere College, the butler (a Mr Vinman – aptly named, the student body often remarked, in view of his large red nose and free access to the college's wine cellar), placed a decanter of vintage port on a little round table next to the Master. The present master invariably filled his glass above the level that most fellows regarded as appropriate if one were to get the bouquet of the wine, and then passed the decanter to his left.

Meanwhile, Mr Vinman set a decanter of old Madeira, usually a Boal, on a similar table placed next to the Junior Fellow, whose first duty was to pass this (after taking what he wanted) to his right – so that the port and Madeira went in opposite directions. The Junior Fellow's more onerous role was to 'complete the circles'. When the port reached him he had to take this, without delay, across the fireplace to the Master's table. The Master then decided when to set it on its journey once again. (At Emmanuel College, where a similar ritual obtained, the somewhat puritan Master would rarely move the decanter after the second round.) Meanwhile, when the Madeira decanter reached the Master's table the Junior Fellow had to keep a constant eye on the Master, and only move it across the fireplace and start it on its next round when the Master gave a little nod in his direction (which at Emmanuel was unusual).

It was this last duty that had most irked Simon when he was Junior Fellow, since on several occasions his mind had wandered from the Master's whim to his own scholarly world. After dinner, except for the rare occasions when he tuned in to the surrounding conversation, he had tended to go into an inner reflection on his most recent work, and until Talworthy's election he had been roused at least a dozen times by a loud cough, that was followed by a frosty stare from the Master.

His present thoughts, however, were not centred on today's translation of Greek text, but on the extraordinary conversation that had taken place in this very room only six days before. Unlike today, the mood had been festive, at least at the beginning, because the Master had brought along an important guest, his friend Viscount FitzSimmons, and although it was otherwise an ordinary Monday, this had called forth special wines from the cellar, as well as the whole complement of fellows and two other guests.

(Normally the two married fellows – allowed under recent changes in university rules – dined with their families in Grange Road. Their presence at hall on that Monday, the result of a request from the Master, suggested that the discussion after hall was to be of importance.)

Monday's conversation was etched in his mind and he was now convinced it had some bearing on the sad events of the day. He recalled it in the most vivid detail:

Shortly after settling down in the Combination Room, Lord FitzSimmons had cleared his throat and everyone else fell silent.

"I know," he began, "that there is some considerable concern within this great institution of learning at the publication of a work that introduces the name of the college in a context that can only cause dismay and discomfort. I refer, of course, to the latest production of the lady novelist Amelia Buzzard, called *The de Vere Papers*. In the first place I should tell you that this new work – or should I say 'piece of scribbling?' – is not licentious in quite the way that the first three offerings by the wretched woman concerned have been, at least with respect to its first half, which is all that I have read. However, the work is deeply offensive for quite another reason."

The noble lord took a generous draft of port (a Taylor Fladgate from the great vintage of 1834) and then continued. "It begins with quite a pretty piece of writing: for let us acknowledge merit where it is due, even from a reprobate. The scene is set at an auction house in a small town in Warwickshire where the contents of a local manor house are being sold off following the death of the last in a line of country gentry. Among those examining the items to be sold is a young schoolteacher, a certain Jane Bartholomew. She is attracted to an old chest, dated 1604, and while examining it for worm-holes notices that the inside is full of papers the seller has not bothered to clear out. A cursory look at the ones on top indicates a number of boring and out-of-date legal documents from the late 1700s. She buys the chest for a modest sum, and because of its considerable weight has it delivered to her cottage by horse and cart. When it arrives she looks at the contents more carefully, and underneath the old legal documents she finds the manuscript of a play. She recognizes it immediately as a copy of Shakespeare's *Hamlet* – or rather, on closer examination, of what appears to be a draft of a slightly earlier version of the play we know by that name. To her astonishment, further research shows that this draft is in the hand of Edward de Vere, and appears to have been penned in the fifteen years before his death in 1604. The story then descends into the expected depravity as all kinds of men vie for the affections of the discoverer of this priceless manuscript."

Lord FitzSimmons glanced round the room. "I imagine that several of you know something about this Edward de Vere, since I understand that in addition to being a relative of the founder, he was, for a year or so, a member of this college."

"Yes, I think I can summarize the principal facts that are known about him."

The speaker was Dr Samuel Heatherington, college lecturer in English literature and one of the leading experts on Shakespeare in Cambridge. In his younger days he had been one of the best oarsmen the college had ever had, and now, in middle age, he coached the first eight on the river. Partly as a result of this, despite his rather pedantic teaching style, he was popular throughout the college. As he spoke, he gradually waxed more and more into the lecturing mode that often characterized his after-dinner comments.

"Although I have no time for what some people are calling the 'de Vere hypothesis'," he continued, "it makes more sense than the still wilder claims I have recently heard concerning the alleged true authorship of Shakespeare's plays on behalf of Marlowe and Bacon, and even more absurdly, on behalf of a woman poet called Mary Sidney. These claims seem to have magnified ever since Delia Bacon published her extraordinary book supporting the Bacon hypothesis, back in '57. This Edward de Vere, the person referred to in the title of the novel, is not, needless to say, our founder, who was John, the thirteenth Earl of Oxford. He is the seventeenth Earl, descended from a nephew of our founder, and known in his lifetime both as a poet of some ability and as an important member of the Elizabethan court. Legends aside, quite a lot is known about this seventeenth earl. After youthful affiliations with the colleges of Queens' and St John's, from 1569 to 1570 he was a 'fellow-commoner' at this college: so some genuine connection with this place must be admitted."

Warming to his topic, he added. "As you probably know, fellow-commoners were typically rich and aristocratic young men who wanted some of the status that went with being a college fellow, with little if any of the academic responsibilities. Most colleges were happy to oblige because of the reflected glory this might bring, not to speak of future legacies. But in 1570 the young Edward de Vere left this college and went to live under the watchful eye of Sir William Cecil, later Lord Burghley, whose daughter he married in 1571. What is more relevant – and makes his claim more feasible than the others – is that it was also known that he wrote comedies and 'interludes', at first, no doubt, for a group of travelling players whom he supported financially, called 'the de Vere boys', or 'the Earl of Oxenford's lads' and later for other groups. None of these plays has survived; that is, unless one supports the de Vere hypothesis. It was common knowledge at the time that de Vere wrote his plays under a false name so as not to jeopardize his position at court. I am personally certain that these plays simply perished, along with many other writings of the time, but of course, for those who wish to spin fanciful tales they provide a marvellous background for a grand conspiracy. According to this conspiracy, William Shakespeare was simply a second-rate actor, who, in return for a considerable sum of money, agreed to lend his name to the plays, thereby assuring their production while protecting the earl's position at court. Later on, according to this tale, it became quite natural to assume that the sonnets too were written by the actor."

Lord FitzSimmons furrowed his forehead. He seemed to be reflecting on what to say next when Simon, who normally did not engage in the more general conversations of the Combination Room, found he could not resist imparting a bit of further information.

"Two years ago," he said, "while I was visiting Oxford, I was asked to a feast at New College. I sat next to a Mr Hammond, who, it appeared, supports the de Vere claim. He argued that if you looked carefully at the plays and poems there are all kinds of cryptic clues hidden in them. I'm afraid I can't remember most of the clues he mentioned, but I do recall one that he thought highly important. However, this really isn't my field, and I'm certainly not one to back his strange views."

"I would hope not," said Lord FitzSimmons. "I should think it could only be in a place like Oxford that any fellow would believe such nonsense!"

A polite titter went round the room. The amusement was only in part a matter of paying suitable flattery to the Master's guest: any remark that put the great rival Oxford in a poor light tended to be received in the same way. Lord FitzSimmons smiled and then added: "As a matter of curiosity, what was the alleged clue that this Mr Hammond emphasized?"

"It's when Hamlet pleads with Horatio to make sure that one day the truth will emerge. Apparently there was a real Horatio, actually a Sir Horace Vere, a first cousin and a close friend of the earl's whom his friends normally called Horatio – perhaps because of his valour on the battlefield. The claim is made that in this speech there is, in reality, an urgent appeal to this Horatio to publish the truth after his cousin's death when the risk of penalties or disapproval at court would no longer matter."

Heatherington, who was proud of his memory, immediately supplied the lines:

> *O good Horatio, what a wounded name,*
> *Things standing thus unknown, shall live behind me!*
> *If thou didst ever hold me in thy heart,*
> *Absent thee from felicity a while,*
> *And in this harsh world draw thy breath in pain,*
> *To tell my story.*

"But really," Heatherington added, "there is absolutely no need to see any reference here to something outside the play. I can't think what induced this Oxford fellow to read the matter otherwise."

Despite Heatherington's disclaimer, Lord FitzSimmons seemed put out at the mention of any possible support for 'the de Vere hypothesis', and Simon, who had already taken a dislike to the peer's pomposity, was amused to see his discomfort. Inspired, as he admitted to himself later, by a certain malicious sense of humour, he replied.

"I do happen to know the answer to that, although the explanation is more in terms of Mr Hammond's character than what we might call a good reason. Apparently, a few months before the feast where we met, he had been to a lecture in All Souls by the famous Shakespearean scholar, Professor Alfred Towse. The lecture had ridiculed the de Vere hypothesis, using as a principal argument the claim that all great literature was produced by men, like himself, who were products of the great grammar schools, and not aristocrats like de Vere. Aristocrats, he said, never achieved artistic greatness. The more Professor Towse argued this case, the more Hammond felt inclined to believe the opposite, in the light of the absurdity of the argument! Had he never heard of Philip Sidney or George Herbert or Byron? And what about the great French nobles, Condorcet and Montesquieu? Of course, I don't accept Hammond's conclusion, and in this case it's possible he is not altogether unbiased, since I gathered he is the younger son of a baron, and likes to be addressed as 'The Honourable Henry Hammond'. However, I have known other situations where the more one listens to someone arguing a case, the more one is inclined to believe the opposite."

Simon was inwardly amused to see Lord FitzSimmons' dilemma. As the Fifth Viscount of his line (which began with a natural son of George the First, born 'the wrong side of the blanket'), he clearly did not want to espouse Professor Towse's view of aristocrats, but at the same time he was fervently in favour of Towse's conclusion! There was an awkward silence, broken by the Master who turned to Talworthy, the official 'keeper of the college paintings'. "Do we have any portraits of this Edward de Vere in the college?"

"No Master," replied Talworthy, who was pleased to be brought into the conversation with an expertise he could parade. "So far as I know there is only one known painting of the Seventeenth Earl, and that is in Lord Portland's seat at Welbeck Abbey. Our inventory of 1652 – the oldest we have – does not mention any portrait, so I don't think the college has ever possessed one."

After another pause in which no-one seemed quite sure how to steer the discussion, Dr Higgins intervened. Somewhat oddly, in view of his profession, he had a passion for old books and manuscripts, and for this reason he had been happy to accept the role of college librarian, even though a fellowship in medicine would normally have been considered a full-time occupation. He was well known (in both medical and bibliographical circles) for a certain crankiness and outspokenness, which included a delight in espousing unpopular views. In the past five years Simon had observed that he was the only fellow who had the courage to disagree publicly with the Master. Sometimes, as in his support for the authors of *Essays and Reviews*, this was the result of real conviction, but at other times he seemed to get a sort of perverse pleasure by putting forward views the Master was bound to oppose, regardless of his personal beliefs. The present discussion, it now seemed, was going to provide just such an opportunity.

"I hear word," he said, "that the citizens of Stratford-upon-Avon are going to hold a public burning of *The de Vere Papers* next weekend, though I should have thought the only effect of that will be to increase the sales still further. But something else occurs to me. Stratford's loss, if this hypothesis gains any ground, could be our gain. After all, if the real Shakespeare were a member of De Vere College, that would be quite good for us. Perhaps, while not actually advocating the de Vere hypothesis, we should say something to the effect that it's an interesting one, and that in the past history of the college there are many secrets that have yet to be explored. For example, there's the famous Lolworth treasure that's supposed to be hidden here."

Simon felt his grip on the glass of port tighten and was careful to remain absolutely still.

Lord FitzSimmons seized the opportunity to change the subject, since it was clear that his attempt to harness universal support for his condemnation of *The de Vere Papers* was running into trouble. "I've never heard of this treasure," he said, and then, turning to the Master, he added, "Is there any substance in this matter, or is this yet another of the Cambridge legends?"

"Ah, well yes," the Master began, also happy to change the subject in the light of his guest's embarrassment, "Oddly enough there is some plausibility in this matter – unlike the de Vere hypothesis – even though the most common view is that it too is purely a myth. The background to the story is this. Lolworth Abbey was a large Benedictine foundation situated in the village of that name about eight miles away, just off the road to Huntingdon, at the edge of the fens. In 1539, when Henry VIII's men came to close it, they found that the abbot, Henry Courcey, second son of Baron de Courcey, had vanished, along with the treasures of the abbey, which were said to be considerable. The eighteen monks were examined, some under torture, but all seemed to be genuinely innocent. Eventually, most of them went off to live on small pensions while others joined the ranks of the 'sturdy beggars'. Then the king's commissioners turned their attention to De Vere College. The reason for this was that one of the Abbot's younger brothers, William Courcey, although only twenty-eight, had recently been made Master."

With a slight smile, emphasizing his own purely deserved election, he added, "In those days, of course, such appointments were often as much political as academic." He continued in his more serious tone. "Not only was it claimed that the Courcey brothers were close, it was also alleged that two weeks before the king's men came to the abbey, there had arrived at the porter's lodge of De Vere's, after midnight, a cart laden with chests. However, William Courcey denied all knowledge of his brother's recent movements or of the treasure or of the cart. Apparently, a search of the college went on for days, but eventually the hunt was pursued elsewhere, following a rumour that the Abbot and his treasure were on their way to France."

Dr Higgins broke in. "There's another twist to this story. William Courcey was responsible for bringing Edward de Vere to the college in 1569, and there is evidence that he and de Vere remained friends right up to the earl's death in 1604. Courcey lived on in the old keep, which used to be the Master's Lodge, until he died in 1606 at the age of ninety-six, still, it was said, in possession of all his mental faculties. So the two stories could have a connection. If the abbey did hide its treasures here, then William Courcey probably took the secret of where they are to his grave, and if his friend de Vere confided in him, then the earl's secrets also died with him. Then, there's an exciting possibility that there might be yet another twist to the story – though if I say anything about this I must ask all those present to keep what I am about to reveal in complete confidence."

There was a general murmur of assent round the room, and then Higgins continued, enjoying the complete attention which his intimation of a secret had assured, and contemplating, with still greater enjoyment, the likely annoyance that what he had to reveal was going to cause the Master's guest, and therefore, in all likelihood, the Master himself.

"As librarian I have been examining all the old books and

manuscripts in our collection, and only two weeks ago, in a locked cupboard within the room that houses the rare books, I found a large box of manuscripts that had been simply catalogued as 'Courcey – de Vere'. I've taken them all to my rooms so that I can go through them whenever I have time to spare. So far I've only made a quick examination and divided them into three categories: letters from Henry Courcey to his brother, William, Master of this college; letters from Edward de Vere to his friend William Courcey; and other letters or papers. I have already skimmed through two letters from Edward de Vere to William Courcey. Both are from the 1580s, and seem to be of a purely personal nature and not intrinsically important, although they may be quite interesting to biographers. However, I've noticed there are several other letters from de Vere, some of them sent from his retreat at King's Place in Hackney, where he retired after the queen gave him a sizable pension. The last one is dated February, 1604, only four months before his death. I haven't had time to read these letters yet, but when I have I shall look carefully at the whole collection – and who knows, something really exciting might turn up! Meanwhile, I would like to keep the existence of all these papers confidential until I've had time to finish my examination."

Lord FitzSimmons made no reply to this latest contribution, and Simon could guess what was almost certainly going through his mind. His plan to gather support for his attack on Amelia Buzzard's latest book, and in particular, to get the college to disown any suggestion that the de Vere hypothesis might be credible, had run into rough weather, not because anyone present was prepared to back the novelist, but because some of the fellows were not prepared to condemn the hypothesis outright. Indeed, some of them even seemed to savour the possibility that the true author of Shakespeare's works might have a close connection with their college. Much more worrying was the possibility that Dr Higgins might come up with some letter or document that could lend credence to the de Vere hypothesis. Of course, it would not prove such an absurd theory, but it might provide more material that could be manipulated by those who wished to cast doubt on Stratford's local genius. This could have serious implications for the projects he had in mind.

The subject changed, this time to rumours of Charles Darwin's new book that was said to be in preparation, in which his theory of evolution was going to be applied more directly to human ancestry. Once again, however, Lord FitzSimmons found himself frustrated. Persuading people to share his outrage – at whatever his anger was presently directed against – was one of the things that kept the lord in good spirits. However, he found that while none of the fellows was prepared to endorse the Darwinian theory wholeheartedly, Dr Higgins – once again the source of irritation – suggested that the whole issue had been blown out of proportion. "After all," he suggested, "none of us have any problem with the idea that the Almighty governs the way each individual grows or evolves – very gradually – in the womb, so what's so shocking about the idea that a whole species grew or evolved by a long series of steps? Why is this a denial of divine creativity?"

Gathering momentum, Higgins added, "Do you know the new headmaster of Rugby, Mr Frederick Temple, who has been the object of quite a lot of attention?" When FitzSimmons shook his head he continued: "He's been preaching that there's no reason for scientists and theologians to get into a controversy about evolution. They're concerned with different things, and the Bible is a book about morality, not science."

Townend, usually taciturn at the after-hall sessions in the Combination Room, and probably the most conservative-minded of all the fellows, made one of his rare interventions. "Isn't that the Temple who wrote a piece in *Essays and Reviews*?" he said. "I would hardly think that he could be a good person to tell us how to respond to *The Origin of Species*."

The four fellows who had been active in supporting *Essays and Reviews*, sometimes in violent debate in the Combination Room, exchanged glances. In addition to Higgins and Simon these comprised Mr Talworthy and Mr Richard Hughes, college lecturer in Greek. There was a certain understanding between them to come to the aid of one another when someone in the Senior Combination Room – often a visiting preacher or guest – attacked the latitudinarian views of any one of them. However, on this occasion none of them was eager to enter an acrimonious debate with the Master's guest. After a pause Simon thought of a point that might defend their views while taking the conversation away from the bitterly disputed *Essays and Reviews*.

"But Mr Charles Kingsley, who was a Professor of History here a few years ago, takes the same position. He can't see why the church needs to get into a fight with Darwin: both are glorifying the wonders of nature in their different ways."

When Hughes and then Talworthy joined in support for this position Lord FitzSimmons gave up, and shortly afterwards made his excuses. At his departure most of the company dispersed, led from the Combination Room by the Master, who looked genuinely put out at the less than enthusiastic reception of his guest's views. Simon learned later that Lord FitzSimmons had been considering a substantial donation towards the proposed new wing (on the assumption that it would bear his name), and that this donation was now in doubt.

Simon woke from his reverie with a start. Talworthy was pressing the Madeira into his left hand and saying something. The events of the day came flooding back into his mind, and he remembered that he needed to speak to Talworthy and make use of the latter's private interest in painting. It was this interest that had led the governing body to appoint him 'keeper of the paintings', a job that included an annual inspection of all the old paintings in the college's inventory, along with a report on their condition. The position had been instituted under the previous Master when it had been discovered that some of the oldest and most valuable pictures had been neglected and were in urgent need of repair.

He poured himself half a glass of Madeira and passed the decanter to the fellow on his right. Then, ignoring the subject of *The de Vere Papers*, which was being discussed elsewhere, he began to question Talworthy about the college's collection of paintings. With the help of some judicious promptings he found the Junior Fellow more than willing to expound on the subject of the Tudor portraits possessed by the college.

There were, as Simon had guessed, ten in all; nine in the Great Hall – including the rare and unique portrait of the founder painted in the reign of Henry VII – and one in the Master's Lodge. The one in the Lodge, apparently, had been put there because it was so unlike the others that it did not, as it were, sit comfortably alongside them. It was not a simple head and shoulders of the sitter, like all the others, but showed a complete figure against a background of the college. At least, this is what Talworthy believed from brief descriptions of the painting in the archives. He had not actually been able to see it, since every time he asked the Master if he could make his annual inspection he had been put off. Dr James was either too busy, or the portraits in the Lodge were in the process of being rehung, or something else was happening which made it important to postpone his inspection. Talworthy was clearly somewhat irritated. Simon realized he would have to find some way of getting into the Master's Lodge in order to examine this portrait carefully.

He was reluctant, at least for the time being, to let anyone else into the secret of his search. In the case of the Master the reason was quite clear – he simply did not like him. In the case of the fellows the situation was more complicated. He would like to achieve success by his own efforts, but there was more to it than that. Ever since the discovery of Higgins's body he had felt a deep unease. The search might involve danger as well as excitement, and letting anyone else know of his discoveries might carry a serious risk.

Chapter 4

The Dog and Goose, London, the same day, 10.30 p.m.

Josiah Tumbler was already late, but, before going up to Lord FitzSimmons' room on the first floor of the Dog and Goose he fortified himself in the public bar. It was almost exactly four days since he had last seen the Viscount – in another public house – and the commission he was given at that time had not worked out. In fact, not only had it not worked out, there had been a disaster that might well put him in mortal danger of the hangman's noose – innocent as he was. Well, to be more precise, not exactly innocent, but innocent of that for which he might be charged.

That last interview with his master was fresh in his mind. He had been waiting for a summons in his local bar at the Black Bull, only a short walk from his small house in Stratford-upon-Avon, and was half into his game pie, when the landlord approached him respectfully. (Although only the son of a local tailor, having risen to be the right-hand man of the powerful Lord, and organizer of his new property interests in the town, he was used to being treated respectfully, except by the noble lord himself.)

"Lord FitzSimmons has just arrived," said the landlord, "and wants to see you right away."

Tumbler bolted down the rest of his pie, finished a pint of brown ale with almost equal speed, and then went to the private room at the back of the public house which his lordship used on his regular visits to Stratford-upon-Avon. His country house was situated fifteen miles to the south, but in the last two years he had taken to using the room in the Black Bull for his regular visits to the town – ever since he had started to plan a Shakespeare centre near the great dramatist's birthplace.

Several things, Tumbler had learned, converged to make the scheme a consuming passion. One – to be fair to his lordship – was a genuine admiration for the work of Shakespeare; another was the desire to create and run a successful business enterprise; the third – and most important – was the hope of making a name for himself in the higher circles in which he aspired to move. On the last visit Lord FitzSimmons suggested that even Queen Victoria had intimated an interest in the project, and its successful completion would likely bring him into the intimacies of court life. (Tumbler did not know that a large part of the pressure came from Lady FitzSimmons, who felt it high time that her title of 'Viscountess' be turned into that of 'Countess', and her husband's promotion to an earldom was therefore essential. She found it insufferable that her closest associates, the Marchioness of Bristol and the Countess of Hillborough, always left her out of their most high-powered gatherings. Fame and acclaim, she knew, especially in court circles, were the most likely way of achieving the necessary elevation of her husband.)

He found the Viscount sitting at a table. Lord FitzSimmons did not look up but continued to read the papers spread out before him. Tumbler could see that something was wrong, and knowing Lord FitzSimmons' uncertain temper and dislike of interruption said nothing. Eventually the Viscount spoke. "I've got a job for you – or rather two jobs, and both of them will require some of your special skills. One's in Cambridge and the other's in London. Do you know Cambridge?"

"No, my lord, I've never been there."

"Well, you'll need to book into an inn and then prepare the ground for what I want you to do. The matter's urgent, so it had better be this weekend. In your case there's no point in pretending to be a visiting scholar, so make up a story about looking for a suitable college for the son of a gentleman of your acquaintance, or something like that. Join one of the college tours and make sure you have a good look at

De Vere College. While you are there take special notice of the rooms that are used by the librarian, a Dr Higgins – they're on the second floor of staircase B, in the old court. That's where you must break in. I wouldn't undertake the burglary at night because that would mean getting past the porter or scaling the walls. I'm told the wall around the college gardens is not so difficult to climb and many of the students climb it at night when they're out later than they should be, drinking or, more likely, visiting some of the town's ladies. But if you were caught climbing in it would be hard to explain what you were up to, and there's really no need to take that risk. It will be much easier to do the job during the day, provided you make sure Dr Higgins is out, giving one of his lectures, or in chapel, or working, as he often does, in the library, which is in the old keep. You'll need to find some excuse to get into the college, perhaps in a suitable disguise. Then you can knock on Higgins's door to make sure he's out, and use your skill with locks to get into the rooms."

"What about the London job?"

"As soon as you've done the work at De Vere, take the next train to London, carrying the papers I'll tell you about, and meet me at the Dog and Goose – where we met last time you were in London and where I'll have taken a room. I'll be booked in from this coming Saturday and I expect to see you on Sunday afternoon. I'll tell you about the London job then."

The interview had ended with a description of what Tumbler was to look for in the librarian's rooms.

In addition to his being late, things at Cambridge had certainly not gone as planned, but there was still some kind of work to do in London and he'd better find out what that was and face the his lordship's bad temper over the first job at the same time.

Tumbler knocked on the door leading to the room reserved for the Viscount and entered on his lordship's command.

"Well, where are they?" said the imperious voice. "Are there too many papers to carry up in one go?"

Tumbler stammered, and it was then that FitzSimmons noticed the whiteness of his face. After a pause he said, "Sit down and tell me what happened."

"I did as you suggested. After booking into the Chequers I got on a Saturday tour of the colleges and took careful note of Dr Higgins's rooms. Then, this morning, when I knew the chapel service was on at De Vere College, I put on an old gown and mortarboard and passed through the porter's lodge, making sure no-one was looking in my direction. I nearly tripped up a couple of times, because as you know I'm only five foot four, and the gown I borrowed from the inn was for a bigger man, but apart from that it all seemed easy. The outer door was closed, and Dr Higgins was almost certainly at the chapel service. I got to work on the lock, but for a time I had to head off downstairs and take a walk in the courtyard because I heard a student coming down from the floor above. Then I got the door open . . ."

Tumbler paused, and FitzSimmons noticed that he was trembling. "Go on," he said, in a voice that was unusually mild for him.

"When I managed to fix the lock and get inside – there was a body on the floor, right between the inner and the outer doors, all covered with blood. I don't know if it was Dr Higgins, but I think it must have been because the inner door was open, and it looked as if he had let the killer in just a short time before I got there. The back of the poor chap's head had been bashed in. I felt the body and it was still warm – so whoever done it must have done it only a short time before. Then I wondered if the killer could still be in the room, so I quickly drew back, closed the outer door, and made off. I can tell you I was in a pretty state. When I got to the porter's lodge I hung around for a bit, and when the porter was talking to a student I sneaked past and got back to the inn, about noon. I walked to the station, but there was no train till 5.20, so I found a seat and tried to look innocent, reading *The Times* I bought yesterday. At about five I had a real scare when two constables walked up and down the platform and had a good look at everyone waiting there. I went on reading, and they walked right past me. The train got into London just before eight, and then I hot-footed it here as fast as I could."

FitzSimmons digested the extraordinary story in silence, making no comment on the obvious fact that Tumbler had waited some time before coming upstairs. He poured him a generous helping of sherry and then returned to his seat. Eventually he said, "Did you get a chance to look inside the room?"

"Not really, but it didn't seem to have been disturbed – at least, not in any obvious way. I could see the long table you told me about, and I could see it had papers on it, but the room didn't seem to have been messed about like it usually is by thieves."

"You didn't go over to the table?"

"No – I don't mind telling you I was scared – and I don't scare easy. I could see there were rooms leading off the main room, across from where I was, and I was scared the murderer might still be there, perhaps in the bedroom. And I was worried someone might come and think I'd done it. I just took off."

"But you did close the outer door?"

"Yes I did that. But in my alarm I did something really foolish, although I didn't realize it until I was on the way back to the inn. I left my tools inside – between the inner and the outer doors. I'd carried them under the gown and then I put them down when I knelt to feel the body. In my panic I just forgot about them!"

"Idiot! I suppose they've got your name on them?"

"No, no. There's just a plain wooden box, about a foot long. Inside was my special collection of skeleton keys and pliers. They'll be hard to replace, but there's no reason why anyone should link them to me. Perhaps they might at Stratford, but not in Cambridge."

"Well, you'd better set about getting some replacements – and with your contacts in the city that shouldn't be too difficult. You've fooled up on one job and you better not fool up on the next. Come back here tomorrow, at six in the evening, and I'll give you details of the London job you are to do that night."

Tumbler left, and FitzSimmons remained sitting thoughtfully in his chair. Someone else wanted those papers: but surely not for the same reason. Who else would be so concerned to hide any evidence that might link Edward de Vere with Shakespeare? No, it was more likely that something else was going on. FitzSimmons recalled the conversation in the Combination Room and the story that Dr James had told of the Lolworth treasure. That was it. There was more at stake here than the authorship of *Hamlet* and the rest. The ancient papers might indeed provide information that would lead to the discovery of something far more valuable – at least to most people – something hidden in 1539.

Chapter 5

S imon sat at his desk in the room that he was lucky to have been granted on his election to a fellowship. Although the room was probably the finest available for private use in the college – apart from the drawing room in the Master's Lodge – none of the more senior members had wanted to claim it when he became a fellow, partly because of the bother of moving all their books, and partly, he suspected, because of its reputation for being haunted. However, Simon had highly sceptical views on the subject of ghosts, and no experiences in his set of rooms had led him to change them. It was true that during the Commonwealth period a college bursar had committed suicide in them (following the discovery of certain financial irregularities) but he had found no evidence that the fellow's departed spirit disturbed the slumbers of subsequent occupants.

However, recent events had set his mind in a motion that would not allow any sleep for some time, so he decided to work. He unlocked the chest of drawers next to his desk and drew out a file of letters labelled 'Fisher-White'. He read once again the one he had received yesterday from the chief editor, covered as always, in a large brown envelope that was post-marked in London but gave no other indication of who had sent it. Peter Robbins, the editor, had given him the latest sales figures for the first three Buzzard books, and intimated that it looked as if the first printing of *The de Vere Papers* would be sold within a few days. Meanwhile, so the letter went on, he was most anxious to receive the new novel written under the name of Emily

Dove. "Everyone is expecting the literary broadside in which she reacts to *The Coachman and the Countess* with appropriate venom – and the sales will be immense if only we can keep up the public interest in the battle between these two ladies you have so brilliantly engineered." The letter concluded: "Please let me know, by return post if possible, at least the title of the new book by Emily Dove, so that we can keep public suspense going."

Simon rummaged in another drawer and brought out a folder labelled 'Dove no. 2'. He sighed. The four books by Amelia Buzzard and the first one by Emily Dove had all been written quickly, under a kind of intense excitement, first to satisfy a sudden urge to write fiction, and later, he was quite prepared to admit to himself, because of the extraordinary and initially quite unexpected effect on his finances. He continued to wear rather shabby clothes and to give only modest dinner parties in his rooms, but this was all part of the necessary plot if he were to remain anonymous. Soon, he realized, he would have to decide what to do with the wealth that was piling up in his bank. In fact, it was not his Cambridge bank that housed the money, since he feared a leak within the gossipy chatter of the town, but a London bank that Peter Robbins had recommended for its discretion.

But now he faced a new problem. The rush of excitement that accompanied the success of the first books had subsided, and already he had more than enough money to set himself up comfortably for life, so, for the first time since he started to write fiction, he found himself running out of steam. He had originally promised Peter Robbins a sequel to *The Upright Canon* by May, written under the name and in the style of Emily Dove, but so far he had only written fifty pages, and he could not even decide on a definite title. The book had to react in a clever way to *The Coachman and the Countess*, but he could not decide how this was to be. The situation was made more difficult because his large tome on the second book of *Maccabees*, which was mostly written (and which was to be published – as had the earlier one on the first book of *Maccabees* – by Grimage and Sons, under his real name), still needed at least three months of hard work. Even without the complication of the new book by Emily Dove it was going to be difficult to complete it within the extra time he had already been granted.

He opened another drawer and brought out a folder headed 'Grimage and Sons'. The firm referred to was, in fact, a wholly owned subsidiary of Fisher-White and although it employed a separate editorial staff the mother house used the same printing and distribution services. The interconnection between the two houses was no secret, but it was not generally appreciated by the general public, who tended to assume that they were completely separate institutions, with Fisher-White involved in popular literature and Grimage's in academic matters. The literary sub-editor at Grimage's was Jeremy Nogle, and although the *First Maccabees* had only been published in 1867, Simon had been in contact with him since the early days of the Maccabees project, as far back as 1863. It was this connection, along with his growing friendship with Nogle, that had led him to confide in him when the first Amelia Buzzard book was being written, and it was this that had led to its acceptance by Fisher-White.

On the top of the folder was the latest letter from Nogle. It began with a congratulatory note, responding to the award of the degree of Doctor of Divinity to Simon, received last month at an unusually young age, in recognition of scholarly response to *First Maccabees* and of an earlier work on the rebuilding of the temple in Jerusalem after the exile. The letter then turned to business affairs. Yes, Nogle was hoping for the complete manuscript of the title *Second Maccabees* by mid-August at the latest. Then he noticed a paragraph that he had forgotten about, added to the end of the letter. On March 12th, that was the Thursday of next week, he was expected to attend a special luncheon at Grimage's head office in Pall Mall. It was hoped that as many as possible of the authors working for Grimage's and Fisher-White would be there, and would mingle with the leading literary and academic critics, contacts that were important for both presses.

Among the list of guests, which had been included, Simon noticed the names of Sylvia Tyson and Theresa Brown, both of whom were on the staff of the *Old Chelsea Review*, which was probably the most widely read intellectual journal in England, and which covered both fiction and more serious works, although usually not strictly academic ones. Theresa Brown he had not met, but she had reviewed the first three books by Amelia Buzzard for the journal. Sylvia Tyson he had met briefly at a function at Fisher-White's headquarters, and he recalled that, very much to his surprise, his *First Maccabees* had been reviewed by her in the *Old Chelsea Review*. The reason was that apart from being a commentary on the Biblical, or more accurately, apocryphal text, he had included a long introduction that gave an account of the Maccabean revolt. This he had tried to make both readable and interesting – which had not been difficult given the truly extraordinary history of the uprising. The result was that the commentary had sold much better than expected (so far just over 600 copies) and had been noted by a number of people for its historical content. This is what had brought it to the attention of the *Old Chelsea Review*.

In retrospect he was glad that the reviewer of *First Maccabees* had not been Theresa Brown, for it was just possible she might have noticed a similarity of style to at least one of the new women authors! Anyway, he looked forward with some anticipation to his first meeting with this formidable critic, and wondered, if he got into conversation with her, how he would keep his composure if the subject moved towards that of recent novels by women writers, which were her primary interest. After all, it was she who had stressed the importance of the woman's outlook in the Buzzard novels.

He walked to the window that looked out across the river Cam. Opposite his rooms, to the south, lay part of Jesus Green, where, not long after the refounding of the college, a number of Protestants had been burned to death. To his right he could see the south wall of the old court and beyond that, part of the garden that belonged to Magdalene College. Further still he could see the edge of the Pepysian Library that hid from view the south side of Magdalene's old court, parts of which dated from the monastic foundation, and were therefore older than the De Vere first court, which had been built between 1488 and 1490.

He looked back to the fine brickwork of the old court in which his rooms lay. The work had been paid for by some of the wealth acquired by the Thirteenth Earl of Oxford after his judicious, but morally questionable, support for Richmond, later Henry VII, at Bosworth Field, in 1485. To his left, jutting out slightly from the far end of the old court, was the handsome Norman keep – by far the oldest building belonging to the college, whose foundation stones were lapped on one side by the river.

The history of this keep and its connection with De Vere College were interesting, and, he was sure, highly relevant to any attempt to find the monastic treasure believed to be hidden in the college. The old castle of Cambridge, most of which had been located to the west of the present sites of Magdalene and De Vere, and a bit further back from the river, had been a typical motte and bailey affair, constructed in earth and wood late in the eleventh century, before there was any university at Cambridge. About 1130, the sheriff had a stone tower built on top of the motte, replacing the old wooden keep, but soon after the construction the walls of the tower had begun to come apart because the motte had not settled sufficiently to stand the weight of the new building. So, between 1145 and 1150, at the king's command, a new stone keep was constructed at a bend in the river, about three hundred yards from the old motte, on massive stone foundations that brought the floor of the basement twenty feet above the normal water level – and ten feet above it when the Cam was in flood.

Following the famous, or infamous, Oxford riot of 1209, when a number of Oxford students were driven from their university and came to Cambridge, the sheriff of the time lent the old keep, which was then not much used, to his friend, a Master Taverner, who set up a school there, accommodating about a dozen students. At this time the keep housed the complete scholarly establishment of what came to be called 'Taverner's Hall'. The Master lived on the top floor, arranged as a set of comfortable rooms with splendid views of the city and surrounding countryside. Immediately below this was the keep's Great Hall – which was somewhat smaller than the later Great Hall built at the time of the new foundation and which was now the centre of college life. The Norman hall, complete with its gallery was where, in those early days, the students lived, ate, worked and slept. Immediately below it was the entrance floor, entered through a 'forebuilding'. Originally this forebuilding had been reached by a flight of wooden steps that led from ground level, steps which could fairly quickly be dismantled in the case of a siege, but these had been rebuilt in stone towards the end of the Middle Ages when the likelihood of siege was less, and cannons were making all castles virtually redundant, except as handsome dwellings. On the entrance floor, inside the main building, there was the ancient kitchen and guard-room (which became the porter's lodge), below which, in turn, was the vaulted basement, comprising storerooms and cellars.

The old keep, under a series of Masters, kept going as a student house without any official charter, continuing to use the name of 'Taverner's Hall' until, in 1290, it received its first royal charter, and the ownership of the keep, which had outlived its military importance, passed into the hands of the university. Then in 1488 the college was refounded, its name changed to De Vere, and the 'old court', built alongside the keep, was completed in 1490. For a time, the Master continued to occupy the top floor of the old keep but a more expansive lodge was built for him in 1622, along with the 'second court', both buildings being situated to the south-west of the first court and near to the college gate, which let onto Chesterton Road. Thereafter the whole keep was used for the college library and for lecture rooms.

At present Simon had a particular reason for being interested in the keep. The clue he was searching for clearly related to something that William Courcey had hidden in 1539, and this must almost certainly be the famous Lolworth treasure, which, until ten days ago, he had dismissed along with stories of the ghost in his set of rooms. It was highly probable, given the nature of the college at that time, that the hiding-place was within the massive walls of the keep in which Courcey had lived, as – it was said – a semi-recluse.

Simon walked across to the bookcase and took down the item he had borrowed from the college library which contained the extraordinary reference to the clue. It was a slim volume, printed in Oxford in 1590, containing the original Greek text of the fourth book of *Maccabees* (wrongly, as he had come to learn, attributed to the great Jewish writer, Josephus), along with a Latin translation. He had first started to look at the book in order to review his preparation for his later commentaries on the remaining parts of *Maccabees* (that is, books three to five), and early in his perusal he noticed the signature at the beginning of it: that of the old Master, William Courcey, who had probably acquired the volume in 1590. But then, as he began to read the Latin translation, he came across something truly astonishing.

It was amazing, he pondered, that at almost the same time that he had found an indication of where the Lolworth treasure might be, Lionel Higgins had found a possible reference to another mystery connected with De Vere College – one relating to Edward de Vere. Until last Monday evening he had no inkling that there were original Courcey and de Vere documents in the library. Once he knew of their existence he was most anxious to see them, not only for their intrinsic interest, but because they might also have a bearing on the hidden message that he had found. But now, given the theft from Higgins's rooms, he might never set eyes on them.

Simon was anxious to review again the cryptic message he had found but suddenly felt fatigue taking hold. Further examination would have to wait till after his lecture the next morning. Meanwhile, any examination of the painting referred to in the message might have to wait quite a bit longer and, in the light of what Talworthy had told him earlier that evening, this was a pity.

Chapter 6

Cambridge and London, Thursday, 12th March.

S imon had intended to take the 9.30 morning express to London
from Cambridge Junction, which should easily have enabled
him to get to Grimage's for the luncheon which was due to
start at one. However, his plans were spoilt when the Master knocked
on his door just as he was about to leave. All he wanted, it turned out,
was to remind Simon about a proposed meeting in the Master's Lodge
the next morning, but the result was that Simon missed the fast train,
and had to settle for the much slower 9.50. He bought a second-class
ticket, still anxious not to let anyone guess the true state of his finances.
During the journey he had hoped to work on some lecture notes but
found his mind far too occupied with recent events to be able to pay
attention to them.

Not surprisingly, the murder of Dr Higgins at De Vere College
had caused a sensation in Cambridge, but so far no arrests had been
made, and the whole affair appeared utterly puzzling to the ordinary
citizen. The police – at least according to local rumour – were baffled
by the discovery that Higgins, although subject to a high level of
irritableness and outspokenness, had no known enemies. Simon
thought that if they knew more they might make an exception in the
case of Dr James. It was certainly a fact that the Master found Higgins
tiresome, not least because Higgins was one of the most vigorous
supporters of *Essays and Reviews*. In contrast with the liberal opinions
expounded in that volume, the Master expressed extremely traditional
views of Biblical inspiration. However, Higgins had been no more
outspoken on this issue than many others in Cambridge. In general, it

had emerged that the physician-cum-librarian was generally rather liked and admired, especially among the students he taught, several of whom testified to the police about how he would often go out of his way to help pupils who were having difficulty with his lectures. The only clue that had been released concerned a mysterious, gowned figure that had been seen 'lurking' in the first court around the time of the chapel service, and, it was thought, at about the time the murder was committed. The Cambridge constabulary had put out a general request for anyone who had information involving this person to come forward. The whole student body at De Vere College had been questioned concerning this shadowy figure, which two students and one college servant had observed. Unfortunately, however, apart from an agreement that he was short, their descriptions of the person in the gown were too vague to be helpful.

With regard to the missing papers, Simon had decided to maintain his silence, especially following a whispered conversation with the Master after the chapel prayers on Monday morning. "Come and see me in the Lodge on Friday morning," the Master had said. "There are some things we need to discuss, but I really can't talk about them till then."

Another matter on Simon's mind, apart from the forthcoming luncheon, and his first meeting with Theresa Brown, was the absence of all reports on the skeleton keys. To his surprise, the police had made no mention of these in their public statements, and since he and the Master had been asked to say nothing concerning what they had witnessed, this important piece of information was still generally unknown.

On reaching Bishopsgate station (the London terminus for the Great Eastern Railway), Simon would normally have walked the two and a half miles to the offices of Grimage's, but the eventuality of getting the slower train, combined with his new-found wealth, meant that he had no hesitation in taking a cab, although he did look around in case any colleague could see him, and perhaps speculate on his extravagance. However, when he reached Grimage's he found that the luncheon had begun. There were about sixty people already sitting down, half of them authors – a few of whom he knew – and the rest, he presumed, critics, although Sylvia Tyson was the only one he recognized.

Jeremy Nogle spotted him. "I've reserved a place for you – with critics on either side to keep you in order!" He led him to a table where there was an empty chair with a middle-aged man on the left and a young woman who looked to be in her mid-twenties on the right. Simon caught his breath. Although he was not a 'confirmed bachelor' his life-style had only rarely brought him into close contact with the fairer sex, and in Cambridge the few women who attracted him were always married or engaged or for some other reason 'not available': at least, that is to say, if one were acting in a way that was appropriate for a fellow of a Cambridge college, not to mention a clergyman.

The young woman's appearance came as a shock. He had thought that an established critic would be much older, because it took some time to build up a reputation. He had assumed also that critics would be less attractive, because really clever women, in the traditional view, were likely to be bespectacled and earnest looking. But, physically at least, this was the kind of woman who attracted him. As she talked her face was half turned, showing a profile in which perfectly proportioned, clearly defined features were topped by blonde hair that was decorated with flowers and ended in a low knot, or 'chignon'. However, following a style that contravened normal convention, some curls had been allowed to reach down below the knot and beyond the top of the shoulders. As he got nearer he heard her laugh, and there was something in the clear ringing voice that added to the anticipation

of meeting. He suddenly felt acutely conscious of the wart on his left cheek, and began to wish he had taken up Higgins's suggestion, made three years ago, that he should have it surgically removed. Otherwise – so he had been led to believe by his family – he was actually not bad looking. He was slim and of medium height, with a slightly craggy, scholar's face, but overall still very much in his youth. Until last year he had also been quite fit, especially during the cricket season, in which he did fairly well as a medium-fast bowler. He made a mental resolve to get back to the game this summer, despite the pressures of his writing.

Nogle introduced Simon to the middle-aged man who was to sit at his left, a critic called Mr Haverstock, whom Simon had never heard of, and then – after mentioning that he worked for the *Thames Review* – rushed off to meet another late-comer, without effecting any introduction to the blonde critic.

As Simon sat down Mr Haverstock, who seemed to have been left out of the conversations going on around him, began to regale Simon with his views on a new travel book, *The Sands of Egypt*, which had been much discussed in the press, and which he had just reviewed. Simon nodded every now and then out of politeness, thinking the man was a complete bore and waiting for a pause in his monologue which would enable him, with some semblance of politeness, to introduce himself to the attractive woman on his right.

Ten minutes later, when Simon's exasperation was almost at its limit, help came from an unexpected quarter. The soup being finished, the waiter was on the point of serving the Dover sole when another late-coming guest accidentally bumped into him from behind, causing the fish to land with a gentle thud in Mr Haverstock's lap. Huge apologies from the waiter (although he was not really to blame) were met with harsh recriminations from Mr Haverstock, who followed his acid comments with a retreat to the washrooms in order to repair the damage to his trousers as well as he could. The incident caused the blonde lady to turn to her left, and Simon seized the opportunity. He held out his hand. "I'm sorry we haven't been introduced yet; I'm Simon Weatherspoon."

"Mr Nogle told me I was going to sit next to you. I'm afraid I haven't read your *First Maccabees*, but Sylvia Tyson tells me I must, and I intend to as soon as I've cleared the backlog on my desk. She says you've made the history really come alive."

He was just considering how to reply, without lapsing into a kind of common false modesty which would sound all the wrong tones, when she continued: "Tell me, did you have sources for the history outside the Maccabean books, or did you rely simply on the Biblical and apocryphal sources?"

Simon began to explain about the additional sources, and especially about the problem of trying to decide how reliable Josephus was. Her probing questions impressed him; they were, he thought, just what he would hope for from a bright, post-graduate student. As she expanded on one of her points he reflected on his own support, in a number of high table discussions, for the recent introduction of women undergraduates to Cambridge, even though they couldn't officially take degrees. It was a pity, he reflected, that it would probably be a long time before they could become graduate students.

"Well, I gather the first printing of *First Maccabees* is sold out, so I'll have to wait a few months before I can read the second printing."

"Not at all, I have a few copies of my own, and I'll be only too pleased to send you one; especially," he added with a grin, "since I gather that Sylvia Tyson is your colleague, so your journal has already reviewed it. By the way," he added, "I take it from our conversation you are a critic in the areas of Biblical and historical studies."

Her laugh rang out, the same infectious sound that had struck him just after he had first seen her. "No, no, I'm afraid I'm a real amateur in those departments. No, my field is novels – recent ones – especially by women authors."

Simon felt a sudden weight in his stomach, and a second later his suspicion was confirmed. "I'm sorry," she went on, "I just assumed you knew who I was because *I* knew who *you* were. But actually there's no reason why you should ever have heard of me, given the kind of scholarship you're concerned with. My name is Theresa Brown."

Simon almost stammered, but recovered himself quickly. "Oh no, I know your name well. I've read some of your pieces in the *Old Chelsea Review*."

The words were hardly out of his mouth before he regretted them. Now it was almost inevitable that the talk would turn to Amelia Buzzard, and that was a subject he tried to avoid with absolutely everyone other than Jeremy Nogle, in case he let slip some comment that might raise suspicions about his relationship to her. Even within the house of Fisher-White, only three or four people knew that he was their new, best-selling authoress.

"Which review have you read most recently?"

Simon felt himself being dragged, more and more, into a kind of trap – although one that seemed to have been arranged by some evil Providence rather than by Theresa Brown's perfectly reasonable questions. The fact was that the only review of Theresa Brown's he had read carefully was the one on *The Male Courtesan*, and although he had skimmed others in the past, including those of the second and third Buzzard novels, he could not remember enough about any of them to make a rational-sounding comment. At the same time he felt an urgent need to make a good showing in front of this most attractive critic. The result was that he felt forced towards the topic he had hoped to avoid.

"I read your review of *The Male Courtesan* with great interest, and I must admit that one thing puzzled me." Theresa did not ask the obvious question, but inclined her head slightly, indicating she expected Simon to elaborate. "I remember," he continued, "that in that review you praised Amelia Buzzard for representing the authentic voice of women, and in particular, for her insight into the nature of fallen men. I liked that, but I couldn't see why, if a woman can have a genuine insight into fallen men, a male writer couldn't, at least on occasions, have an equivalent, genuine insight into fallen women!"

Theresa smiled disarmingly. "*Touchée*! I see what you mean. Because I am so anxious to expand on the special insights of women writers, I tend to play down the special insights of male ones. Your point, if I can put it this way, is that it is one thing to see men and women having equal, although complementary gifts, another thing to put women in a superior category altogether. This is just to commit the same old fallacy as most men have committed, but, as it were, in reverse."

"Well, yes – that is a good way of summarizing what I was getting at."

"From a strictly logical point of view I think you're quite right. But then you must remember that you write as a scholar and I write more in the style of a journalist. You have to write in measured tones, while I am trying to get an effect, as well as giving a reasonably accurate report. The fact is that there is such a massive prejudice against women that a certain exaggeration is legitimate in order to bring attention to the prejudice."

One half of Simon wanted to argue this point, claiming that deliberate exaggeration was always the enemy of truth, but another half of him wanted to agree. As he pondered his reply he was acutely aware of an ongoing inner analysis of his present thinking, an analysis that he frequently observed accompanying his conversations, especially on serious topics. This second half of himself felt pressured as much by the desire to seem agreeable to Theresa as by an appreciation of the intrinsic merits of the argument.

He had a flashback to one of his days as a first year undergraduate and to a class on St Paul where he found himself uttering an opinion that would, he felt sure, please his teacher, while inwardly thinking that this was not what he really thought. He still hadn't really settled how to draw the right balance between being utterly honest and being polite and, perhaps more sinisterly, keeping one's position in whatever society one walked in. The memory triggered another flashback, with its particularly vivid experience of the combination of inner and outer dialogue. The occasion was one of his lectures on the Jerusalem temple that happened the morning after a college feast at which he had enjoyed himself particularly well. Half way through the session he became aware of what a poor lecture he was in the process of giving, and had carried on only with difficulty.

He came back to reality with a start, finding Theresa staring at him. He hoped his inner reverie had only taken a few seconds. Avoiding the issue on which he felt qualms, he said, "I completely agree about the systematic prejudice of most male writers. Do you know the eminent historian, Mr W. E. H. Lecky?"

"I know of him, although I've never actually met him."

"Well next year he's going to publish his long awaited *History of European Morals*. I happen to have been given a preview of some of the chapters, and he says, in icy cold language, that no-one can deny that from an intellectual point of view, women are generally inferior to men!"

"Good Lord! Does he pretend to give any evidence?"

"Not really – apart from cataloguing male achievements. And incidentally, he goes on to say, with the same conviction, that women are morally superior to men. But, as I'm sure you'll agree, it's remarkable what some women have achieved, given the treatment and status they've been given. Take Hildegard of Bingen, for example, and Hypatia."

"I don't think I've ever heard of Hildegard, but I have heard of Hypatia, though only because of Charles Kingsley's recent novel about her. How much of that was real history and how much was Kingsley's invention?"

Simon launched into what was known, historically, about the extraordinary life and tragic death of the great woman philosopher, murdered by a mob in Alexandria in 415AD. Prompted by Theresa, he then told what he knew about the twelfth-century polymath, Hildegard, and her equally extraordinary life as theologian, poet, mystic, musician, medical scientist and politician, whom even the Pope was said to treat with caution. The conversation turned to other women philosophers known to Simon, including, in the ancient world, Themista, to whom Epicurus wrote letters, and more recently Anne Conway and Catherine Cockburn in Britain. This, in turn, led to a more general discussion of whether the female mind, when given its due rein, would send philosophy and religion in directions that were significantly different from those of the past. Simon was caught up in the dialogue, when, at the beginning of the cheese course, Mr Haverstock – who, after returning from the washrooms, had evidently bored both his other neighbour and the gentleman sitting opposite – forced himself into their conversation. "There are some good women novelists," he intervened (having eavesdropped on the last few minutes of their conversation), "but you must admit, there are no great women philosophers or theologians."

Theresa glanced knowingly at Simon and responded, "What about Hildegard, for a start?"

Haverstock looked put out. It was obvious he had never heard of Hildegard. Theresa followed up with "And what about Philistia, Archella and Probes in ancient Greece, let alone Drusilla, Marcellina and Gorgia in ancient Rome, and of course, Hypatia in Alexandria? How would you describe their achievements?"

Simon had difficulty suppressing his mirth at this sudden and mischievous invention – with the exception of Hypatia – of a whole raft of purely fictitious philosophers. But Haverstock deserved it, for being a bore and for his interruption and for his prejudiced view of women. Simon hadn't actually thought about the role of women in philosophy prior to the present conversation, but it occurred to him that since they could obviously be great novelists, which involved having both complexity and subtlety of thought, there was no reason why they couldn't be great philosophers. But the question remained, would they be *different* philosophers? However, it was likely that the subtleties of the latter question would not be evident to this critic for the *Thames Review*.

Haverstock fumbled with the cheese plate, obviously trying to make up his mind whether to admit his ignorance of these great personages, or whether to invent some clever reply. In the end he came out with an evasion. He turned to Simon and said, "What do you think of these philosophers?"

"Well, the only one I know well is Hypatia." Then, on a certain impulse he decided to join Theresa's invention game. "There's no doubt that her Alexandrine dialogues are important, you know, the ones they teach at school when they reach the higher levels of geometry. Which of them do you think is most interesting?"

Simon felt guilty, but he had already decided how he could defend himself if Haverstock, on a later occasion, and perhaps in the presence of someone who actually knew about the subject, questioned him about these 'dialogues'. He would be hard pressed to defend his claim about what was taught to school children (which he had added in order to increase Haverstock's discomfort), but with respect to the dialogues he had already thought of his defence. "Oh," he would say, "but of course, I wasn't referring to written dialogues, but to the reports of what Hypatia taught, orally, while in Alexandria. I thought the other comments I made about Hypatia had made that clear." Anyway, this new question seemed to have the desired effect, and he even noticed a slight flush in Haverstock's cheeks. "I need to think a little more before I respond to that question," he said, and shortly afterwards forced his way into the conversation taking place on his left. Theresa's eyes were glistening, and both young people grinned conspiratorially.

The port was about to be served, signalling the departure of the five women present. This event, Simon reflected, both in terms of the number involved and of the very act of withdrawal, provided an interesting comment on the conversation Theresa and he had been having. Just before leaving Theresa scribbled a note on a piece of paper. Aloud she said, "I intend to hold you to your promise to send me *First Maccabees*. Here is my address." Then, with a slight hesitation she added, "Do you often come to London?"

Simon was about to reply, having decided that he now had an added reason to make the journey, when Sylvia Tyson came up, took Theresa by the hand, and led her away to the ladies' drawing room.

Chapter 7

Grimage and Sons, Pall Mall, a little later the same day.

Simon had been somewhat dreading the port, not because he disliked the drink, but because it might mean facing Haverstock again, and in addition to having to listen to his monologue he was already feeling a little guilty about his own elaborations on the history of philosophy. Fortunately, Jeremy Nogle came up and led him to a side-table. However, his relief was short-lived for Nogle looked worried and evidently had a serious matter on his mind.

He spoke in a low voice, even though the nearest table with other diners was some fifteen feet away. "I'm afraid I've got rather unfortunate news which I think you should know about immediately," he said.

"What's happened? Is it to do with *Second Maccabees*? I'm truly sorry it looks like being late, but I'm afraid my other commitments have made things really difficult, especially" (and here he lowered his voice even more) "trying to get the sequel to the Dove book ready. I'm afraid that threatens to be delayed as well."

"No, no, it's nothing to do with that. And incidentally Mr Robbins is greatly pleased with the way all the novels are going. I understand he'll be sending you another large cheque early next week. It's nothing to do with the novels, at least not directly. The fact is – well, on Monday night, we had a break-in at the head office – on the ground floor, where we keep the author files for both Fisher-White and Grimage and Sons. Nothing seemed to be missing – at least at first sight – but a window that leads into a passage-way had been forced open and the appearance of the archive room indicated that someone had been inside. This is really surprising because the lock on the door to this room is quite special and wasn't damaged, so we suspect the thief must somehow have got a key to the room. Perhaps someone from inside the company may be involved, but so far we have no grounds for questioning anyone we employ. Anyway, at first it didn't look as if anything important had been taken, even though in the archive room we keep some rather nice porcelain that was left to the firm by a grateful author, but yesterday, after carefully checking all the files, we found that some of the papers in yours were missing. It's odd and rather worrying. So far as we can see nothing else has been taken."

Simon stared at Nogle in silence. Now there had been two unusual burglaries, both leaving behind the most obvious things to take, one in Higgins's rooms and one in London, and both with a suspicion of skeleton keys. Could there be a connection?

"So someone knows about Amelia Buzzard, in addition to you and me and a couple of other people at Fisher-White!"

"Yes, I'm afraid so and, come to mention it, about Emily Dove as well. I can't say how sorry I am, but believe me, we've really taken more than the ordinary precautions. It looks as if someone is determined to find out about the authorship – and now I'm afraid they know."

"Were the files under my name, or under that of Buzzard?"

"Unfortunately we had files under both names, otherwise it might have taken the thief several days of searching to make the connections."

"What have you told the police?"

"On Tuesday morning we told them about the break-in, and today, when we found out about the missing files, we got one of the Scotland

Yard detectives to come down and we put him in the picture. He pointed out that the thief will have to be careful how he leaks the information, assuming that is his intention, since if we can trace the source of the leak, then the trail will lead to the thief."

Simon was reminded of a seriously ill patient asking a doctor how long he had left. He found himself framing the analogous question. "How long do you think I've got: I mean, before the storm breaks?"

"It's hard to say. The detective reckoned two or three weeks, but he was guessing. He seemed to think any newspaper hoping to make money by using the story would look for other evidence before running it. That way they would never have to admit how they came by the story in the first place. In the meantime, is there anything we can do to help?"

Simon thought for a while and then said, "As a matter of fact there is. But before I come to that let me say that you mustn't feel too bad about all this. I've always felt that one way or another the truth was bound to come out sooner or later, and when it did, I'd simply leave Cambridge – that is, if I'm not forced to leave! For some time now I've been planning a different kind of life, away from the university, but near enough to a big library so that I can go on with my scholarly work in my own time, as a gentleman of leisure rather than as a college fellow. Oxford is out, because I know too many people in that relatively small city, and I hate being a centre of attention. The obvious thing to do is to buy a nice house in London, preferably within easy walking distance from the British Museum library, and preferably under an assumed name. Here I am known by sight to very few, and I can live more or less anonymously, at least most of the time, which is what I want. Then I can divide my time between writing more novels, carrying on with my research into the Maccabees, which I really enjoy, travelling on the Continent, and going to the theatre and to concerts in London. All in all it doesn't sound like a bad life!"

"I must say you've taken it remarkably well. But you haven't made clear what we can do for you."

"It's a matter of finding a suitable house, along with very discreet staff. Not a large staff, perhaps a butler, a cook-housekeeper and two other domestics. The house doesn't have to be grand, but not too far from the museum and large enough to bring up a family, in case anything were to befall my bachelor status!"

Nogle smiled, not a little relieved at the way Simon had reacted to the news.

"And you'd want the house bought under a false name? I'm afraid I've no idea of the legalities of that, but I can speak to Grimage's lawyers, and I can certainly start a private search for the kind of house and the kind of staff you would like. It's the least I can do for you in the circumstances. I take it the price is a secondary consideration?"

"That would be most helpful. I'm generally free on Thursdays, so may I suggest that I come to London next Thursday, when there is another matter of business that may take up the luncheon period? Then perhaps we could meet in the afternoon, and I'll stay overnight in a hotel. With a bit of notice I can rearrange my lecture for the Friday that follows, and perhaps look at some properties then."

For the return journey Simon succeeded in catching the express, the five o'clock from Bishopsgate. At the only stop on the run (at Bishop's Stortford), he began the letter that had been forming in his mind, taking advantage of the possibility of a steady hand while the train was in the station. He had the address in his pocket, and with luck Theresa would be free for luncheon next Thursday, and perhaps, for a concert or a theatre in the evening; but he thought it would sound too forward of him if he were to suggest an evening encounter in this letter. He would see how the luncheon went before making any suggestion along those lines. But, he wondered, was there some way of preparing Theresa for the revelation that might soon strike the literary world? Since Theresa had been heralding the genius of a woman writer – and her particularly feminine insights – she might not be very happy about this particular thunderbolt!

Chapter 8

De Vere College, Friday, 13th March.

On Friday, along with all the fellows who lived in college, with the exception of the very elderly Townend, Simon went to Morning Prayer in the chapel at 7.00, and then to the fellows' breakfast in the Combination Room. The sky was overcast, which was appropriate, not only because it was Friday the 13th, but also because at noon there was to be the funeral of Dr Lionel Higgins. The ceremony in the chapel had originally been set to take place two days earlier, but the police had not been prepared to release the body until yesterday, when they concluded that it had nothing more to tell them.

Once back in his rooms, Simon had a few minutes to spare before walking across the courtyard to the Master's Lodge for the meeting that had been arranged, and he decided to look again at his transcription of the secret message he had found: a message which he might be able to understand in the next hour if the painting it referred to were indeed in the Lodge, as he suspected following his talk with Talworthy.

Early in his reading of the fourth book of *Maccabees* he had compared the Latin translation of the original Greek, provided in the edition before him, with his own translation into English, made some time before from another edition of the Greek text. He noticed that, on the second page of the Latin, one letter was underlined in ink, for no obvious reason. Then, two pages later he had found another underlined letter, and then more. Curious, and following a sudden hunch, he had made a copy of the underlined letters in the order in which they came, and it was then he found that they spelled out a message!

In Latin the message read: *'Videte sub anulo socii episcopi facti'*, and after the final 'i' no letters appeared to be underlined anywhere else in the book. The Latin could loosely be translated: "Look beneath the ring of the college fellow who has been made bishop."

The message could, in principle, have been put there at any time after the book's publication in 1590, and by any number of people; but several things led Simon to the conclusion that it was almost certainly William Courcey who had done the underlining. In the first place, the ink was clearly old, and looked very similar to that used in the signature at the front of the book. Secondly, this was a volume that exceedingly few people would be interested in, and Simon had ascertained that only one other college library in Cambridge contained it. It was quite likely that he, with his particular and somewhat recondite interest in the later Maccabean books, was the first person to open the volume since Courcey. Thirdly, and most importantly, the message seemed to make sense if one put it into the context of Courcey's connection with Lolworth abbey and the mysterious disappearance of its treasure.

He did not immediately connect the underlined letters with a college portrait. His first act had been to go to the college chapel and look at the tomb that was placed to the north of the altar and which had immediately occurred to him as the most likely source of the reference. The tomb was that of a bishop during the reign of Edward VI, Henry Winterton, who had been put out of office by Queen Mary in 1554 for refusing to return to Catholicism. However, perhaps because of his ill health, he had not been executed, but allowed to live quietly at De Vere College, where he had formerly been a fellow and where he died shortly before the queen's death. Winterton's family had paid for the fine alabaster carving early in the reign of Elizabeth.

As he had remembered, the right finger of the effigy did indeed carry a ring, but it seemed to be of no significance, even though he pushed it hard to see if there were some secret catch. His thoughts turned to the crypt immediately below the chapel, in which, so he assumed, the bishop's coffin lay, along with the bodies of a number of early masters and fellows. The crypt, like the chapel, dated from 1489, and was both lit and ventilated by small openings, placed just above ground level – so that the floor of the chapel was raised to about two feet above the general level of the ground floors of the first court. As a result of these miniature windows, the crypt would not be anything like as damp as the wine cellar under the Great Hall (that had no windows of any kind), and it might, perhaps in a walled-off section, provide a place for hiding valuables. He had never been in the crypt, which could only be accessed – so he had been told – by lifting a large stone in the chapel floor, a stone identifiable by a big iron ring set into it. He wondered what excuse he could invent to call in a mason and then for him to go down. Perhaps the portrait in the Master's Lodge would show that it was imperative that he find a way of getting into the crypt and indeed soon, if Nogle's prediction were accurate.

He had looked up at the stained glass, which included two representations of bishops, but he remembered that all the chapel glass either dated from before the re-foundation (some pieces of glass having been brought from Lolworth Abbey after its dissolution), or from a restoration in the 1750s. None of it was Tudor. Then he had noticed the portrait of a bishop in the ante-chapel, complete with an episcopal ring. With a surge of excitement he had examined it, only to see the date, 1694, making the portrait too late to fit the clue. However, it was then that he had gone to the inventory of college paintings, having realized that the clue could most easily refer to a portrait.

Since the visit to the chapel, Simon had made cursory examinations of the Tudor portraits that were in the Great Hall. None of them showed a fellow in bishop's robes, but this did not necessarily rule them out, since he had not yet discovered how many of them had become bishops at a later date. (Timpson, he had learned, was made a bishop in 1593, although the portrait had clearly been done some years earlier.) Two of the portraits, including that of Timpson, showed rings, but there seemed nothing special about where the rings were placed. Eventually he decided it was essential to get a glimpse of the portrait in the Lodge, and only then return to a thorough examination of the other portraits if it turned out not to be the one he sought.

The chapel clock chimed ten, and it was time to go to the Lodge.

The building of the new Master's Lodge in 1622 had been occasioned, in part, because the majority of post-Reformation Masters were married, and, unlike the case of fellows, the college was expected to provide accommodation for the Master's family and servants. However, the present Master, the Reverend Dr Arbuthnot Oliver James, lived alone except for two servants who had rooms in the attics. (For these, the Master had been careful to pick exceedingly plain women, in their sixties, being highly sensitive to any assumptions that might otherwise have been made.) There was also a valet, Lovelock, who came in on a daily basis.

When he arrived it was Lovelock who led him into the waiting room on the ground floor. Simon reflected that this was the first time he had ever entered this impressive Jacobean building, which was a shame, since the general assumption throughout Cambridge was that the palatial residences normally provided for the Masters were not only to enable them to live in style, but to entertain, and generally assist the social life of the college. But Dr James was an exceedingly

private man and, so far as Simon was aware, in the six years of his mastership only three or four formal luncheons or dinners had been given in the Lodge, on which occasions Vinman had been pressed into service.

The waiting room contained three portraits, but, to Simon's disappointment, the style indicated they were all from the late eighteenth century. There was also a glass-fronted cabinet that contained a selection of fine chess pieces, some beautifully carved in ivory and others made of porcelain or hardstone. He examined them with interest, and noticed there were three incomplete sets, and a number of individual pieces, obviously chosen because of their beauty or interest. He did not hear the Master enter the room, but turned round on hearing his voice.

"Ah, Weatherspoon, I see you find my chess pieces interesting."

"Yes, I've never seen anything quite like them."

The Master displayed a willingness to talk that Simon had never witnessed before. "I've been collecting for almost twenty years now," he said. "When I was young I used to play the game enthusiastically, but after I became a fellow at Pembroke I found I was just too busy to play seriously, so I started to collect the pieces as a kind of substitute for my former love of the game. The five pieces on the top shelf are Wedgwood, from the Flaxman models made in the late 1700s. They're some of the most interesting pieces I own and I only wish I had a complete set."

The Master crossed to the cabinet and pointed to one of the porcelain figures. There was a light in his eyes that indicated a true collector's passion. Simon had come across this passion once before in his life when he had been introduced to a collector of Greek vases for whom the drive to possess a particularly rare specimen had become an obsession.

"You see that jester over there, next to the queen? That's what the French call a '*fou*'. It's their name for the piece we call a 'bishop', which shows that the set from which these pieces came was made for the French market. The sets for the English market have regular bishops. I know of one complete set, owned by a duke, that has thirty-six instead of thirty-two pieces, because it contains four bishops and four jesters, so that it could be used in either country. I think it must have been specially ordered from Wedgwood."

"I knew that in Rome English bishops aren't thought to be real bishops, but I didn't know that French bishops aren't really bishops either!"

"Well, it's most interesting." The Master did not smile at Simon's weak joke, and he wondered whether it had passed him by or whether it was just a case of choosing not to respond to wit. Instead, he went on with his account of the pieces. "Some of the old Indian sets have elephants where we have bishops, while most German sets have 'runners'. However, the Swedish and Spanish sets have bishops, just as we do. Come upstairs to the drawing room and you'll see some more."

The Master led Simon up the staircase and into the spacious drawing room on the first floor. At one end there was a fine bay window that looked out over the river, while at the opposite end two windows looked over a small courtyard. Near one of these windows was a large desk and next to it another glass-fronted cabinet containing six complete sets of chessmen. Just to the left of the cabinet was the portrait that Simon had been looking for!

He realized immediately that this had to be the right painting. The sitter was un-named, but was clearly a Tudor bishop, seated on a window seat. Behind him was a stone wall and to his right there was painted the inside of a double window, divided by a stone column, thicker than a standard mullion, each half of the window being shaped in the Norman style. The window in the painting was glazed, the original wooden shutters having been replaced with hexagonal pieces of glass that were typical of the Tudor period. It was strikingly similar to the eight windows that ringed the gallery in the Great Hall of the keep, three of which still had their Tudor glass. The bishop's right hand was resting on the end of the seat and displayed a large ruby-coloured ring. On either side of the portrait there were two narrow panels, making the whole painting look rather like a triptych, except that the three sections were all on the same piece of canvas, separated only by narrow margins, painted in black. From where he stood it was difficult to make out what was in the panels, but nevertheless Simon was sure this was the painting he had been looking for. He longed to see exactly what lay behind the bishop's ring and what was painted in the side-panels, but he was anxious not to display any undue interest.

He forced himself to concentrate on the Master, who was describing a beautiful chess set on the top shelf of the cabinet. "This is a rare and exquisite example of Spanish chessmen. As you can see, each figure is set in a kind of pulpit – which is why these sets are often called 'pulpit pieces'. In this case, the pulpits are all of silver on one side and silver-gilt on the other, and the figures inside them are carved ivory. Usually both the pulpits and the figures are made from dried animal bone."

The Master unlocked the cabinet and opened the case. Very carefully he took out the king with the silver-gilt pulpit and handed it to Simon. "Look underneath it," he said.

Simon saw a neatly carved inscription cut into the silver; 'TF – Madrid – 1719' "It's the only dated Spanish set I've ever seen," the Master added proudly.

Simon pointed to the set that was immediately below the Spanish pieces. It was clearly Chinese, with each piece delicately carved in ivory and set on a kind of spherical stand. One side was in its original white and the other was stained red. Seeing his interest the Master took out the red king and continued with his exposition. "As you can see this is Chinese, with each piece set on top of what is called a 'devil's ball' – with one ball carved inside another. In this set there are nine concentric balls under the kings and queens, and I know of other sets where there are even more."

"It's incredible! It must have taken years to make a set like this."

"With a large example, like this, you're probably right. But oddly enough, sets like this are not nearly as interesting or valuable as the Spanish set. In the first place they're nothing like as rare; in the second, they're not as old. This one, I happen to know, was carved in Canton only five years ago. In the third place, from a collector's point of view they are just too fussy, like a lot of sets made for the export market rather than for local players. No-one would ever play with one of these sets, whereas the Spanish set is both beautiful and practical."

The Master replaced the chessman and took out a piece from another set, carved in the shape of a boat. "Can you guess what this is?" he asked.

"Well, I saw that you took it from one of the ends of the lines of major pieces, so it's got to be what we call a rook, but I've never seen a piece like this before."

"Not many people in England have – but in Russia it's the standard example of what we call a rook, which actually comes from a Persian word for a chariot. Some old sets have chariots for the corner pieces, while others have towers or a variety of other things, including ships, in Bengal and Russia. The variation adds to the interest in collecting chess pieces. This set was probably made in the province of Archangel in the mid 1700s, and it's carved from walrus ivory, like most Russian sets. Look, you can see the coarse grain at the  bottom of the piece where the nerve runs through the centre of the tusk. Elephant ivory is quite different in that respect."

The Master replaced the boat and motioned him to a chair. The portrait of the bishop was almost immediately opposite where he sat, and Simon decided he could risk one observation concerning it without raising too much suspicion.

"I see you have a portrait that includes what looks like part of the gallery in the old keep."

"Oh, yes," the Master replied, "When I first moved into the Lodge and saw this portrait I assumed it had been painted in the

63

keep, though this puzzled me because if the portrait were painted from life the painter would need to be on a piece of scaffolding, high above the floor of the old hall! But later I realized that it can't be a picture of our keep here at De Vere, but of the almost identical one at Hedingham. Do you know Hedingham castle?"

"I think I may have heard the name, but I've certainly never seen it."

"Well it's the ancient seat of the de Vere family, or at least it was until they lost most of their money in the sixteenth and seventeenth centuries. It's in Essex, only a little over twenty miles to the west of here. The similarity is very likely due to the interest taken in both buildings by the builder-Archbishop, William de Corbueil, who was said to have been consulted over the designs of both Hedingham and Cambridge castles – as well as the huge keep at Rochester – being something of an architect as well as a churchman. I've never actually been inside the keep at Hedingham, but I've been in the gardens, and look, here they are in the left-hand panel."

Simon reflected that William de Corbueil was not the only clergyman to combine differing professions. Seizing the opportunity provided by the Master's words, he walked right up to the painting. The Master joined him, pointing to the two views, painted on either side of the portrait. The one on the left showed a distant view of the whole castle, including the grounds, and the scene was clearly not that of any part of Cambridge. Moreover, the castle's forebuilding was half fallen down, which was certainly not the case at Cambridge. Also, he noticed that the windows in the top storey were large, single lights, rather than the double windows that adorned the top floor at De Vere's, copying the double lights of the gallery to the Great Hall, set immediately below them. The right hand panel, also painted in a kind of miniaturist style, showed the interior of the Great Hall, with a small representation of the same bishop that was painted in the main picture, seated in one of the gallery window seats and looking upwards, as if in prayer. Of course, Simon realized, this arrangement allowed one to see which of the eight windows the subject was sitting in, and thence to help anyone who found the clue to unravel it.

"The painter at Hedingham would have the same problem of where to sit while he did the painting," commented Simon.

"Yes, you're right. I presume the painting was done first, somewhere else, and then the background was added later. But it is rather odd."

Simon wondered whether he might have gone too far, for the last thing he wanted to do was draw attention to the painting, and especially to any oddness about it. He glanced quickly at the episcopal ring, confirming that it lay right at the end of the seat, close to the window, and then forced himself to turn away and walk back to his chair. To cover any apparent interest in the painting he changed the subject. "I've never seen such beautiful chessmen," he said.

"Yes, yes, some other time I will be happy to show you the whole collection; but we have something urgent to discuss. As the two people who witnessed the scene in Dr Higgins's rooms we have to reach a common mind. I've been considering the matter, and I'm sure that whoever did this terrible thing came from outside the college."

"But, as I remarked when we met just after the murder, if that is so, why would the murderer only take the old papers and leave all the seemingly more valuable things untouched?"

The Master embarked on one of his narrations characterized by his habit of starting almost every utterance with 'yes', or 'ah yes', and which formed the butt of many jokes within the university.

"Ah, yes, that's what led me, originally, to wonder if the murderer could be one of our colleagues. But look at the evidence that points the other way. First, there are those keys – surely, the property of some professional thief – and surely not the kind of thing one of the fellows would have. Second, just go through the list of fellows and of the guests that were there when Higgins talked about the Courcey documents. Can you really imagine any one of them doing something like this? Then, third, and I think most importantly, remember that Higgins was not one to keep everything to himself. I was talking to the librarian at Trinity Hall, Mr Bambridge, only two days ago, and out of the blue he asked me if I'd had a chance to see the Courcey documents. Evidently Higgins had talked about them, at least to some

65

fellow librarians, so all kinds of people outside the college may have got to know about them. Given the fascination with any story to do with treasure you can easily see how some villain may have decided to get his hands on the papers."

Simon was uncertain. It was true that Higgins had a close circle of friends, mostly lovers of books, and he might have talked to some of these about the papers, or even perhaps have actually shown the papers to them. On the other hand, Mr Bambridge – whom he had met on the two occasions when he had dined in Higgins's rooms – was a very shy man, and certainly not one to spread what might be considered confidential information. It was more likely, Simon thought, that some of the other fellows had loose tongues, notwithstanding the request to keep the finding of the papers confidential, and so the news about the treasure might well have passed beyond the college this way. All in all the Master could be right about the murderer being an outsider, but this led him to voice the obvious question that arose.

"Last time we talked you suggested we might have to do some detective work ourselves in order to protect the good name of the college. Are you saying you no longer think this is a good idea?"

The Master looked uncomfortable. "Ah, well, yes – well, I'm not really sure. Perhaps a little very discreet inquiry about who else knows about the Courcey documents – but nothing that makes it look as if we're not happy with the official investigation. Perhaps I was too hasty when I made the suggestion about turning detective – and too much under the shock of finding poor old Higgins like that."

"Do you have any idea what was in those de Vere papers, apart from the hints that Higgins gave us?"

"No, I've absolutely no idea."

"Well, I suppose it's obvious that there are two very different possibilities. The first concerns an interest in the treasure. Following this idea, either the thief was party to the discussion that took place in the Senior Combination Room, or, like Mr Bambridge, he heard about the Courcey documents from Higgins and suspected a possible clue to the Lolworth treasure. The second possibility, instead of focussing on the treasure, takes up the possible implications for the new venture at Stratford-upon-Avon. Perhaps the thief was anxious to see if there were anything in the de Vere papers that might cast doubt on the Shakespearean authorship of the plays, since that could have worrying implications for the Stratford venture."

The Master looked shocked. "Surely you're not suggesting Viscount FitzSimmons could have anything remotely to do with this outrage?"

Simon lied. He had taken a dislike to the noble lord, and although he couldn't imagine him being involved in the murder in person, he could conceive of a plot to which he was privy. "No, no, of course not. But there could be other, less reputable people, who had an interest in the affair, for business reasons."

"But you don't give any credence to the ridiculous hypothesis about de Vere's authorship of *Hamlet* and the other plays?"

Simon found himself lying again, and noticed, in another of his interior reflections that went side by side with his speaking, how much this was becoming a habit since the onset of the whole pretence that Amelia Buzzard had got him into. "No, no, of course not. But the point isn't whether you or I give any credence to the de Vere hypothesis, it's whether other people, including complete madcaps, do so. Also, one has to remember that there are many people out there, especially in the popular press, who would like any excuse to poke fun at the literary establishment. Now I come to think of it, there are a number of journalists who might have good reasons for trying to get a look at those papers. I don't suppose they would kill for them, but one of them might have been surprised while breaking in, using those keys we found, and then there could have been some kind of unfortunate accident."

To Simon's surprise the Master seemed to take this last suggestion seriously. After a pause he said, "That's an interesting idea. Perhaps you are right and it's the journalists the police should be looking at. But in any case, I don't think it's a job for you and me."

The Master got up, indicating that the conversation was over, and after a few formal exchanges Simon went back to his rooms. As he walked across the court he wondered how quickly he could arrange a visit to Hedingham castle and what excuse he could find for going there. Hedingham castle was, it appeared, a sort of twin to the keep at de Vere. Moreover, not only was it a mere day's journey away: it had been in the hands of the de Vere family for all its early history, including the time when Edward de Vere and William Courcey had been friends. Perhaps Henry VIII's men could not find the monastic treasure because they were looking in the wrong castle. He had to examine the gallery that ran round the Great Hall of that keep, and in particular the seat in the window above and to the left of the fireplace.

Chapter 9

The train from Cambridge to London,
Thursday, 19th March.

S imon took the early train to Bishopsgate, and in addition to a
spare copy of *First Maccabees* he brought with him the most
recent edition of the *Old Chelsea Review* that had arrived by
post the morning before. Among the reviews was one by Theresa,
which he read for the second time, in anticipation of their meeting
for lunch. (The review was of a recent book by a little-known woman
novelist, and his curiosity arose simply from his new interest in the
reviewer and in such insights into her way of thinking as might be
given.) In her letter, responding to his invitation, she had written "I
would be delighted to come", and although her reply had been brief,
the evident warmth of tone led him to hope that in the evening she
could be persuaded to come to the concert at St James's Hall, where
the great German violinist Herr Joachim was scheduled to give a
recital that included Bach's Chaconne.

He put down the *Old Chelsea Review* and looked out at the passing
countryside. They rattled past a village church, and the graveyard
alongside it set him thinking about Higgins's funeral, six days before.
It had been a sad occasion, with the sister and her young children on
the verge of tears throughout the ceremony. What made the service
particularly stressful for him was the fact that the eulogy had been
given by the Master. Everyone in the college knew that Dr James
disliked Higgins intensely, and his sanctimonious talk was a classic
case of hypocrisy.

To wrench his thoughts from the painful scene, he pulled from his pocket the small notebook he had purloined from Dr Higgins's rooms. He had already looked at it many times, and had been disappointed at how little helpful information it gave. He decided to scan it again in case there was something he had missed.

The notebook contained three sections, corresponding to the three divisions in which Higgins had evidently placed the documents. The first section was headed 'Henry Courcey' and listed eighteen letters written by Henry to his younger brother, William, Master of De Vere College. The list simply gave the dates of the letters, in historical order, with no indication of the contents. The second section was headed 'de Vere' and listed seven letters written by Edward de Vere to William Courcey, again with their dates, but also giving the addresses from which they were written. Simon had noted that the last three were sent from Hackney, which fitted well with what Higgins had said when he described his discovery of the papers. Again, there was no indication of their contents and no copy of any reply made by William Courcey. The third section was headed 'Miscellaneous' and began with a list of letters written by five additional correspondents, one of whom was known by name to Simon: John Aylmer, an Elizabethan Bishop of London. Following this was written 'A list of books owned by William Courcey, ten of which are marked with a star'. Unfortunately there was no identification of these books in the notebook, and no indication of why some were starred.

Simon returned to the end of the first section where, after the list of letters, were two short and puzzling entries. One read: 'Number 17 from Henry Courcey lent to A.O.J.'. The initials, which he recognized immediately, were the same as those of the Master, and led to all kinds of possible speculations. If, as seemed probable, the letter had been lent to the Master it was odd he hadn't mentioned the matter at the time of their joint discovery that all the other papers had been stolen. The other entry was truly baffling. It contained six lines of what looked like nonsense, the first of which read: 'Dpoufout pg wfoufe dibncfs'.

He looked yet again at this strange entry. At first, he had thought the words were written in some foreign language, but he soon decided it was probably a code, composed either by Higgins in order to hide the nature of the papers, or possibly by Courcey himself. For the twentieth time in the eleven days since he obtained the notebook he tried to make sense of the words – and then it hit him. He had been looking for some complex code, like the one in which a key word indicates how the first letter of a message should be moved forwards or backward in the alphabet, in accordance with the number in the alphabet of the first letter in the key word – and then how the second letter should be changed, and so on, until all the letters in the key word had been used. Then one started the whole process again, using, for the second time, the first letter in the key word. But now he saw that Higgins's code was much simpler, and once seen, perfectly clear. It was almost certainly designed by Higgins, not to confound someone who had leisure to work at it, but to prevent the meaning being obvious to someone who had the opportunity to glance at the entry in the notebook, such as the servant, or 'gyp', who cleaned his rooms. Each of the letters in the original had simply been raised to the next letter as it occurred in the order of the alphabet.

Two minutes of work with a pencil, placing the correct letters below the coded ones, revealed how the six lines should be read. The result ran:

Contents of vented chamber

Four chests of reliquiae, with holy relics
Eight illuminated manuscripts
Wooden chests, with sundry items of gold, silver and ivory
Two wooden chests containing nine sets of pieces for chess
Bishop Odo's mace

Simon felt his heartbeat rising. The documents included an inventory of the treasure hidden in 1539, most likely a list found by Higgins within the letters written by Henry Courcey, and to his amazement, in addition to the relics and the reliquiae (probably jewelled boxes holding the relics), which would be the expected content of any medieval abbey's treasure, the other items in the list included not one, but nine sets of chessmen!

Simon's mind went back to the Master's passion. Could this be coincidence? Surely, it had to be, since the Master had begun his collection twenty years ago when – as Simon recalled – he had been a fellow of Pembroke, and could have had no possible idea about what was hidden at De Vere College or, as now seemed likely, at Hedingham castle. But Simon had an instinctive dislike of coincidences, and in fact one of the things that irritated him most about some of the novels he had read before turning his own hand to the art was the artificiality of so many coincidences that seemed essential for the weaker plots. No doubt it was a coincidence that the Master collected some of the things that happened to be in the treasure, but if he knew about the Lolworth chessmen – perhaps from the letter 'lent to A.O.J.' – then all kinds of connections became possible.

His eyes returned to the list, and especially to the last item, Bishop Odo's mace. Churchmen, he recalled, were not meant to draw blood; however – especially in the middle ages – by a strange irony it was considered quite proper for prince-bishops to carry maces into battle with which they could crush an opponent's head. He recalled the medieval history he had been taught as a boy by a gifted teacher at Manchester Grammar School. William the Conqueror, he remembered, had a half-brother called Odo who was both Bishop of Bayeux and, later on, Earl of Kent; a prince-bishop if ever there were one. He had been at the Battle of Hastings, wielding a mace and helping to rally the Norman soldiers. With a slight grin he remembered one of the anecdotes told by his teacher. According to the story, some years after the great battle, Odo was in dispute with the King, who arrested him in person and put him in prison for four years. When the Pope complained about the arrest of a bishop the King replied that he had arrested the earl but not the bishop! Whatever the truth of this matter, there was no doubt this

Odo had a mace, and that this could be it, even though it was quite likely there were other bishops who had borne that name.

Thinking about Bishop Odo stirred something in his conscience. Was his own dual life – as a clergyman and a novelist – so very different from Odo's double life as both churchman and warrior? Perhaps, if his novels had been what the general public would call 'elevating', there would be a case for saying they were just an extension of his regular profession, but given their content, let alone the financial motive that, at least in part, was their motivation, this would be a hard case to defend.

His inner reverie returned to the inventory of the treasure. The mace was an odd thing to be kept at the abbey, although, perhaps, no odder than the chessmen. On the other hand Simon recalled some medieval writers complaining about the lax life-style of certain monasteries, and including in their complaints the claim that the monks played chess when they should have been at their prayers. Even so, having nine chess sets seemed strange. Perhaps one of the abbots had a collecting instinct that included both chess sets and historic pieces of armour, or again, in the case of the mace, perhaps Odo's family had some connection with the abbey.

His thoughts were interrupted by the guard's cry 'Bishopsgate! Bishopsgate!' It was time to prepare himself for his second meeting with Theresa Brown.

Chapter 10

Le Français, London, the same day, 12. 30 p.m.

Theresa and Simon lunched at Le Français, in a little sidestreet off the Strand, and the meal was a great success. Both – so it turned out – enjoyed French cooking, and as they pored over the menu they quickly got onto the subject of French wine, on which, to Simon's surprise, Theresa was well informed. She turned Simon's surprise into a friendly rebuke. "Why should you be amazed that I know something about French wines, when you would not be surprised if one of your male friends showed a similar expertise? Isn't this just another indication of the false assumptions that underlie our culture?"

It was said in a friendly way, but Simon felt a slight edge to the question, and remembered hearing how Theresa could be quite formidable when roused.

He thought of a way to re-establish his radical credentials. They were still looking at the menu when the waiter approached with the wine list and Simon indicated that it should be given to Theresa. The waiter hesitated, his face a study in puzzlement, but when Theresa put out her hand he gave it to her and left.

"What are we going to eat?" she asked.

They both chose Boeuf Bourguignonne. Theresa glanced at the waiter, who came over to them, his now impassive face a testimony to his professional manner. She ordered the 1864 red Corton.

"I think it will be a bit young," she commented, "but it's one of my favourite Burgundies, and it should go well with the meal. I hope you will allow me to pay for the wine – after all, and let's be quite frank about this – I probably earn quite a lot more than you do as a fellow of De Vere. Also, you can think of it as a kind of return gift: I mean for the copy of *First Maccabees*."

Simon felt stumped. He had never known a woman make such a suggestion, and he certainly didn't feel comfortable with it. At the same time he found himself analysing his discomfort and wondering whether it was, in reality, a symptom of prejudice. After all, if the woman were richer than the man, why shouldn't she pay, whatever convention laid down?

He told a half-truth. "No, no, please, let me pay – and really it's no problem. I don't only rely on my fellowship stipend: I have some private means, though I don't let on about this at De Vere in case it would cause envy among the other fellows."

"Well, I'll agree to let you pay for everything on condition that I pay for the meal next time."

A sudden sense of happiness filled him. There was likely to be a 'next time'. "I'll agree to that," he replied, "but under protest, since I can perfectly well afford it." He grinned as he added. "I nearly always travel second or third class even though I can afford first class. When I do travel first I find myself looking round to see if anyone I know can see me. I suppose it must look rather like a kind of reverse snobbery, but actually it's not that, or at least not only that. I really don't like the idea of standing apart."

"What about being a doctor of Divinity when you're still in your twenties?"

"You've been checking up on me! But the answer is that in Cambridge it really doesn't matter; and I was lucky at my school, because there you weren't considered peculiar just because you liked books and did well in exams."

As in their first conversation at the reception, Simon wished he could take back some of the words he had just uttered. They could easily be misunderstood, as if he were saying, "I know I'm really clever, but I try not to show off", and, for good measure, he had also suggested "Even though I'm only a Cambridge don, I do have private money." Both indications could easily sound quite the wrong note, perhaps not to most women, but to someone of Theresa's discernment.

Then his inner voice came back in another mode. "No, you're exaggerating the problem. You're simply expressing what you think – or rather the half-truth that's now becoming your trade-mark."

To Simon's relief the conversation turned to the relative merits of claret and Burgundy, Simon generally preferring the former and Theresa the latter. Half way through the bottle Simon felt bold enough to ask about the evening. He was spending the night at a hotel so that he could hear Joachim; and would she be interested in joining him for the concert?

"I'm afraid I can't," she responded. "Really I'd like to, but I have promised to join a party – eight of us from the staff of the *Old Chelsea Review*. We're going to *The Lady and the Devil* at the Royal St James's Theatre. I've heard mixed things about the play, but it sounds fun. Come to that, why don't you join us? We could almost certainly get another ticket?"

Simon hesitated. His real reason was a reluctance to be in a large group, partly because he wanted to speak more privately with Theresa, partly because, at this stage of their relationship, he would rather not provoke gossip. "I'm tempted," he said, "but I had set my heart on hearing Joachim, especially as he's going to play Bach's 'Chaconne'. Do you know the piece?"

Theresa did not, and the conversation turned to music which Theresa enjoyed, although not a regular concertgoer. However, under some gentle pressure she agreed to go with Simon the following Thursday night to Handel's *Acis and Galatea*, which was due to be performed in St James's Hall. Somehow the conversation changed to architecture, and in the process, during the cheeses, Simon mentioned that he was planning to visit Hedingham castle over the weekend. His stated reason, still another half-truth, was that he had only recently learned how similar it was to the keep at De Vere, and this had aroused his curiosity. Theresa's response was unexpected.

"How extraordinary!" she said, "I've been there several times, although I don't think I've ever been inside the great tower. I have an uncle who lives in Sudbury, which is only a few miles away from Hedingham, and when I was little we sometimes had picnics in the grounds."

"Can one go inside the castle? I really would like to see if there are any differences from De Vere's keep."

"I'm sure you can, although I seem to remember that one needs to make arrangements with the custodian beforehand. It's not a ruin, although it's pretty shabby inside, and the battlements as well as the whole forebuilding are fallen down. I don't think anyone has lived there for a long time. My uncle knows the owner, and I can easily write and arrange for us both to see the old place."

Provisional plans were quickly made. Next Thursday they would meet again in London and after dinner they would go together to *Acis and Galatea*. After staying the night in a hotel, Simon would spend the Friday working in the British Museum Library, and on the next day Theresa and he would travel to Sudbury together by train. Meanwhile, Theresa would ask her uncle to arrange their trip by horse and trap from Sudbury to Hedingham. All things considered, even if the Joachim concert had not worked out, everything else had exceeded Simon's expectations.

Chapter 11

London, Friday, 20ᵗʰ March.

On the Friday morning Simon woke early in his hotel room, his mind awash with conflicting thoughts and emotions, most of which were the result of happenings on the previous day. First, there had been the meeting with Theresa. After the lunch she had had to go back to her office, but now he was looking forward with eagerness to his first evening alone with her. He only wished it could be sooner than the six days his return to Cambridge necessitated. Then, there was last night's concert, which had filled his mind with the opening theme from the Chaconne, a theme which came again and again – both within the piece itself and in his memory of the concert – each time with a sort of increased intensity of emotion in a way that parallelled his repeated imaginings of encounters with Theresa. Finally, and in a less happy vein, was the meeting with Nogle in the afternoon. Nogle, as always, was friendly, and had arranged for a property agent to meet him at his hotel immediately after breakfast in order to show him some likely houses. Also, he had spoken to the firm's lawyers, and there appeared to be no reason why Simon could not buy a property in another name, provided this did not involve any kind of financial fraud. The worrying factor was an approach to the publishing house by a journalist from one of the popular papers, the *London Echo*, in which some suspicious questions about the true authorship of the books by both Amelia Buzzard and Emily Dove were raised.

Nogle, to whom the journalist had been referred, had vouchsafed nothing, but by judicious questioning had gathered that the paper had inside information that might be sensational. It was clear the editor was trying to get some confirmation of this information before going to press, being aware that if he got things wrong there could be heavy penalties for libel. This had given Nogle an idea. He had intimated that if the journalist would come back in two weeks, he would see what information he could give him, but if anything were written before, then absolutely nothing would be forthcoming. At the end of the conversation Nogle had expressed himself to Simon in these words. "I think this is the best we can do. The matter's virtually certain to come out soon, and now it looks as if whoever stole the documents is trying to make money out of them. If he's shown the papers to the *London Echo*, which is what I suspect, they will be very nervous about legal action, especially since they must suspect the papers were acquired by theft, so I think they're playing a clever game so that they can use the information without quoting the source directly. If

I'm right, we can play for time – holding out the carrot of more information – and I can probably put the man off a little beyond the two weeks. I'm thinking of having a convenient case of influenza when the journalist comes back and postponing the meeting for a few days, but whatever we do they're going to find a way of leaking the information sooner or later, even if they don't quote the stolen papers. In fact, they may not bother to check back with me at all. I think you had better prepare for an explosion. It looks as if De Vere College is soon going to make the headlines again."

After breakfast Simon looked at four properties, and given the urgency of the situation he decided, then and there, to make an offer on one of them, a Regency house that stood in the middle of a crescent-shaped terrace, which, among other attractions, had a pleasant garden at the back and a spacious, well-ventilated cellar. Within two hours the contract was signed, thanks to Nogle's introduction to a discreet firm of solicitors, 'Booth and Rankin'. Because he had immediate cash available, the house was to be his with vacant possession in a matter of days, registered under the ownership of Mr Simon W. Spoon.

Chapter 12

De Vere College, the same day.

S imon got back to his rooms in De Vere College in the late afternoon, and was just debating whether to attend the chapel service before formal hall when there was a knock on the door. To his surprise it was Mr Bambridge.

Nathan Bambridge, the librarian of Trinity Hall, was a man of unusually small stature, now in his mid fifties, having been a bachelor fellow of his college for over twenty-five years. His academic subject was Roman law, but his passion, like that of Higgins, was for old books. Simon recalled that at the dinner parties where they had met it had been hard to get the conversation going on any other topic. Bambridge now seemed embarrassed, and the slight stutter he often displayed was more pronounced than ever.

"I'm truly s-sorry to disturb you," he said, "but do you think I c-could come in and ask you about something."

"Yes, of course." Simon steered him to a chair and poured out a glass of dry sherry – which he remembered was to Bambridge's liking. He decided it might reduce his visitor's evident agitation if he anticipated the likely reason for his call.

"I expect your visit has to do with the tragic events of the past fortnight. I think we both held Dr Higgins in high regard, and I must tell you that his death remains a complete mystery."

"Thank you." Bambridge swirled the sherry in his glass, smelt it carefully, and then continued. "I think this is the same F-Fino that dear old Higgins used to serve. Yes, it - it is in connection with his death that I have come to see you." After a pause he continued, "How much do you know about the Courcey documents?"

It was not a question Simon had expected, and he collected himself before answering, "Only a little. A few days before his death Higgins told all the fellows about finding the documents; but he didn't say anything about them except that they were mostly letters, including some to William Courcey from his old friend Edward de Vere."

"He told me of letters around the same time, probably the next day, but I got the impression that apart from the fellows in his own college no-one else knew, and that for the time being he wanted to keep the discovery quiet. But he did promise to let me see them, and, well, I just wondered if there were some way I could look at them. I understand you have been made librarian 'pro-tem' – until an official appointment of a new librarian has been made, so I presume the papers are now in your charge."

"Well yes, I am temporally in charge of the library." Simon paused, wondering how much more to disclose. He decided that despite his recent resort to mendacity, as far as possible he should try to keep to the old adage 'if in doubt, tell the truth'. Almost always, keeping to this rule made things simpler, partly because you didn't have to keep remembering all the lies you had told.

"Can I trust you with another confidence?"

Bambridge nodded.

"The papers have gone. Whoever killed Higgins took them, except, so far as I know, for one letter from Henry Courcey which he lent to the Master."

Simon stopped suddenly. Of course, he only knew about the letter lent to 'A.O.J.' from the notebook he had taken. His determination to tell the truth was certainly going to be stretched if the source of his knowledge were asked!

Bambridge was staring at him. "Stolen! But that's extraordinary. Was anything else taken?"

"The police have asked me not to say anything, but since you know about the papers you might as well know the rest but, let us agree, in strictest confidence."

Simon thought of a way of covering his mistake in letting slip about the letter lent to the Master, and added, "In fact, if you don't mind, I must ask you not to let the Master know that I've spoken to you, either about the theft or about the letter in his possession. He and I were together when the police cautioned us, and if they find out I've been telling you things I may get into trouble. But to answer your question, no, nothing else seems to have been taken, and as you say, the whole thing is very odd."

"What do the police say – I mean about the missing papers?"

It was Simon's turn to feel embarrassment, but he decided to keep going with the truth unless the conversation involved the notebook.

"Well, er, as a matter of fact we – that is the Master and I – didn't tell them. We felt the papers were very much a matter for the De Vere community to think about, and we simply didn't want anyone outside the college getting hold of some idea that might seem sensational."

Bambridge looked hard at Simon, and it was evident he suspected that the whole truth had not been told. Not telling the police about what had been stolen, was, after all, a pretty strange thing to do, and it would be no wonder if it looked suspicious. Simon wondered if Bambridge had made a link with the story of the treasure, or just possibly, whether Higgins had discussed a possible connection with him. Was Bambridge just interested, as a scholar, in some newly discovered Tudor letters, or was he specially interested in what they might reveal?

The college bell sounded. Evensong in the chapel would now be drawing to a close, and dinner would begin in a few minutes. After some polite exchanges Bambridge excused himself and Simon picked up his M.A. gown, ready for the evening meal at high table. He was hoping to arrange things so that he could sit next to Talworthy again, and see if he could steer the conversation in such a way that the keeper of the paintings would enlarge on the subject of the Tudor portrait in the Master's Lodge.

Chapter 13

De Vere College, later the same day.

Simon was the first to arrive in the Senior Combination Room, where the fellows assembled before dinner at the high table. On Friday evenings, as a recognition that most of the week's work was done, sherry was available before the meal, and this tended to bring a number of the fellows into the Com-bination Room earlier than would otherwise have been the case. When Mr Vinman entered at half past seven to announce that the students were assembled and ready for the Latin grace which preceded the meal, there were nine fellows present and two guests, but, to Simon's surprise, no sign of the Master. In term time it was most unusual for him not to be at formal hall, and on the few occasions when he had to be absent – usually because of a feast at another

college – he always warned the Senior Fellow. However, on this occasion Professor Townend indicated he had had no warning. Following tradition, he did not delay, but led the other fellows into Great Hall, himself taking the seat at the far end of the high table. There was no special order in which the other fellows were expected to sit – unlike the more formal seating in the Combination Room – and Simon had no difficulty finding a seat next to Talworthy. By the end of the soup, he had got the Junior Fellow talking about the portrait of the bishop in the Master's Lodge.

"You're right," he said, "according to the description in the inventory the painting is unusual because not only is it a full-body portrait, but also because there are panels on either side of the main section. I would like to know if they are really part of the original painting or were added later. I can probably tell when I see it."

"When do you think you'll be able to examine it carefully?"

"Well, actually it's a little difficult. There are about twenty paintings in the Lodge that I ought to look at properly in case any repairs are necessary, but, as you know, Dr James does not like people coming into the Lodge. When I tried to make a quick tour, just to confirm the pictures listed there were all safe, he wouldn't even let me go up to the first floor, where most of the pictures in the inventory are said to be. He said he had very private papers in both the drawing room and his study, and for the present I would just have to take his word that the paintings were there."

The conversation turned to a more general discussion of painting, and Talworthy and Simon shared experiences of visits to Italy, where, on different occasions, both of them had been overwhelmed by the galleries of Florence. Simon's inner thoughts noted how commonly senior members of De Vere seemed to have private obsessions; Higgins with books, the Master with chessmen, Talworthy with paintings, and perhaps he should add himself, with his secret life as a novelist. He wondered if an inventory of university fellows would highlight a general tendency to such passions, perhaps engendered by the cloistered life so many led.

After hall, over the port and Madeira, their conversation continued. At 11.00 there were just the two of them still there, the port almost finished, and a pleasant and companionable atmosphere abounding.

When there was less than an inch of wine in either decanter, the college tradition allowed Mr Vinman to finish it. However, it was said that his measurement of the inch was not very accurate, and the two of them, in the interests of humour rather than real detective work, decided to leave exactly one and a half inches of each wine, and then to check the decanters after breakfast. Since all the decanters – those in use and those in reserve – were kept in a small room that could only be entered from the Combination Room, along with the less valuable high table silverware that was in daily use, this should not be difficult. After they had made as careful measurements as they could, given their somewhat unsteady hands, Simon decided to return to his rooms with the hope of summoning up enough energy to continue his work on *Second Maccabees*. However, just as he stood up to leave there was a loud knock on the outside door of the Combination Room, and without waiting for a reply, the porter on duty, Finton, came in.

He looked worried. "Excuse me sirs, but I thought I'd better find someone in authority. I think there may be something wrong at the Lodge."

Simon, as the senior fellow of the two, got up quickly. "What's wrong? Has the Master called you?"

"No, sir. Two of the students came to me just now. They were passing the Lodge and when they looked up towards the large windows of the drawing room they saw that one of them was broken. They called up to ask if everything was all right, but there was no answer. They came to me and I went to see the broken window. Then I rang the doorbell at the Lodge but there was no reply. I don't know quite what to think, or what to do, sir."

"I think Mr Talworthy and I had better take a look. The Master was not at hall, and it's possible he may have been taken ill. Please get the emergency keys and meet us at the entrance to the Lodge."

The news seemed to have driven the effects of the alcohol from their blood, and the two fellows went quickly to the Lodge, and themselves tried the bell. There was no response.

As they waited Talworthy speculated, "Perhaps Dr James had some kind of heart attack and fell, breaking the window as he did so. But if that's the case why doesn't one of the servants come?"

"I think I can answer that," said Simon. "I happen to know that Mrs Jenners is away, visiting her even older mother, who's something well up in her eighties. As for the other one, Mrs Cartwright, she sleeps right up at the top, and she's been almost totally deaf for the past two years."

Finton arrived and Simon took the key labelled 'Lodge – front door'. Fortunately the door was not bolted on the inside and they were able to go in. The gas lights were on and by their light they made their way upstairs to the drawing room, Simon calling out as they went, "Hello, hello, is all well?"

The three men entered the drawing room. The first thing they noticed were the papers scattered all over the floor. The drawers of the desk and of two cupboards were open, and showed ugly marks where the locks had been hurriedly broken. Then, initially hidden from them by the overturned chair, they saw the Master by the broken window – but he had not been taken ill. He was lying full length, with the desk chair on which he had evidently been sitting broken by his fall. There was a large gash in the back of his head. Sitting on the middle of the desk was a bronze statuette, its base covered in blood. What had happened, at least in general terms, was clear. As he sat at his desk, which was set at a right angle to the window, the Master had been struck from behind. It looked as if he must have half risen before falling, breaking both the chair and the window as he fell. The attacker had then calmly put the weapon, probably seized from somewhere on the ground floor, onto the desk and begun to ransack the room. Simon felt the Master's neck, acutely conscious of having made the same action only a few days before in Higgins's rooms. But this time it was not quite the same: the Master was unconscious, but still alive.

Simon thought quickly, and then spoke to Finton. As night porter he would have no colleagues standing by, and therefore he should not be asked to stay away from his post for long.

"Finton, please rouse two of the students in staircase C, the one nearest the gate. Get them out of bed if necessary. Send one to Dr Carrs in Bridge Street, and the other one to the police station by Parker's Piece. Then keep your station in the porter's lodge until they come. Mr Talworthy and I will stay here and see to the Master as best we can."

Finton left hurriedly while Simon and Talworthy knelt by the Master. "I don't know if we should move him," said Simon. "When Higgins was attacked the Master and I moved the body and the police were not pleased because we might have destroyed evidence."

"But Higgins was already dead," Talworthy replied. "Dr James is still bleeding and we've got to try and prevent more loss of blood."

Without further discussion they carried the Master to the day couch near the bay window and propped up his bleeding head, placing a towel from the downstairs bathroom under it. The blood was congealed, and although there had been a significant loss the flow had now almost stopped. It looked as if concussion rather than loss of blood was the main cause of concern. He was breathing heavily but regularly, and Simon suspected he would come to within the hour. However, this surmise, he admitted to himself, was based more on his reading of recent fiction, part of the preparation for his own novels, than on any real knowledge of medicine.

Five minutes passed without any change in the Master's condition and Talworthy's eyes started to wander round the drawing room, looking at each painting in turn. Sensing there was nothing more to be done before the doctor's arrival, he stepped over the scattered papers and went over to the portrait of the bishop and looked at it closely. Simon joined him. "Look," said Talworthy, "this panel on the left isn't by the same hand as the main painting, nor, unless I'm very much mistaken, is the panel on the right, which looks to me by the same hand as the left panel. Both are less well executed than the main painting, and the brush strokes are quite different."

"Do you think they were added much later?"

"No, I don't think so: they look, from the style and from the general condition, to be of a similar period."

"Is this unusual?"

"Not really. There could be several explanations. One is that the original panels got lost or damaged quite soon after they were done, so they ordered replacements from whoever was around. But I think it more likely that the original painter, who looks to have been pretty skilled, just became caught up in other work and never completely finished the commission – that is, assuming there were always meant to be the two panels on either side. That sort of thing – I mean not finishing a commission – happened quite often, and there was probably some kind of fight about the final fee."

"Do you want to seize the chance to look at some of the other paintings? I know it seems a bit mean to use this opportunity – but after all you are the keeper of the paintings. I also think that we ought to check on the rest of the Lodge to see if anything's missing and whether Mrs Cartwright is safe."

Simon led the way and they went together to the attics. From a bedroom door, half open, they could hear loud snoring so, satisfied that the servant was all right, they had a quick glance inside all the other rooms. Nothing seemed to have been touched in the attics, but on the bedroom floor below it all the rooms had been ransacked, with the locked drawers forced and every cupboard door left open, with the exception of those with glass fronts. It was the same story on the first floor, where in the study, opening off the drawing room, they found the greatest confusion. It contained another desk, from which all the drawers had been taken right out and their contents spread over the floor. The ground floor rooms had been given similar treatment, with every drawer and cupboard opened in the dining and in the reception room where Simon had waited for the Master only a few days before, but again, the glazed cupboards were untouched.

Almost as soon as they returned to check on the Master the doorbell rang and Talworthy went down. Simon lingered, staring round the Master's study. On the mantelpiece was a silver porringer, dating from the late seventeenth century, and two eighteenth-century silver tankards. He shivered slightly. There was something sinister here, and an unpleasant reminder of the theft at Higgins's rooms. The thief was leaving valuable things behind, including, it would appear, all the chessmen, because he was after something that was, for him, still more valuable and which he could see was not in the glass-fronted cupboards. In the last few days he had begun to wonder if the Master had some involvement in the affair, for he was one of the few who knew the potential value of the Courcey documents and there were several suspicious things about his behaviour. But now it looked as if the suspicions were misplaced. It was almost certain that whoever struck Higgins had also struck the Master. But who on earth could it be?

Chapter 14

De Vere College, later the same evening and the two following days.

Talworthy brought Dr Carrs upstairs, and barely had the examination of the Master begun when he came to. His first act was to vomit all over the couch and his suit. As he started to sit up Dr Carrs supported his back and began to wipe his suit with the towel that had been under his head, but the Master, almost rudely, waved him away. After quickly looking round him, and despite the protests of Dr Carrs, Talworthy and Simon, he got up and walked, albeit shakily, straight to the adjoining study. On seeing the disturbance, he immediately got on all fours and started to scrabble through the papers on the floor. After a minute he uttered a groan. He then got up and, ignoring further protests, went back into the drawing room and checked his precious chess sets. As Simon had already seen, they were unharmed. Rather shakily, and holding on to the arm of the doctor, the Master went downstairs and into the waiting room. Seeing the glass-fronted cabinet undamaged he seemed to relax, and only then, sitting on a chair in the same room, did he allow Dr Carrs to examine him carefully.

During the examination Simon and Talworthy waited in the drawing room above, saying nothing. After about five minutes they were joined by Heatherington. He had been out late at a feast in Queens' College and on passing through the gate had been told by Finton about the incident at the Master's Lodge. The three of them talked quietly for a few minutes, and then Talworthy, true to his enthusiasm and bored with the delay, started to inspect all the paintings

89

in the room, concentrating on one of the few college paintings that was not a portrait. This one, hung over the fireplace, was a handsome seascape showing a British man-of-war in heavy seas. Earlier Simon had noticed that Heatherington had been eyeing the portrait of the bishop, and while Talworthy looked at the seascape he went over to the portrait and started to examine it in a way that made Simon uneasy. He certainly didn't want anyone else taking an interest in this particular painting. His unease was increased when Heatherington took a magnifying glass from his pocket – a glass that Simon had seen him use before when he was examining manuscripts or books with small print. At first, his attention seemed focussed on the panels on either side of the painting, but then it switched to the figure of the seated bishop.

Talworthy and Heatherington were still examining the respective paintings when two constables arrived, shown upstairs by Finton, and shortly afterwards Dr James and Dr Carrs joined them, the Master looking amazingly recovered. Simon recalled that as a younger man he had been an expert fencer and that he continued to keep fit, partly by vigorous walking, and partly by regular visits to the fencing club in town. As for the attack, the Master, it appeared, remembered virtually nothing of it. He had been working at his desk when he thought he heard a sound. He began to stand up but before he could even look round everything had gone black. The next thing he remembered was Dr Carrs holding smelling salts to his nostrils. The police were told about the chaos on the first two floors and asked what was missing, and then, after a pause, the Master said. "I've briefly inspected this room and my study and so far as I can see nothing has been taken. It does look as if the thief wanted something in my desk, but until I've had a chance to go through all the mess I can't be absolutely sure what – if anything – is missing."

Carrs, Talworthy and Simon exchanged glances. The Master's reaction to the papers on the floor certainly did not accord with this account, but it was not up to any of them to say otherwise. Statements were taken, and shortly afterwards they all dispersed, leaving a series of questions unanswered.

Most of the fellows knew nothing of the attack in the Lodge until breakfast. This was served, as usual, by Vinman, along with one of his assistants, while Simon and Talworthy recounted their experiences of the night before. However, Simon decided to say nothing about the Master's odd behaviour in the study, when he had seemed to be aware that something important really was missing. Talworthy too made no mention of this matter and Simon wondered why. Was it possible that the Junior Fellow had a special interest in what was stolen and did not want to draw attention to it?

Right at the end of breakfast Talworthy began to whisper something in Simon's ear, and he was wondering if he were going to refer, privately, to this odd episode when he found that the reason was much more prosaic.

"I've had a look at the decanters," Talworthy said, "and they're both empty!"

The following two days only deepened the general mystery concerning the incident in the Lodge. The Master was said to be much better, but he kept to himself and was not seen in the Combination Room. The official word was that the thief had been hunting for valuables when he was disturbed by the shouting of the two students who had seen the broken window from the courtyard. Nothing, it was said, was missing. However, there was also talk of two gowned figures, one very short and one quite tall, passing quickly through the entrance gate, evidently at about the same time as the students raised the alarm. The rumour mill quickly recalled the short figure seen at the time of Higgins's murder, and common speculation assumed that the person seen on this occasion was the same.

When the rumours reached Simon his thoughts turned to Mr Bambridge, who was certainly short, but, he remembered clearly, was not wearing a gown when he called on him. On the other hand, the librarian of Trinity Hall was one of the few people who were party to the importance of the Courcey documents, and he had had reason to think that an interesting letter that had been withdrawn from the papers was in the Lodge. After all, if the letter were not of special interest, why would the Master have borrowed it?

It was also true that Bambridge was in the college at about the time the Master was attacked; indeed, it was possible that he could have gone straight from his rooms to the Lodge. Moreover, dons who visited a fellow informally often left their gowns on one of the hooks that were placed outside the 'oaks' of most sets of rooms, unlike students who were compelled to keep theirs on; so it was quite possible that Bambridge had come with a gown. Nevertheless, it seemed inconceivable that he should commit such a crime, especially just after visiting Simon, who would know of his presence in the college. It was all very strange.

Chapter 15

From London to Sudbury, Saturday, March 28, 9. 00 a.m.

Simon waited for Theresa to join him in the station tea-room, located on one of the platforms. He arrived early, just as the male heroes in his novels did when they were anxious to keep a rendez-vous. For a few minutes he watched the platform, eager to see the slim figure for whom he was waiting, but then his mind started to wander to the memory of his researches in the British Museum Library the afternoon before, shortly after his arrival in London.

As a scholar he knew about the one and only person who had ever been made an official 'Antiquarian' to the sovereign. A few years before the dissolution of the monasteries this highly unusual person, John Leland, had begun an inventory of monastic books and manuscripts, along with other items of interest. The printed editions

of Leland's *Itinerary*, as it was called, had only a few pages devoted to Cambridgeshire but, as he had hoped, the original manuscript in the British Museum had more. Shortly before the library closed he had found the reference to Leland's visit to Lolworth Abbey in 1538, and the brief entry held him spell-bound. Forty rare and precious printed books and manuscripts were listed, and a note was added: 'Sundry sets of pieces for chesse'. In the strange sequence of events, at least some things were beginning to add up, thought Simon.

There was still no sign of Theresa, and feeling restless he took from his bag the review of *The de Vere Papers* that had come out in the *Lambeth Literary Gazette* a few days before. He read it through for the third time. The reviewer, James Halford, who was unknown to him, had very mixed views of the novel, disliking, in particular, the implication that Edward de Vere might be the true author of Shakespeare. Since for the purposes of the novel this was part of the plot, Simon found that criticism irritating. The book was, after all, a work of fiction. At the same time, however, while writing it, and long before any intimation of the actual existence of de Vere papers in the college library, he had formed the view that the possibility of Oxford's authorship deserved serious attention. It was, at the least, a more plausible hypothesis than those concerning Bacon or Marlowe. He grinned inwardly at the discomfort that would be caused to Mr Halford and many others if the revelations from De Vere College should actually end by substantiating the de Vere hypothesis. The rest of the review was a kind of damning with faint praise, giving Simon the distinct impression that the reviewer envied the huge popularity of the book along with the money it was making for its author.

He did not want Theresa to find him reading the review in case this showed too great an interest in a topic he wanted to avoid, so he put the *Gazette* in his bag and again watched the platform for her arrival.

Although his eyes were focussing on each woman that came into view, he still found his mind going over the extraordinary happenings of the past week. In particular he rehearsed the events that had taken place in the Master's Lodge, trying to recall if there were anything important he had overlooked. Despite the Master's protestations it was evident something important had been stolen. Could it, perhaps, be the letter he had borrowed from the Courcey documents; and if so, why was this letter so important to him?

Theresa was now more than ten minutes later than the time they had agreed to meet and, since the train was due to leave in only five minutes, Simon began to fret. However, it was unlikely she would not come. Yesterday's lunch had gone well, as had the evening at *Acis and Galatea*. In the interval they had met some of her friends, a married couple, and that had led to the only disappointing part of the evening. At the suggestion of the couple the four of them shared a cab on a roundabout journey that ended up at his hotel, which it turned out involved taking back Theresa before going on to the friends' house. This had prevented any chance of a romantic good night at the front door of Theresa's apartment. But with luck, today would allow for something of the kind.

"Hello – I'm sorry to be late. We must hurry to platform four or we may miss the train."

Theresa's sudden appearance caused Simon to catch his breath, rather as it had done when he first saw her at the publisher's luncheon.

That event had been only a little over two weeks ago, and yet they seemed like an age, so much had his priorities changed since then. Theresa was dressed more conventionally than he had seen her before: perhaps, he thought, out of respect for her aunt and uncle, whom she had described as 'somewhat old-fashioned'. Her chignon was a little higher, and no curls could be seen below it; she wore a long tweed dress, topped with a blue bonnet, and walking boots. In one hand she held a picnic basket, covered with a white linen cloth. Why was it, he thought, that this more traditional presentation had stirred him again so powerfully? Perhaps it was because of Theresa's ability to look beautiful in different settings, or perhaps – he wondered – it was the change of scent; something that reminded him of wild flowers, but delicate rather than overpowering.

It was a stopping train, which took two hours to reach Sudbury. On the journey they talked about writing styles, and Simon was unable to prevent Theresa getting onto the subject of the *The de Vere Papers*, which, it appeared, she herself had just been reviewing for the *Old Chelsea Review*. In fact, it was the act of dropping off the finished article at the company offices that had led to her almost missing the train.

"You should read the book," she said. "After all, your college ought to be interested in the hypothesis – you know – the one about Edward de Vere being the true author of Shakespeare. Didn't he actually have something to do with your college? Although I know he wasn't the founder"

"Around 1570 he was a fellow-commoner for a year or so, shortly before he married Sir William Cecil's daughter." Simon found himself unable to resist the question on his mind: "What did you think of the novel?"

"Well, to start with, I don't think the case for seeing de Vere as the true Shakespeare is as strong as it suggests. Have your read Delia Bacon's book?"

In fact Simon had, as part of his background reading for *The de Vere Papers*, but he did not want to admit this in case his research in the subject led to surprise at his interest in the topic of Shakespeare rivals, which, in turn, might lead to suspicions about his own involvement. If possible he wanted to avoid any more direct lies, but a kind of half-truth might suffice.

"I seem to remember someone referring to the book. Is she one of the people who claimed Bacon was the real author of Shakespeare's work?"

"Yes. It came out, I think, in 1857, and seemed to make a good case. But the trouble is that once you really believe in a theory it's easy to find evidence for it and to ignore the equally good evidence for another theory. It's rather like the current row about what to make of the new fossils people keep finding. All in all, I think there's more to be said for the view that Shakespeare was Shakespeare. But to return to *The de Vere Papers*; it's quite fun, but not really good writing. It gets by through the use of a lot of clever ideas and exciting events, but in terms of actual writing, well, it's just not in the same league as, say, George Eliot."

"What are its main faults – as literature?"

"Well there are two. The first is that the characters are not deep enough. At the beginning one tends not to notice as one gets carried along by the story, but when you sit back, say, after finishing a chapter, then you realize there's a certain hollowness in all the main players. Then – and this is my second main criticism – the descriptions, I mean the accounts of human interactions and perhaps even more, the accounts of scenery and background, nearly all make the classic mistake of lesser writers. They try to get an effect by naming it, rather than by, as it were, evoking the effect, indirectly."

Simon found it hard to analyze his feelings. His pride felt hurt. He admitted to himself that since the extraordinary success of the books, he had begun to believe he really was a gifted writer. At the same time he realized that here was a most unusual opportunity. Most successful writers rarely had genuine criticism of their work made to their faces: there was too much toadying to success. Certainly, there could be hard, and often painful written reviews, but honest criticism one could discuss openly and freely was hard to find. It was a truly odd situation, and perhaps, despite the pain, he should take advantage of it. He knew he would like, one day, to write a novel that Theresa really approved, even if it were not a financial success.

"That's interesting. Perhaps I should get a copy of *The de Vere Papers* and read it through to see if I notice the same faults. Did you know that the Master of De Vere has banned all Amelia Buzzard's books from college? But of course such a ban only applies to students: there's no reason why fellows can't get a copy."

"Well look, take this one." Theresa drew a slightly battered copy from her handbag. "I've finished my review, and you're most welcome to it. You can take it as a small return for your gift of *First Maccabees*, which I'm sorry to say, I haven't had time to read yet. But by the way, you never signed it, and I've brought it with me so that you can do so, perhaps while we're having dinner tonight."

Theresa opened a bag that contained both *First Maccabees* and *The de Vere Papers* and handed him the latter. Simon surveyed the unexpected juxtaposition of the two books and accepted the novel from Theresa, feeling more than a little guilty because he hadn't told her that he already had copies, in case the possession of them might raise suspicions. He opened the cover and his heart missed a beat. At Robbins' request he had signed quite a few copies 'Amelia Buzzard' before they had gone to reviewers, and this was one of them.

He was thinking fast. To his eyes, there was a worrying similarity of style between the false signature he was now staring at and the genuine ones in the two letters he had sent to Theresa. When, later in the day, he signed the copy of *First Maccabees*, he would have to make the hand-writing as similar as possible to that of the genuine signatures in the letters but, at the same time, as different as possible from that of the false signature in the copy of *The de Vere Papers*! On the other hand, he had half decided to confide in Theresa about his secret life, for after all, it would be much better coming from him now than from an exposure in the papers. He felt Theresa's gaze on him as he was lost in thought, trying to decide how and when to broach the subject. Certainly, with other people in the same carriage this did not seem the right time, and he quickly thought of an appropriate question that would get them back to the main topic.

"Can you give me a particular example to look for – I mean, of trying to get an effect by naming it?"

"Well, take the opening passage of the book, which describes how a school-teacher discovers a de Vere manuscript in an old chest. Amelia Buzzard wants to build a sense of tension in the auction room, but she does so by saying things like 'Jane Bartholomew' – that's the heroine – 'could feel the tension in the air as the bidding began'. A better writer would note the agitated words and actions of those around the heroine and lead the reader to sense the tension in the atmosphere, rather than simply saying that there was tension. You can get away with naming the effect now and again, but most of the time it's a cheap way of avoiding the real challenge of descriptive writing."

Simon nodded, well aware that he was frequently guilty of this fault, and grateful for having it pointed out. Like so many things, it was pretty obvious once it was seen but, typically, lots of things didn't seem obvious until something brought them to one's attention.

"I'm busy finishing my *Second Maccabees*, and I'll try to bear what you say in mind. Of course it's not a novel, but there is some descriptive writing, and I think the same rule should apply."

"Yes, I do too, although it's only in imaginative fiction that the fault really stands out. It's one of the things that separates a first-rate from a second-rate or a third-rate novel. A first-rate novel keeps you enthralled by the power of the descriptive writing, especially of the characters, and the novel can be first-rate even if the plot is a little thin; a second-rate novel – as I would classify it – keeps most people reading by a good story line, but the descriptive writing is poor; while a third-rate novel has neither good writing nor a good story. Unfortunately this doesn't stop some of them being read; but that's because they rely on filth or sensation and because so many readers don't have real standards."

"Some people, I gather, regard the Amelia Buzzard books as filth and sensation."

"Yes, indeed they do, but they're quite wrong. You should see some of the filth that gets published nowadays: not so much by the regular press, but by what in the trade we call the 'underground'. You don't find them in most bookshops unless you ask – in a meaningful sort of way – for something 'a little more interesting'. I'm sometimes asked to review them, but my journal won't touch them – and for good reasons. A good novel always asks the reader's imagination to come into play, but this is much less so in these books, where the explicit accounts of intimate relationships and brutality undermine their value as good literature."

"So you're more conventional than I thought, after all."

"It depends what you mean by conventional. What disgusts me about the underground press is not the carnal imagery, though this often goes way beyond what you find in Amelia Buzzard, but the way in which women are nearly always portrayed as spineless victims. As you've heard me say before, Amelia Buzzard represents something of the authentic voice of women writers, but these writers of filth are almost always men, and they show no respect for the intrinsic dignity and worth of women."

As Theresa warmed to her subject Simon reflected that by her standards he was generally content that his novels, or at least those under the name of Amelia Buzzard, could be considered 'second-rate' rather than 'third-rate'. Nevertheless, he would like, some time in the future, to write something that was, by her standards, 'first-rate'. Perhaps what she said could also be applied to his sermons. He didn't preach very often, perhaps twice a year in the college chapel and about the same number of times as an invited preacher in local churches, but his sermons often included a descriptive element, for example, of a Maccabean battle scene, and he decided that next time he preached he would consider how to evoke the effect he wanted rather than simply name it.

Theresa was expostulating on the nature of some of the 'fourth-rate' novels she was expected to read for review when they pulled into Sudbury station and the conversation had to be postponed. They were met by Theresa's uncle, Colonel Reginald Brown, and his friendly, rather plump wife, whom Theresa addressed as Aunt Wilhelmina. They were escorted, on foot, to a comfortable tea-house situated near the station, and Colonel Brown explained what he had planned.

"Dr Weatherspoon, I've arranged for a pony and trap to pick both of you up from here in about half an hour. The driver knows the way to Hedingham Castle, and you should be there before two. It seems it will be fine, so you can enjoy your picnic while you wait for the custodian to show you round the castle."

"When will the trap come back for us?" asked Theresa.

Her aunt replied. "We've asked Mr Porlock – that's the man who owns the pony and trap – to pick you up again at four. That should give you plenty of time to see the castle, and then to have tea with us before you take the 6 o'clock for London."

Not only had Colonel Brown already seen to everything: he would not hear of any payment for the journey or the custodian, in fact he seemed genuinely pleased to be able to do something for his niece.

At tea they chatted in a rather stilted and formal way. Simon was asked about his family, and although he was normally reticent on this subject he felt it would seem impolite not to respond. His father, he explained, was the younger son of a clergyman, but although pressed to follow him in the same profession had chosen to be a schoolmaster. He taught classics at Manchester Grammar School, where he still remained. This had enabled him to take advantage of the special fees for sons of teachers. His mother had been the youngest daughter of a country squire, but all the family money had gone to pay the debts of an improvident elder brother. She had died when he was fourteen, leaving himself and an older sister, who was married to one of his father's colleagues.

In the subsequent conversation Simon noticed that Mrs Brown kept glancing at him. He overheard one whispered comment to

Theresa that much amused him. "He's a clergyman you say – well, a most welcome change from that friend you introduced us to in London last month. What was his name – Marcus Peabody, I think – you know, the poet-fellow who dresses like a sort of canary?" Theresa, he had gathered from Nogle, had a certain reputation for unconventionality, and this evidently applied to her choice of friends, to the chagrin of the very obviously conventional colonel and his wife. His own background was certainly conventional, if a little modest by their standards, but he wondered what they would say when the Amelia Buzzard business broke!

Shortly afterwards Colonel and Mrs Brown had to go, having arranged to have lunch with friends in the town, leaving Theresa and Simon alone to wait for the trap. They sat next to each other, watching an elderly man at a table near the far end of the tea-house. He was casually dressed and seemed almost too scruffy to have been allowed into this high-class establishment. However, what caught their attention was the enormous black dog he had been permitted to bring with him. Simon had always known that Newfoundland dogs were large, but this one was the biggest and fattest he had ever seen, with a huge, sloppy mouth which was busily masticating a large cream cake which the owner, in defiance of the normal rules of propriety, had set on the floor in front of him.

The scene was in total contrast to that at the very next table where an exceedingly genteel-looking lady, probably in her early sixties and dressed in widow's black, was neatly nibbling a lettuce sandwich while she read from a small leather-bound book. The contrast was the more evident because of the way she handled both sandwich and book with the very tips of her fingers, suggesting a special fastidiousness, if not primness. As they watched, the dog at the nearby table got up and shook itself, in the way that some dogs do when bored or, perhaps, irritated by a flea. The huge, froth-covered jaws vibrated as the head went from side to side, and to their horror, they saw a large chunk of half-chewed cake take flight from the side of the dog's mouth. It flew, in a kind of arc, right across to the prim lady's table, and with a slight plop! landed in her teacup.

The lady looked up, aware of the sound, but evidently not aware of its source. She glared at another table where some children were noisily stirring their milk, and then went back to her book, quite oblivious of the new addition to her menu, and clearly putting the sound down to the children's antics.

Simon glanced at Theresa and saw her grin. Together they watched the old man, who half rose, as if to go to the lady and apologize. But

he stopped – and Simon could almost hear the working of his brain. What should he say? How should he put it? He sat down again. The lady took up the teacup and raised it to her lips. Simon felt Theresa's hand slip into his – and a kind of trembling anticipation passed between them. The lady took a sip of tea, and grimaced, conscious of a foreign object slipping down her throat that had been mysteriously concealed at the bottom of the cup.

Theresa stuffed her handkerchief into her mouth, her body convulsed in suppressed laughter. It was infectious, and Simon, not having time to reach his handkerchief, coughed and spluttered into his table napkin. Colonel Brown, they knew, had already paid for the tea, so holding hands, they passed rapidly from the tea-house, their mirth largely covered by a show of coughing. Outside, and clear of earshot, they burst into laughter. The trap was already there, and the driver recognized the colonel's niece. They mounted, holding hands and laughed riotously for the next three miles, even though the driver glanced back at them twice, evidently mystified by their behaviour.

As they recovered their composure Simon realized that one of his problems was solved. He had wondered and wondered how to break the ice and enjoy a first moment of physical contact, given his inexperience in matters of the heart, the results of the isolated nature of his family background and of his employment, leading together to a total lack of personal familiarity in the area of romance. But the first physical contact had been achieved in the least predictable of circumstances.

Chapter 16

Castle Hedingham, early afternoon the same day.

They reached the village of Castle Hedingham just before two o'clock and, passing over the handsome Tudor bridge which, Theresa remembered, had been built at the time of Henry VII, they came to the large garden that surrounded the ancient stone keep. At one time the garden must have been magnificent, but it was now largely spoilt, partly by neglect, and partly by a series of diggings

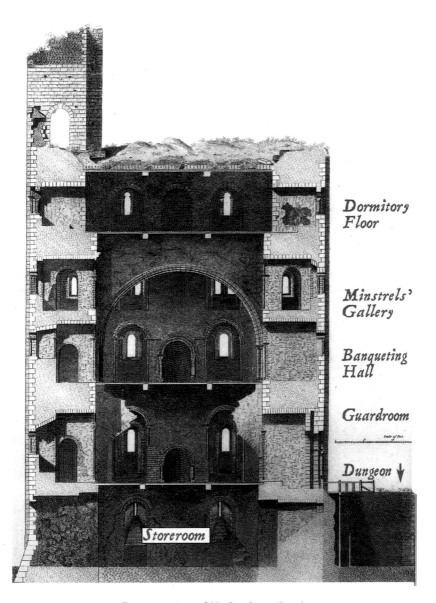

Dormitory
Floor

Minstrels'
Gallery

Banqueting
Hall

Guardroom

Dungeon ↓

Storeroom

Cross section of Hedingham Castle

evidencing the beginning of some kind of archaeological exploration of the inner bailey.

Since the weather was unusually warm for the time of year, they spread out their picnic in one of the grassy areas and sat down on cushions. The driver withdrew, promising to return at four o'clock, and reminded them that the colonel had arranged for the custodian to be there at 2.30 to show them round, which would give them an hour and a half to explore.

The castle was impressive, and, as Simon had learned from the Master, built on almost exactly the same plan as the keep at Cambridge. The nearly square tower was fifty to sixty feet in breadth and length, with slight thickenings at the corners, and a 'splay' or 'plinth' round the bottom courses of stone. (The plinth rendered attack with battering rams much harder and, at the same time, caused rocks thrown from the battlements to bounce off the stonework and fly straight at any enemy who was near the base of the tower.) Another similarity was not obvious at first sight, but Simon had read about it after deciding to gather more information on the keep at Hedingham. Both castles were provided with fireplaces (two at Hedingham and four at Cambridge) and instead of flues that ran right up to chimneys at roof level, as in most castles built after the middle of the thirteenth century, the relatively short flues led directly to holes in the walls, set immediately above the fireplaces. This was a system that produced a lot of internal smoke when the wind was in the wrong direction, as Simon knew from the rare occasions in winter when they lit fires at the De Vere keep. In order to prevent this smoke some fellows had suggested putting in flues that ran right to the battlements and then to chimney pots, but others had objected to such a drastic change to an ancient fabric. In the end nothing was done, not least because the mason's estimate for the work was huge.

The basement had small ventilation slits, above which the entrance floor had modest windows, above which were the windows of the Great Hall, doubled in the case of the gallery. On the top floor there was one more set of windows, placed immediately above the others, once again in the round style of the Normans, but here at Hedingham they were crowned with fine chevron carvings that typified the period.

Despite the similarities, four things made the exterior of this tower different from the one at De Vere, with which he was familiar. The first he had noticed on their approach: the presence of large and ugly holes made into the basement on the east side of the keep, which Theresa told him had been put there in the eighteenth century to make easier access when the castle was used for storage. The second was

that the forebuilding here was a ruin, while at De Vere both storeys were still intact and comprised the old dungeon underneath the entrance way, only reached by an exterior door and now used as a storeroom, and the entrance way itself, which had its own set of battlements and a high-pitched wooden roof. (The ruined forebuilding at Hedingham, Simon recalled, was exactly what the left-hand panel of the portrait had indicated.) The third difference he had spotted when he first saw the distant view of the castle in the painting in the Master's Lodge. At De Vere, the windows at the top level were doubled, in exactly the same way as in the gallery, which, Simon thought, gave a particularly pleasing appearance to the Cambridge example. Finally, the battlements at De Vere had been restored, whereas these had disappeared.

The custodian, a pleasant woman in her forties, who introduced herself as Mrs Pine, turned up on time and led them to the entrance. They climbed the outside staircase (the upper part of which would originally have been within the forebuilding) and a huge, old-fashioned key was turned in the lock. Before going in she pointed to the gardens below. "I'm sorry about the mess. It usually looks much tidier than this, but Mr Majendie – that's the present owner – has agreed to an exploration of the site. There used to be many other stone buildings round the inner bailey and they're trying to find out where."

Theresa was running her hands over the outside stone, and admiring the carving above the main door. "This stonework seems to be in excellent shape. Is it the original material?" she asked.

Mrs Pine was pleased to show her knowledge and to stress the impressiveness of the castle.

"Yes indeed. This is the original ashlar, brought here all the way from Barnack quarries in Northamptonshire. The entire exterior of the keep is faced with it, which must have been an extraordinary expense at the time. It explains why the basic structure is still in such excellent condition, despite the vandalism such as those dreadful openings on the other side."

As they passed through the door she added, "Perhaps we should begin with the Great Hall. It's the most impressive part of the castle, and still beautiful, despite the years of neglect."

Once inside she led them through a short passage on the left that entered into the great spiral stairway, some thirteen feet in diameter, that ran from the basement to the top of the castle.

"I can't help thinking of all the people who have climbed these stairs, ever since around 1140," said Simon. "How worn they look."

"Yes, they're well used," replied Mrs Pine, "but in fact you're not walking on the original stones. They were so badly trodden that these red bricks were set into the stone about the time of Henry VII: but now even these are badly worn."

After a whole turn the staircase opened directly onto the Great Hall, and they stepped inside.

Theresa gasped. The room was sensational, even though it was unfurnished, its walls covered with decayed whitewash, and the windows dirty. It was roughly forty feet long by thirty wide, with a great stone arch, decorated in the Norman manner, dividing the ceiling into two equal sections, allowing wooden beams crossing from the walls to the top of the arch to bear the weight of the floor above. Simon later measured the arch to be twenty-eight feet in span. Each of the four sides of the hall had two windows, with single lights on the lower floor, while the gallery – which ran right round the upper

floor – had almost identical windows immediately above them except, as Simon had noticed from the outside, these each had two lights. On the south side – facing the arch – was a fireplace, and Simon felt his eyes drawn to the gallery window above it and to the left. This was where the clue told him to look!

"Can one walk round the gallery?" asked Simon.

"Yes, of course. Just follow the staircase and it opens onto it."

Leaving the two women to continue their admiration of the great arch, Simon climbed the stairwell. Theresa seemed to have sensed something of his inner excitement, since, just as he set off, she glanced at him with a puzzled expression. However, for a minute or two he wanted to be alone in that window, to put his hand exactly where the bishop's ring had been, and – perhaps – to see if the top of the window seat could be moved. He had envisaged how an expert mason could have used a stone seat as a kind of door: one that slid outwards as one pulled on the curved end of the stonework, and he had almost convinced himself that this would be the entrance to a secret room that held the Lolworth treasure. If he found a door, he would have to come back again, and he would have to provide some explanation why he needed time alone in the castle. Perhaps, he thought, he could say that he needed to take a whole series of careful measurements so that he could write an article on the relationship of the two keeps.

As Simon mounted the stairs he felt a tightening in his chest, and he knew that his rapid breathing was not caused only by the exercise. Once at the level of the gallery he went quickly to the window indicated in the painting.

There was the double window, but, unlike the situation at the De Vere keep, there was no window seat! He crouched down and examined the stone floor. There was no evidence that there had ever been a stone seat, or of any interruption in the fine stonework that could indicate the presence of a secret door. Moreover, because the gallery pasage at Hedingham was considerably broader than the one at De Vere, there was, in fact, almost no room for a seat between the passage and the window. Either the painter of the Tudor portrait had invented the seat, or this was not the right castle!

Simon recalled what it had felt like as a boy when one was bitterly disappointed. There was a lump in his throat which, when he was younger, would have been the prelude to tears. He heard the approach of the women and quickly stood up, making a show of looking at the view from the window. This view, he realized, was similar to that shown in the left-hand panel of the portrait. Despite the recent decay he could see that the general outline was the same. But how could this be? How could the painting be so right about the view of the castle, including the layout of the gardens and the poor state of the forebuilding, and so wrong about a vital detail of the interior?

The others joined him at the window. "It's funny you should come straight to this spot," said Mrs Pine. "That's exactly what the gentleman did who came here on Thursday!"

Theresa looked at Simon while he stammered slightly. "H- how odd," he said, "I thought you had very few visitors until the summer season got under way."

"That's right, but this was a gentleman from Cambridge – like yourself sir. He was a Dr Jones, but I don't know from which college he came. Mr Majendie passed on his letter to me asking if he could see the castle as soon as possible, and I showed him round all by himself. He went all over the castle, but this is where he wanted to go first."

"I know one Dr Jones, a rather large man, I mean both tall and with a large figure – about sixty I should think. He teaches Latin at St John's College."

"I don't think that could be him. This man was about average height, and looked quite trim, and I don't think he could have been more than forty-five."

Simon said nothing more, but he was both worried and puzzled. It couldn't be just by chance that another Cambridge fellow should be anxious to see Hedingham Castle and, it would seem, pay special attention to the same window in the gallery! Was Dr Jones his real name? It was possible, since he certainly didn't know all the dons in Cambridge, but when he got back he could soon check up on how many Dr Joneses there were among the fellows of all the colleges.

They continued with the tour. The top floor, to Simon's surprise, was arranged differently from that at De Vere's. Here, there was simply a large open space with thick wooden posts supporting the roof. In earlier days, as Mrs Pine explained, the space would have been divided up by partitions or curtains in order to make private sleeping quarters for the Earl of Oxford and his family and retainers. However, at De Vere's the top storey was divided by a stone wall, three feet thick, placed immediately above the arch. The roof beams there ran from the exterior walls to the top of this dividing wall.

There was one other significant difference that Simon noticed. At Hedingham there was just the one large spiral stairway that ran from top to bottom, whereas at De Vere's, in addition to an equivalent large stairway, placed right by the entrance, there was a much narrower spiral staircase in the opposite corner that also ran from the basement to the battlements, a mere six feet in diameter and used, he presumed, as a kind of servants' route between the floors.

They went to the roof level, and walked carefully right round the castle, keeping well back from the edge because of the absence of battlements, Mrs Pine, meanwhile, indicating how easy it would be to see enemies approaching from any direction. Then they went down to the entrance floor which, as at De Vere, contained a guardroom and a kitchen (although at Hedingham they were not separated by a wall); then they surveyed the vaulted basement.

"At one time," said Mrs Pine, "there used to be a well here, but for some reason it got blocked up, perhaps when they started using this place for storage in the eighteenth century and made those horrible openings. We're not sure where the well was."

"I seem to remember being told there was once a secret passage," said Theresa. "Perhaps, if there were one, it ran from the well shaft, as it does in the great Norman keep at Bamburgh."

"Yes," said Mrs Pine, "that's possible. The story goes that the passage ran from somewhere down here to the fishponds in the outer bailey, and that during one of the famous sieges of the castle, the soldiers on the battlements fetched some fish and threw them down onto the attackers – just to let them know they weren't short of supplies. The idea was to make them give up. I don't know that I believe it, but it makes a good story."

They went back into the garden, and chatted while they waited for the pony and trap. Theresa was clearly aware that Simon had a special agenda and was anxious to quiz him about it, but while Mrs Pine was present she contented herself with asking whether there was a similar story of a secret passage at De Vere's keep.

"No," said Simon, "I've never heard tell of one, and I don't think it's really a possibility, as it is here. Our keep is built right by the river, and although the floor of the basement is above the water level I don't think you could build a secret tunnel out of the keep that wouldn't get flooded. The setting's quite different here, with the castle on top of a small hill – partly natural, by the look of it, and partly built up from an early earth-work. Here, I could imagine a passage to the fishponds, but not at De Vere."

Chapter 17

Sudbury and London, later the same day.

In the light of Simon's behaviour, Theresa was far too intelligent to believe he just happened to be interested in Hedingham castle, especially when she saw his reaction to the visit by another don from Cambridge who was anxious to see exactly the same place within the keep. But the air was still, and on the return drive to Sudbury the driver could hear anything above a whisper, so serious conversation had to wait. Later, at the colonel's house, it had to wait again. They had a friendly, though rather tedious tea, making small talk about Hedingham and Cambridge. The colonel and Mrs Brown were clearly fond of their niece, but disapproved of her life-style in London, and avoided talking about it. On the train to London, Theresa was frustrated yet again as they had to share a compartment with other travellers. However, while the others in the carriage were involved in a lively conversation about a new play, she did feel free to respond to a question about how she got into the profession of reviewing books.

"My father," she explained, "is rather like my uncle. He's a country physician; a thoroughly decent person but, quite frankly, rather dull. However, there's a good library in the house, and both my father and mother read a lot, mostly historical works and more sober and 'proper' novels. One day, when I was about fifteen, I was sitting in the library, preparing some work for my governess, when my father made an angry sound and threw the book he had been reading into the waste-paper basket. I was intrigued, and early next morning, before the housemaid had time to empty the basket, I retrieved the offending item. It was a copy of Mary Wollstoncraft's *A Vindication of the Rights of Women*. Have you read it?"

This was a time for honesty, Simon decided, in part because any claim to detailed knowledge would very likely be exposed by some probing questions. He answered, "I know of the book, and something of the furore it has caused over the years, but in truth I've never actually opened it."

"Well, I can easily lend you one of my copies – I have got several slightly different editions. Anyway, I loved it, and I must admit the fact that my Tory father hated it was part of the initial attraction. I was fond of my father, particularly after I left home and became a governess myself – when I found I missed arguing with him – but my own views differed more and more from his."

"I must admit, I just can't see you as a governess."

"It certainly didn't suit me, and I certainly met no Mr Rochester, but for three years it gave me some independence and a quiet place to begin my own writing. I tried my hand at novels, with several started and none finished, all in the style of Elizabeth Gaskell, and then I had an unexpected success. I knew that Mrs Gaskell used to write for the *Analytical Review*, and, inspired by her, I sent two of my own reviews of recent novels to the *Old Chelsea Review*. To my amazement they were accepted, and within six months I had joined their staff."

The opportunity for Theresa to question Simon properly came only after they had ordered their meal at 'Le Français' (which, it was agreed, Theresa was to pay for, although it was Simon's turn to choose the wine). On the journey Simon had decided that now was the time to make a clean breast of things, both about the treasure and about his literary activities, and also, in the light of the latter, about his proposed move to London. He decided to start with the treasure story, since it involved the least embarrassment.

"I suspect you think I've been hiding something from you, and you're right. I've been waiting for the right time to tell you, and I think that time is now. In fact there are really two things I want to tell you about, but I'd better begin with the one that's easier to explain – although, in a way, it's more fantastic than the other."

Theresa put her elbows on the table (one of her many unconventional manners), and her chin in her hands. "Yes, I really would like to know what you're up to."

Simon began with his discovery of the clue in the old copy of *Fourth Maccabees*. Theresa didn't interrupt, so he went on to tell of the evening when Lord FitzSimmons had tried to enlist support for his condemnation of the de Vere hypothesis and of Higgins's subsequent revelation about the Courcey documents. Then, "I've told you a little about the murder," he said, "but what I haven't told you – or come to that, the police – is that something was stolen from Higgins's rooms. The Courcey documents, including the real de Vere papers, were all stolen!"

"Good heavens! This is sounding more and more like a Gothic novel. But why haven't you told the police?"

"The Master specially asked me not to."

"Why ever not? Could there be any conceivable reason why he might want to keep the theft secret?"

"As a matter of fact there is." Simon went on to tell Theresa about his first visit to the Lodge, and the Master's passion for collecting chessmen. Then he added, "The fact is I happen to have found a note about what may be in the Lolworth treasure and it appears that one of the abbots, perhaps Henry Courcey, who was the last abbot, and I think more of a nobleman than a churchman, also collected chessmen. Apparently the treasure includes nine complete medieval chess sets."

"Good Lord! So that makes it look as if the Master – if he knows about this – has a very special interest in the treasure. I know something about collectors and how some of them become absolutely fanatical about whatever it is they collect. I remember a friend saying about one book collector that he would kill for a first folio of Shakespeare. But do you think the Master would kill to get his hands on chessmen? How rare are medieval pieces?"

"Actually I've been looking into this ever since I found out about the possible contents of the treasure." (Simon was relieved that Theresa had not asked how he had first found out about the chess sets at Lolworth, since he would prefer not to mention his taking of the notebook.) "I can't be certain that the Master knows about the chess sets in the Lolworth treasure, but I suspect he does, because Dr Higgins almost certainly knew about his collection, and given this knowledge it would have been very odd, when he told the Master about the treasure, not to mention them. In fact, I suspect that one of Henry Courcey's letters refers to them. As for medieval chessmen, they are extremely rare. There's only one complete set recorded in the known collections, and that's a simple one, in turned bone. A French museum has a splendid set in silver and quartz from about 1400, but it's missing a queen. Then there are the Lewis chessmen, found in a cave in the Outer Hebrides nearly forty years ago. They are probably twelfth century – but it's not certain they're what we would normally call a set, with matching pieces; the collection is more like part of a merchant's stock from which three or four sets could be made up. There are also quite a lot of important odd pieces in museums and private collections, and a few part sets – but a complete medieval set, if it were finely carved, would be of enormous value and interest. As for nine sets, it would just be amazing. Putting it all together, along with the Master's odd life-style I had begun to think Dr James might be guilty of the theft – although I couldn't quite figure out why he had to go so far as to kill Higgins. But then came the attack on the Master I've told you about, and now it looks as if I must look elsewhere. It's possible, I suppose, that there are two completely different criminals at work, and that the Master is just one of them, but that seems far-fetched."

At eleven they were still discussing the strange events surrounding the murder of the librarian, and the even stranger context of a medieval treasure hidden, in all probability, in a Norman keep, which led Theresa to repeat her comment on the Gothic nature of the whole affair. Simon decided it was time to broach the more sensitive subject, but that it might be easier to tell her first about his proposed move to London, and then to explain the real reason for it. He told her about the house he had bought and about his plans for moving most of his things the coming weekend. The Lent term was due to end on Friday, 3rd April, in only six days time, after which Simon would be free of teaching until the Easter term began, and he planned to take advantage of the break to move most of his belongings from his rooms at De Vere to his new home. However, he would leave a few clothes and books behind so that he could continue to live in college until the end of the academic year. (Simon did not add that if the news broke before then, which was likely, his final move would be much more precipitous.) For Saturday 4th April, he had hired a horse and cart to do most of the moving, while he went ahead by train in order to meet the driver at his home in the late afternoon. On the Sunday he planned to set the house in order and he would like to know whether Theresa would agree to be his first guest at his new home, coming for tea on the Monday afternoon?

Theresa sat staring at Simon. "You did tell me that you had a private income," she commented, "but I'm still amazed that you plan to give up the life of a Cambridge don for a life in London. Are you anticipating finding this treasure as part of your plan, in which case isn't it a classic case of counting the chickens before they're hatched?"

"No, no, it's not like that. In the first place, if I find the treasure that doesn't mean it belongs to me. There might be some kind of reward – though I'm not sure what that would be – but I can manage a modest life in London without counting on anything from that. I have been thinking about a move to London for some time, but by staying on in Cambridge till the summer I hope to give myself a good chance of solving the riddles. But you haven't said whether you can come to tea at my new home on Monday week."

"Well, I'd love to come and see what kind of house you've bought, but . . ." – In mid-sentence Theresa looked at the watch that hung from her necklace. "I must go," she said, "I've got an early start tomorrow at the office; but I'm glad we can meet again soon. Write down your new address before we leave."

Simon realized he had not broached the second, and more difficult disclosure. It would have to wait for the meeting at his new house. Meanwhile he hoped fervently that the dreaded revelation would not come before then, from another source. As they drove to her apartment in the cab all he was able to say was, "Theresa, there's another

116

matter I need to talk to you about – but now it will have to wait for nine days."

Leaving the cab in the road he saw Theresa to her door, conscious of how easily his last words could be misunderstood, and trying, in vain, to think of something else to say that might correct any possible misunderstanding. He might indeed want to propose to Theresa in due course, but he wasn't ready for that yet. He liked her very much and, perhaps more to the point, he felt physically excited by her presence as never before; except for one powerful memory of himself as an undergraduate when a friend's sister cornered him in the house he was visiting, and suddenly put her arms round his neck. As her lips sought his he had drawn away guiltily, but not without an inner struggle. On that occasion, one part of him had been eager for physical contact, while the other, and more puritanical part of him had already told him that this girl was not a suitable partner for life.

There was indeed an extraordinary contrast between the lives of the characters in his novels and his own life experience. Could this be true of other novelists? When he first read their convincing accounts of romantic encounters he assumed they wrote from experience – but perhaps many of them did not – but rather from pure imagination. Could it even be that the very lack of a longed-for experience tended to trigger the imagination? Could Jane Austen and the Brontë sisters have found in their novels a compensation for unsatisfied longings?

Theresa looked at him, aware that he was yet again in one of his internal reveries that both attracted and puzzled her. The pause was too long, and before Simon could find out whether she might have offered the doorstep embrace he so hoped for, she had opened the door and waved goodbye. Disappointed, he returned to the waiting cab and was driven to his hotel, tingling not only with the imagination of closer contact with Theresa, but also with the hugeness of the life-changing decision he had to consider. He was realistic enough to see that Theresa – if she accepted him – would not be your conventional don's wife. She would not docilely arrange the dinner parties and look after the children. She would surely want to continue her own life as a successful critic but, more importantly, she would not want to be dancing to all his whims. If anything she would be the one to organize him: and much as he was attracted to her, he wasn't sure he was prepared for that.

Two voices seemed to be at work in his mind. One came from the part that was Amelia Buzzard. This was saying, "Forward – now is the time to take risks. This might be the one real chance you ever have of true love". The other came from the part of his mind that found expression in Emily Dove. "Be careful. Does Theresa Brown represent a suitable partner – for a don and a clergyman? Do you really want your ordered life to be turned upside down?"

Chapter 18

London and Cambridge, Sunday, 29th March and Monday, 30th March.

For most of the Sunday Simon relaxed. He went to a service in St Paul's cathedral in the morning, which he did not enjoy, largely because of the narrow-minded sermon in which the canon in residence seemed more interested in damning the Roman church than in saying anything positive. The preacher's tirade confirmed his intention to focus his next sermon in the college chapel – if there were to be one – on one of his heroes, the seventeenth-century bishop, Jeremy Taylor (who had been imprisoned two or three times under Cromwell), and his grounds for supporting full toleration, inclusive of Anabaptists and Roman Catholics, which was a brave position to take in his day. If possible he would also try to bring in

Taylor's progressive view of women, and in particular his claim that in an ideal marriage a wife should be a man's 'best friend'.

The afternoon and evening he spent with friends from his undergraduate days, after supper enjoying an informal concert at their house at which a comely red-headed girl played the flute. If it had not been for his interest in Theresa he might have tried to strike up an acquaintance. On the Monday morning he settled matters relating to his new house, formally taking possession, arranging for some furniture to be delivered on the following Saturday (in addition to that which was to come by cart from London) and hiring the cook-housekeeper recommended by Nogle: a middle-aged widow whose children were all grown up, called Mrs Peters. He gave her authority to hire cleaners and provided her with money for this and other necessities. Finally, he just had time to visit the representative of his favourite wine-merchant, Mr John Clarke Avery of Bristol, who, as he had previously ascertained, was on one of his visits to London. De Vere College had bought most of their fine wine from this merchant's business since shortly after the firm's foundation in 1793, and he felt happy to continue this connection with his old life. He arranged for an initial supply of claret, port and Madeira – some for immediate drinking and some for laying down – especially, in the latter case, clarets from the great vintages of 1864 and 1865. If the scandal erupted earlier than expected, he now had a place to hide, with suitable fortification for the inner man. The very next day he planned to begin the packing up of his books, ready for transfer to the library in his new house, a handsome first-floor room that overlooked the back garden.

In the afternoon he travelled back to Cambridge deciding to go

119

first class since it was only a matter of weeks, at the most, until he was likely to change his style of living, and any observation of extravagance was now a risk worth taking.

In some ways he was sorry about the prospect of leaving Cambridge – especially his circle of friends, the libraries and his students. In the time that was left he was anxious he should prepare his close friends for the news that was soon likely to burst upon them and make time for a special and very private visit to the college library. He was now pretty certain that the clue did refer to the keep at De Vere, especially in the light of the proximity of the bishop's ring to the window seat, which would have no equivalent in the college chapel or crypt. It was true that the panel on the left of the painting referred to the castle at Hedingham, partly because of the garden setting, and partly because it did not show the double lights in the top storey which were a feature of the De Vere keep. However, he now knew, from talking to Talworthy, that this panel was not part of the original work, and he suspected either that it had been added to throw people off the scent, or that the painter had simply assumed that Hedingham castle was the setting for the portrait. As for the right-hand panel, here he was not sure, but he suspected that the artist had been told what to illustrate, and that either keep could have been his source. In any case, now he was in charge of the library he had a unique chance to examine the appropriate window seat, perhaps that very night. It was probable that whoever had come to Hedingham before him was on the same quest – and there was the worrying possibility that the mysterious Dr Jones might have come to the same conclusion concerning which castle was more likely to hold the treasure.

At formal hall the Senior Fellow presided, since the Master, they were informed, had gone to a feast at Trinity Hall at the invitation of the head of that college. Apparently he was now much better, and had been back for the college dinner on the Sunday night. Professor Townend took charge of the port. It was a specially good one (a Warre's from 1853, which two of the fellows, after tasting it, said should be put away for another ten years), but Simon had other things on his mind and made his departure after one glass. Back in his rooms he removed his gown and picked up the librarian's set of keys to the old library, along with a candle and a box of phosphorus matches, because the gas lighting might not be adequate for a detailed examination of the stone window seat in the gallery. He began to walk to the keep, but noticing a number of students in the courtyard he decided to wait, hoping to keep his late night visit a secret. There was no reason why, as acting librarian, he shouldn't work late in the old library, but it would be preferable, he decided, to keep this visit unknown.

It was nearly midnight when he mounted the exterior stone steps that led to the library. The forebuilding, reached at the top of the steps, had originally been entered through a portcullis, lifted and lowered by a windlass, but both iron gate and windlass had long since disappeared, and now there was simply a fine, open Norman archway. Beyond this was the even finer archway that led into the main body of the keep and within this second archway was set an ancient wooden door strengthened with iron. He unlocked the door and, after entering the keep, locked it again and put the key in his pocket. Since no-one seemed to have observed his entry he decided not to use the gas lamps but to rely entirely on the candle. There was a slight draught, which blew out the first match he tried, and when he got the candle alight he felt unsettled by the flickering shadows. As he mounted the worn steps (still made of stone, unlike the brick steps at Hedingham), he shielded the candle from the narrow windows. Already there was talk of ghosts in the college, and not only in his rooms, and he wanted no mysterious lights to be reported. He could well understand how the ghost stories arose, for there was indeed something eerie about the old building, especially when no-one else was about and when the candle seemed to produce fleeting images in every corner. He was trying to step softly, but was still conscious of the slight sound made by his shoes on the old stone.

After reaching the Great Hall he went on up, leaving the stair where it led to the gallery. He followed the narrow passage that joined the windows, each of which had an opening onto the hall that was as wide as the window, that is, about six feet; this passage in ancient times had been used by the sheriff's minstrels. After taking a few

121

steps he froze. There was – or so he fancied – a light footstep in the hall below. He held his breath, holding the candle in front of him. There was a double window immediately to his left which faced the river, so there could be no sight of the candle from within the college, but anyone looking at the keep from Jesus Green, on the other side of the river, would see a flickering light. But that couldn't be helped: he wanted to know who, or what, was on the main floor of the hall.

As his eyes adjusted to the gloom he could just make out the whole shape of the hall. There was the fine arch, very similar to that at Hedingham, although a little thicker, because of its need to support the stone wall immediately above it which divided the top storey. There, on the floor, were the rows of bookcases that spoilt the symmetry of the rectangular room. Everything was still. Perhaps it hadn't been a footstep at all, but the creaking of an old piece of wood in one of the cases as it dried out. But there did seem to be a shadow in one of the windows – in fact the one to the left of the fireplace, immediately below the window that he was anxious to examine. Gritting his teeth he decided to go down and confront whoever was there or, more likely, the image that his imagination had conjured up. He turned back to the stairwell, but just as he began to descend, failing to shield the candle-flame from the draught made by his movement, the candle went out. In the dark he swore under his breath and searched for the matches.

The sound of a soft footstep came again, and this time he felt sure it was not just his imagination.

Without the candle he found he could still see a little. Outside it was a clear night, and it was only a week before the paschal moon. Since the windows had neither shutters nor curtains the starlight, combined with the light from the half moon, made it possible to make out the opening from the stairway to the hall. However, if there were someone lurking in the shadows, then, with the absence of a candle, their eyes would have adjusted to the dim light better than his. They might well have been observing his movements.

He passed into the hall and stood perfectly still, forcing himself to control his breathing as he recalled that in different parts of the college two people had recently been struck from behind, one fatally. He turned quickly, sensing something behind him, but there was nothing except an old bookcase. Then there was a blur of movement – or so it seemed – in one corner, the one from which the smaller staircase ran, exactly opposite the main staircase. He fumbled with a match and relit the candle. Forcing himself to overcome his fear he went systematically between all the standing bookcases and into each of the eight window areas. There was nothing. Either his imagination had played tricks or there really was a spiritual presence or – though this was the idea he disliked most – there had been another person in the hall, a person who had observed his entry, and who had then retreated by means of the secondary staircase.

Simon's nerves began to settle and he returned to the gallery, once again shielding the flame from the windows. He reached the upper gallery window to the left of the fireplace and set the candle on the floor so that he could carefully examine the right-hand stone seat. It ran for four feet, from the beginning of the entry off the passage to the window. The top corner, underneath where the bishop's ring had been placed, was rounded, and gave a good grip. He pulled with all his strength, but nothing moved. He moved the candle nearer to see if there was any small gap in the stonework, but there was none.

However, there was something there that did not belong – candle wax on the floor – immediately below the end of the seat, and it was still flexible and slightly warm! It had been dropped within the last few minutes! He was not the only person examining the window-seat tonight. It was evident that whoever it was had then turned their attention to the window below, in case there had been some mistake, and, perhaps, in the realization that despite the discrepancy of the single window, the lower hall would have been a more natural place for the portrait to have been painted. In any case, it looked indeed as if Dr Jones, or whoever used that name, had followed his inspection of the window at Hedingham with a similar search here.

Simon descended the stairs, and again, his candle blew out. This time it was not because of his failure to shield the flame: it was because of a sudden draught that ran up the stairwell.

He was pretty sure what had happened. There had been no spiritual or ghostly visitor but a very human one, and whoever it was had opened the door to the outside and retreated, thus producing a rush of air. Quickly he went down to the entrance. The door was shut, but now it was unlocked. Whoever had been there had a key, both to gain entrance and to escape, but had forgotten, or been in too much of a hurry, to lock the door on departing.

Simon locked it again, this time leaving his key on the inside, thus blocking the key-hole and making it impossible for anyone else with a key to unlock the door from the outside. Then he returned to the window on the lower level of the Great Hall where the shadow had been. There was no sign of wax but there was a faint whiff of candle smell. The other person had been to this window after examining the gallery, and he must have put out his candle when he heard Simon coming up the stairs.

The stone seat here was similar to the one above it, but longer, because of the absence of a gallery. Again Simon felt the rounded end and pulled and pushed with all his might, with the same result as before. If this were the way of opening up a secret chamber, then it would require more than his effort, possibly because a hinge or catch had become rusted up over the years. As with the window seat above, either this was not the real entrance, or he would need the help of a mason.

The window area where Simon stood contained part of the catalogue, placed in a cabinet so that the drawers containing the cards could be pulled out as one sat on the stone seat. An idea occurred to him. One drawer contained references to all the books published before 1600, and he recalled that each entry mentioned the previous owner of the book, if known. By candle-light he looked through the list, noting several that – according to the catalogue – had William Courcey's signature on the title page. He noted the position of one of these, a first edition of the first book of Richard Hooker's *Laws of Ecclesiastical Polity*, printed in 1593. This was in the rare books section on the top floor, so there he went, going into the room that had once been the chapel. He sat at the table in the middle of the room and examined the edition of Hooker.

On page six he found what he was looking for, an underlined 'v'. Two pages later there was the expected 'i'. He found the rest of the word, *videte* and then returned the book to its shelf. Now part of the mystery was solved. The secret message he had found was not only in the book he had borrowed. William Courcey had placed exactly the same information in some of the other books he proposed to leave to the college, including at least one that was not written in Latin, possibly in all of them, that was something he must check. Perhaps, Simon thought, he had put the message in all his favourite books, assuming that whoever first came across it would be a person who shared some of his interests and with whom he might have something in common. At about the same, probably only a few years before his death, he arranged for the unusual portrait of the bishop to be painted: thus providing the second half of the clue to the treasure.

Simon decided to check another entry. According to the catalogue, another book bearing William Courcey's signature was one titled *Master Broughton's Letters*, printed in London in 1599. Simon retrieved the book, and began to search for the underlined words. He got to page nine and was then struck by a particular sentence. Broughton's pretentiousness, so the anonymous editor said, was "like an old bottle with new wine, unless you should vent, you would burst". He paused at the use of the word 'vent', recalling the description of the secret chamber, and noting a contemporary use of the same word. There was a clue here that he had not thought of carefully enough, although when he had first considered the possibility of the hiding place being in the crypt under the chapel he had realized the possible significance of the small windows. The person who hid the treasure probably wanted a flow of air so that damp would not destroy the manuscripts.

He read further, but no letters were underlined. Simon remembered the entry under 'papers A' in the notebook. A hundred and fifty books were mentioned, against ten of which Higgins, presumably following some indication in the Courcey documents, had put a star. Perhaps there were just these ten books that contained the clue he had found. Although the notebook gave no indication of which these were, when he had time he would need to check all the books that Courcey had left to the college. If his suspicions were correct, then anyone who had actually been able to see the Courcey documents, and to see which of the books had been starred, might well have been given a short cut to the clue that he had found by chance. They would carefully examine one or more of the starred books, and sooner or later they would probably stumble on the clue that he himself had found.

Simon returned to the hall and went to the main catalogue that stood near the centre, between the rows of bookcases. On a table was the book in which all borrowings from the library were recorded. In the back was a place for the rare books, which only the Master and fellows could borrow, unless there was special permission from the librarian. These books were sometimes consulted within the library, but only very rarely taken out. In a normal year there would probably be only one entry, but presently three were out, including his own borrowing of *Fourth Maccabees*. Both of the others, he noticed, had been borrowed after the meeting in the Senior Combination Room when the Lolworth treasure had been mentioned and the Courcey documents discussed for the first time.

He returned to the catalogue of old books. His suspicion was confirmed. The two recently borrowed rare books had belonged to William Courcey. Heatherington had one (a collection of Virgil's works printed in London in 1580) and Talworthy had one (a copy of Euclid's *Elements* printed in Paris in 1573). Perhaps one or both of them had decided to investigate what William Courcey had left behind, in addition to the recently discovered papers and found, in one of the books, the clue that he had come across by chance. Both of them had seen the portrait in the Master's Lodge and had found it interesting, so it might have been one of them, perhaps partially disguised, who had decided to check out the Hedingham connection last Thursday and who had come to the same conclusion as himself. But it seemed unlikely that either of them could have been the person who attacked the Master. In the case of Heatherington, at the time of the attack he had been at a feast. Of course, Simon only had his word for this alibi, that is, at present, but it would not be difficult to confirm this matter.

However, even if he had been at the feast, it was just possible that, if he left a bit early, he could have had time to go to the Lodge before walking to Queens'. Moreover, he might have left the college through the door that linked the garden with the outside, to which fellows had a key, and this would mean that the porter on duty could not have noted when he left.

There was of course another factor to consider. Heatherington was a well-known Shakespearean scholar, and it could be that, like Lord FitzSimmons, he had a vested interest in discrediting the de Vere hypothesis. Certainly, quite apart from any interest in treasure, Higgins's discovery of the letters from Edward de Vere must surely be of more concern than he had led anyone to believe.

Simon's consideration turned to Talworthy. In his case he had been at dinner in hall, but it was just possible that he could have attacked the Master before they assembled in the Combination Room, prior to going in to dine. In the ten minute period between the end of chapel and the beginning of formal hall some fellows, usually the older ones, used one of the lavatories, and if Talworthy did so, or pretended to do so, it was unlikely that anyone could verify exactly where he was during that time.

All things considered, Heatherington and Talworthy were both possible but unlikely candidates for the attack on the Master. But if they were innocent there had to be someone else who was interested in the Courcey documents, and it would certainly make sense if that person also visited Hedingham in order to check on any clues found in the papers.

In addition to a mystery concerning who was actually on the trail of the treasure, or indeed whether there might be several people on the trail, all the searchers, including himself, had a problem. If the stone seat could be moved, then it would take a stonemason to move it. But perhaps he – and whoever else was in the hunt – had got it wrong. He had a strong feeling that he had missed something.

The candle was burning low, and despite his disbelief in ghosts he didn't fancy spending any longer in the lonely keep, particularly without a light. He went back to his rooms.

Chapter 19

Simon found it impossible to sleep. In his own mind he was certain the Lolworth treasure existed, and almost certain that it was somewhere within the De Vere keep, although neither Hedingham castle nor the crypt under the chapel could be ruled out absolutely. The keep at De Vere College remained his first choice because William Courcey, whenever he wished, could have had the whole place to himself, and – over against the chapel possibility – because the extreme thickness of the walls provided so much opportunity. The walls were about thirteen feet thick at the basement level (not including the additional stonework provided by the plinth), and still eleven feet at the level of the top floor. At every level there was plenty of space for a secret room within the walls.

Set against this conclusion, however, was the problem of how to vent such a room without giving its presence away. Also, the mention of an underground passage at Hedingham did raise the possibility that the secret room might lie under the castle and form part of an ancient escape route, perhaps, as at Bamburgh, running from the well. There was a well in the basement of the Cambridge keep, not filled in, but covered with an iron framework for reasons of safety. But he remembered that it only ran down for thirty feet before the water level was reached and, when the Cam was in flood, the water actually rose to only ten or twelve feet below the floor. This fact, he realized, did suggest that the well was connected in some way with the river, either by a series of fissures or by a passage. However, he did not think this was a likely place for the Lolworth treasure to be, in part because of the evidence of the portrait and in part because any hiding place connected with the well would be most unsuitable for the valuable manuscripts, which would quickly suffer from the damp. Nevertheless, in addition to the crypt, he ought – if he could – to check this possibility. It was conceivable that the hiding place for the Lolworth treasure had been intended to be only temporary but that there had never been an opportunity to find a dryer place.

His mind turned to the question of library keys. There were four that he knew of. The librarian had one – which was now in his possession. The porter had one, and this was used to open the library in term time between morning chapel, at 7.00 a.m. and formal hall, at 7.30 p.m. At other times, the porter had to be asked to open it specially. A third was kept in the entrance tower, along with all the other duplicate keys that could be used in emergencies: as when they had needed to get into the Master's Lodge. A fourth, Simon happened to know, was kept by the Master. However, although this might point to Dr James as the most likely suspect with regard to the midnight visitor, it was perfectly possible that there were other keys, or that one of the fellows had arranged to make a copy, possibly from a wax imprint. Then, recalling the box of skeleton keys left by Higgins's oak, he realized that the door could have been both opened and locked by someone who had no library key at all. The key was not like the huge, old-fashioned one still used at Hedingham, which would have been exceedingly difficult to copy, and where the lock would be very hard to force by a skeleton key; it was a relatively modest key, probably made for a new kind of lock put into the door in the past twenty years or so. This meant that anyone borrowing a key, perhaps from the porter's lodge, could fairly easily take an imprint of it, and then have it copied for personal use.

The reading room and rare books room, he recalled, used quite different keys, copies of which were provided to the Master and all the fellows, so that, once the library was open, they could work quietly on the top floor in either room, and take away any volume they wished, provided they entered it in one of the borrowers' books. (There was one for books printed before 1600 and one for others.) However, there was no evidence that the intruder of last night had been inside the rare books room.

Still unable to sleep, Simon started to imagine the whole plan of the keep, trying to work out the most likely site of a 'vented' secret room. When, in his mind, he came to the top floor he recalled how he had described it to Theresa the week before. At Cambridge, instead of there being one very large space, as at Hedingham, one half of the top floor, accessed from the main staircase, comprised a spacious drawing-room or 'solar', complete with fireplace, with stone walls on all four sides – the stone wall opposite the fireplace being placed immediately above the arch that spanned the hall below. This solar had originally been the main private room used by the sheriff, or by the king on one of his occasional visits, but was now a reading room, sometimes used for meetings or lectures. The walls were lined with books but the main space was left open, rendering the whole room one of the finest in Cambridge. The other half of the top floor was divided into two smaller rooms by an ancient wooden partition, with doors leading from each room, through the stone partition above the arch, to the solar. One of the smaller rooms was the original chapel and now held the college's collection of rare books. For the most part the walls of this room, once again, were lined with books, but there were also several locked cabinets, one of which had contained the Courcey documents. The central part of this room contained two tables and some chairs reserved for the use of fellows. The other room was furnished with a small fireplace and had originally been the sheriff's, and later the Master's, private sleeping chamber. Leading off one of its two windows was a twelfth-century garderobe that had been turned into a small bathroom and toilet. This chamber was now an office for the librarian and, in addition to a desk, contained stacks of books waiting to be catalogued or repaired.

There was another difference between this top floor and the one at Hedingham. At De Vere College, in addition to stone window seats on both levels of the Great Hall, the top floor had ones made of wood, although they were certainly not part of the original construction, having been added in Tudor times. At Hedingham there were no such seats.

Still restless, Simon decided to get up and return to the library, where he could try out two ideas that had come to him during the sleepless hours. First he found the list of Cambridge fellows and scanned it for all those called Dr Jones. There were three. One was the Jones at St John's College that he knew, and whose description certainly did not fit that of the visitor to Hedingham. Another was a fellow of Queens', and Simon realized that he did know him after all, at least by sight. He was an extremely old and bent theologian, who, once again, did not fit the description. The third was unknown to him, a certain Dr Hywel Jones who was a fellow of St Catharine's College and, it appeared, a mathematician. He decided that he had better find out more about this person.

Next, he turned to explore his other idea. Going to the catalogue of old books he scanned all the entries to see how many bore the signature of William Courcey. There appeared to be one hundred and fifty-eight. Evidently the former Master had left his entire library to the college, and eight of these must have been acquired after he made the list referred to in the notebook. Simon wrote down the names of twenty of them, picked at random, and then went to the rare books room to look at them systematically. The first one was a Latin grammar; and after a few minutes he was satisfied that none of the letters was underlined. The next was an edition of Horace: and again there was no underlining. One thing was already certain. As he had suspected, only some of the books had been furnished with the clue. He found Courcey's copy of Aristotle's *Metaphysics* (a Latin translation of the original Greek). Yes, starting on the eighth page some letters were discreetly underlined, spelling out the same message as before. It did indeed look as if Courcey only wanted people who read certain books to be exposed to the clue.

It was now breakfast time and, as he had hoped, Talworthy and Heatherington were both in the Combination Room. He approached Talworthy first. "There's a small favour I want to ask you. I'm trying to take my duties as librarian seriously, and I'm making an inventory of all the books that William Courcey left to the college. I have a list, but I don't think it's complete, and I would be grateful if I could have a quick look at the copy of Euclid you've got out, since it might be one of them."

"I'm pretty sure it is," said Talworthy, "because I noticed his signature on the title page. But you're welcome to come and take a look – and actually you might as well take it back to the rare books room since I only wanted to check a small matter and I've finished with it."

Heatherington was sitting at the other end of the long table and Simon approached him with the same request, respecting the collection of Virgil's poems from the rare books room. Heatherington, quite out of character, seemed a bit flustered. "I really don't know if it belonged to Courcey," he said. "Of course you're welcome to see it, but I'm very busy just at the moment. Can I bring it back to you when I've finished with it?"

"Yes, that will be fine," said Simon, not meaning anything of the kind, since he really wanted to know right away whether Heatherington had access to the clue and, as a result, whether he could have been the visitor to Hedingham and, perhaps, the late-night visitor to the library.

When breakfast was over he followed Talworthy to his rooms. Despite the early hour Simon was offered a sherry, and he sat down to continue their earlier talk about the college paintings. He had not been in this set of rooms since Talworthy took them over and he was interested to see a number of fine photographs set out on top of the mantelpiece and desk. Photography, it turned out, was Talworthy's second 'obsession' (as he himself described it), the first being paintings. "Good paintings," he explained, "I simply cannot afford to buy; I just have to get along with admiring them on the walls of museums or other places; but photographs I can begin to collect for myself."

Talworthy, in the true spirit of an enthusiast, launched into an account of the development of photography from the early camera obscura, known to the ancient world, to the addition of lenses to these cameras in the sixteenth century and later, to the photographic plates made popular in the Daguerreotype process of the 1840s. Talworthy pointed to a big camera placed near the window, mounted on a large wooden tripod. It comprised a brass box, forming a cube about twelve inches each way, to which was attached what looked like a kind of bellows made of folded leather. "That's what I use," he explained, "along with what are known as 'wet plates'. Then I do the development in the small kitchen which I've turned into a dark room."

Next to the camera Simon noticed a large brass telescope, also mounted on a tripod, the latter – like the one on which the camera was mounted – having adjustable legs.

"Is the telescope also part of your photographic apparatus?" Simon asked.

"Yes and no. It's a straightforward telescope set up for terrestrial use, that is with an 'erector' to make the image come the right way up. I bought it because I'm interested in the idea of taking photographs through the telescope, setting up the wet plate where the eyepiece is so that I can take long-range pictures. But I'm having trouble getting it to work properly. The difficulty is that the exposure through the telescope has to be even longer than with a regular camera, and the result is that any slight shaking gives a blurred image; but, as you probably know, when you crank up the magnification you nearly always get some shaking, especially if you're out in a wind. I've got to find a way either of having an absolutely steady stand, or of taking a faster picture."

In ordinary circumstances Simon would have been interested, but in view of his present preoccupations he was getting impatient. He was about to take possession of the Euclid and leave, when Talworthy showed him a recent photograph he had been asked to take by Lionel

Higgins, shortly before his death. It showed Higgins with three of his friends, all in Cambridge M.A. gowns. Two of the subjects, Higgins and Heatherington, were fellows of De Vere, while the other two he did not recognize, although one of them looked vaguely familiar. They must be from other colleges. Simon had a sudden idea.

"I wonder if I could ask a favour. I would really like to show this photograph to a friend who is interested in portrait photography."

Simon observed, internally, that he was lying once again, but continued, "He's interested in making a record on photographic plates of all the members of his club, and this would give him an idea of what can be achieved."

Talworthy was happy to agree, and Simon promised to return the photograph after his next visit to London. Shortly afterwards he was able to leave, carrying both the photograph and the Euclid. When he reached his rooms he examined the book carefully. It was 'clean': there being no underlining. Talworthy did not seem to be in the hunt – although perhaps that was not too certain. After all, it was odd that he should borrow one of Courcey's books so soon after the revelations about the old documents, and with access to the rare books room allowed to all fellows, Talworthy could have looked at several other books when he found nothing of interest in the Euclid. As for the photograph, this might help to solve the mystery of the visitor to Hedingham castle. Term ended on Friday, and Simon had teaching engagements till then, after which he had arranged the moving of his things to London on the weekend, followed, he hoped, by a meeting with Theresa. So it would have to be Tuesday of next week before he could show the photograph to Mrs Pine and see if his suspicions were justified.

He decided to go for a walk, crossing the river at Magdalene as he headed into the town, then taking the back route to King's. After crossing the river again at the end of King's garden he could walk along the 'Backs' and return via Silver Street and St Catharine's College, where he could try to get a glimpse of Dr Jones.

When he reached Trinity Hall he noticed that the flag on the gatehouse was at half-mast. He passed into the first court and saw a small group of people talking, including Mr Arthur Young, a former student of his who had recently been elected to a fellowship at the college. As he approached the group Young detached himself and came up to him.

"Have you heard the sad news?" he asked.

"No; I just noticed the flag was at half-mast and thought I would inquire."

"It's Mr Bambridge, the librarian. I think you may have known him – for I believe you share at least some of his interest in old books. He was found dead, early this morning. It looks as if he fell from the roof of the chapel some time during the night."

"I'm terribly sorry to hear it. I did know Mr Bambridge, although not well: we sometimes met in Dr Higgins's rooms. Is there any suspicion of foul play?"

Mr Young looked shocked and surprised. "No, none at all – though I suppose in view of what happened to Higgins you might be led in that direction. No, the official view is that it was just a tragic accident, since it seemed he had imbibed fairly heavily last night, when we had one of our major feasts. The general belief is that he went for a breath of fresh air combined with a view of the stars, and just failed to keep his balance."

"You seem to be hinting at another, less official view."

Mr Young lowered his voice. "Well, there are one or two of the fellows who think he may have jumped. Mr Bambridge did suffer from depression from time to time, and particularly in the last few days he seemed to have had something on his mind. He was also a rather lonely and isolated person, and I believe the death of Higgins affected him badly. But still, I think that theory is unlikely, and I would certainly ask you not to suggest it to anyone you meet."

Simon didn't ask if Dr James – who he knew had been at the feast – had been sitting near Bambridge, or had been seen speaking to him, since in view of his earlier question about foul play he didn't want to say anything else that might be taken amiss, but he was worried. Here was another coincidence – and the past few weeks had seen too many.

After a few more polite words he continued his walk in thoughtful and sombre mood. Bambridge had not been exactly a friend, but he was sorry to know he was dead, especially in tragic circumstances. In a way, he reflected, he would prefer to think he had been killed than that he had been unhappy enough to take his own life. But in any case, being a librarian at Cambridge was beginning to look like a hazardous occupation!

He walked along the Backs to Silver Street, then, after crossing the river, he passed Queens' and entered the front court of St Catharine's. He went casually round the court, noting the names on the staircases, and found what he was looking for in one of the corners. Dr Jones, it seemed, had rooms on the ground floor. Then he had a piece of luck. The door leading to the staircase attached to Jones's set of rooms opened, and out walked a man of middle height, probably in his early thirties. Almost immediately he was accosted by a friend. "Jones," he said, "are you going to the river?" The reply came in a broad Welsh accent. "Yes, I'll be there in an hour or so, I've a couple of things to see to first."

Simon carried on with his walk. It was just possible that the Jones who had visited Hedingham castle had disguised both his age and his accent, but it was much more likely that he had given a false name, or perhaps made a false claim about his connection with Cambridge. In either case, this confirmed his suspicion that the person Mrs Pine showed round the castle had been on a quest for the treasure and was prepared to lie and perhaps to do other, worse, things in order to pursue his goal. Already there had been one murder, one suspicious death and one physical assault. He would have to be careful.

Chapter 20

Darlingscott Manor, Warwickshire, Wednesday morning, 1ˢᵗ April.

Viscount FitzSimmons sat at the large table in his library on the second floor of his fine Elizabethan manor. The window-shutters were open, on two sides giving a view of the expansive park that surrounded his home near Stratford-upon-Avon, bought by the first Viscount FitzSimmons shortly after his ennoblement. Formerly, it had belonged to a recusant family and the priest-hole, which could only be accessed from the library, had provided a useful resting place for the Courcey documents when he was not examining them.

Shortly after Tumbler had brought him the papers from the Master's Lodge he had realized they were incomplete. When Higgins had broken the news of his discovery to the assembled fellows of De Vere College he had spoken of three sets of documents and it looked as if Tumbler had only found one of these. Suspecting that the papers might well be in the Lodge he had persuaded him with great difficulty to attempt one of his more ambitious burglaries. Although a highly competent thief, Tumbler never used violence and, in the end, he had agreed to do the job only on condition that he could bring a colleague to strike a blow, if it should prove necessary to do so, a colleague who knew how to use force without causing death.

After the blow had been struck both men had searched Dr James's desks and drawers and table-tops. But all they had found with respect to the Courcey documents was a folder containing seven letters from

Edward de Vere to William Courcey. These had been in a locked drawer of the desk in the study.

In a way this did not matter, since it was the de Vere letters that were the Viscount's principal interest and, in any case, he expected that most (perhaps all) of the other letters would be in Latin. Although he had the usual schoolboy's background in the language, he had not pursued the subject and this, combined with Tudor hand-writing, would probably have meant that he could make little sense of them. Moreover, if he had the other letters, he certainly wouldn't want to show them to anyone else, not even someone who could help him to make sense of them. However, the absence of the major part of the Courcey documents was puzzling. His best guess went like this:

It was probably not Dr James who had killed Higgins. Not only did this seem quite out of character for someone he had known for years, but the fact that he seemed not to have most of the old documents pointed to someone else being the murderer. Some other person, someone intent on finding out more about the Lolworth treasure, had struck Higgins and then taken the papers that interested him, including the letters from Henry Courcey to his brother. Subsequently, Dr James, who probably had access to all the keys he needed, had entered Higgins's rooms, perhaps in the process of making a friendly call so that he could have another look at the papers. When he had no answer he used his own key and found the dead body. Anxious about the papers he left the body where he found it and then himself took the de Vere letters left by the thief. This still left a puzzle about the third category of papers that Higgins had referred to: letters by people other than Henry Courcey and Edward de Vere, along with other papers, but perhaps the murderer had taken these as well. This was one of several things that didn't altogether make sense, but it was still the most likely scenario he could come up with.

Among the possible murderers Dr Simon Weatherspoon had to be included. The discovery that he was the true author of the books by both Amelia Buzzard and Emily Dove had come as a complete surprise. Here Tumbler had been at his best, not only for finding the files at Fisher-White, but also for his delicate negotiations with Sir

Edward Featherstone, managing editor and part owner of the *London Echo*, negotiations which would keep the Viscount at arm's length from all agreements. On the negative side this meant that Tumbler was to receive half the money that was to come from Sir Edward, and would then be well enough off to become independent of himself if he so wished, but on the positive side he would achieve three things: first, a tidy sum that would help many of his schemes that were currently in need of an injection of money; second, a legal distance from any awkward repercussions that might follow from the disclosures in the *London Echo* and third, a way of dealing a blow to Weatherspoon.

In truth, however, his initial dislike of the scholar – particularly after the unsatisfactory conversation in the Senior Combination Room at De Vere College – had given way to a certain degree of admiration. Weatherspoon was clever and, so he reckoned, unscrupulous, but he acknowledged to himself that he was hardly in a position to condemn someone else for these qualities. Moreover, none of Dr Weatherspoon's dubious activities really provided evidence that he was a murderer. Furthermore, the real challenge to the Viscount's schemes at Stratford did not come from the novel, but from the papers that were now spread out before him. His unmasking of Weatherspoon would be sufficient satisfaction for any ill feelings he had harboured, and if the author of *The de Vere Papers* were as rich as the press claimed, this would hardly be a personal disaster for him.

He was now reading the de Vere letters for the third time. They had proved both fascinating and worrying. Fortunately they were all in English, although, as one would expect, of an archaic kind. The first five were of minor interest, except for one reference concerning a trip to Cambridge to see a performance by the 'de Vere Boys' of one the Earl's plays. However, when he reached the last two his attention was fully engaged. Here was evidence of a kind he had hoped not to find and which might indeed put his plans for Stratford-upon-Avon in jeopardy. William Courcey had actually been asked to hide some manuscripts that were to be entrusted to him. Exactly what they were was not clear: they might have been miscellaneous poems or plays that had no connection with the Shakespearean canon. The only indication of where they were hidden was de Vere's thanks to Courcey for agreeing to put them in a secure place within his college. FitzSimmons knew that the old Master had his private rooms in the ancient keep, so that pointed to one of the likely hiding-places.

Youre most assured and louinge Brother .

Edward Oxenford

Carefully he replaced all the papers in the priest-hole and then went over to his writing desk. He would post a letter to Dr James that morning, accepting his invitation to come to De Vere College for Easter with a view to renewing discussions on the possibilities of funding a new building. In truth, in part because of his annoyance with the reception of his ideas at the college, he was no longer interested in helping to fund any such building, but he would like the opportunity to take a closer look at the old keep where, he knew, William Courcey lived until his death at a great age.

Chapter 21

Cambridge and London, Saturday, 4ᵗʰ April.

By special arrangement with the porter, two horses and a substantial cart, along with two strong men, came to the gate of De Vere College at six in the morning. The cart was loaded under Simon's direction and then trundled off on its twelve-hour journey to London, which included a change of horses.

For two reasons the loading caused little surprise. Term had ended the day before, so there was quite a lot of coming and going as many of the students had boxes to collect. In addition to this, in order to avoid comment, Simon had let it be known he had found a pied-à-terre where he could work quietly in the long vacations, and that he was arranging to move some of his things to this hide-away ahead of time. Among the fellows the idea had got around that this pied-à-terre was in the countryside, and Simon did nothing to prevent this misconception. The moving of his possessions meant that anyone having cause to visit his rooms would now be amazed at how bare they were, in fact, with only a few pieces of furniture left, all of which belonged to the college. Mindful of this he had asked his manservant, Humphreys (who saw to the needs of six of the fellows), not to clean his room for the next two weeks, on the excuse that he was involved in some work that required absolutely no disturbance to his papers. He also intended, if possible, to put off potential visitors.

Simon breakfasted in the Senior Combination Room and then took a morning train to London. On the journey he found himself nodding off, which was not surprising. He had been in the old library from just before midnight till 3 a.m. checking on the entire list of books donated to the college by William Courcey. One was still out, the one borrowed by Heatherington, but he was able to examine the other one hundred and fifty seven. As he had suspected, nine of these – including the *Fourth Maccabees* that he had only just returned – contained the Latin clue. This meant that the book now held by Heatherington almost certainly contained the clue, and that the reference to ten starred books was explained in the way he suspected.

It was nearly noon when he reached Bishopsgate station and he decided to visit the tea-room before going on to his house, where, as he waited for the cart, he planned an enjoyable afternoon arranging within the cellar the fine wines that should have arrived from Averys of Bristol.

A paperboy was calling out, "Amelia Buzzard sensation – read all about it!"

The boy was selling the *London Echo*, and Simon felt his heart sink. Nogle had thought it likely the storm would not break for another

few days, and he desperately wanted this time, partly to finish settling his move, but more urgently so that he could smooth the way with Theresa. He was still fearful of what her reaction would be to the discovery that he was the author of the books she had described as typifying the woman's viewpoint. It was going to be bad enough if the news came first from him, but much worse if it came through the *London Echo*.

He bought the paper and sat down in a corner of the tea-room, thankful that accurate newspaper illustrations of people which used photographic techniques instead of purely hand-made engravings were still uncommon in the London papers.

This reflection prompted the memory of a recent event. Only two days ago a photographer from London had knocked on the outer door of his set of rooms. He was, so the photographer's story went, taking part in a scheme to take professional photographs of all the college fellows in Cambridge. There would be no initial cost, and only if one liked the result and wanted a copy would there be any charge at all. He had the camera already set up in the courtyard and if only Dr Weatherspoon would oblige everything was ready. Simon had refused, not having any wish for a record of his face to be made, but only now did he connect the incident with the *London Echo*. It could well have been a lucky escape, and the photographer's visit part of a plot by that paper to show a representation, or even an actual photograph of his face, alongside its sensational story.

In their conversations about photography Talworthy had given him an enthusiastic and, as it now turned out, a useful introduction to the art. On the worrying side, Talworthy had told him how the French, since 1848, had been developing a technique to print actual photographs directly onto newspapers, and that this technique was beginning to be used in England. On the more hopeful side of things, he had also said that, at present, making a portrait, even in good light, took him eight or nine seconds. Although there were some newer techniques that required less time, they still demanded that the subject be still, and this meant that a snooping photographer would have been unlikely to get a usable picture without Simon's knowledge and consent.

He turned to the article. It was guaranteed to create public interest but, to Simon's great relief, it was only stage one in what was intended to be a three-instalment thriller, designed to sell as many copies of the paper as possible. His identity had not yet been made public.

Page one of the paper carried a huge headline – "Amelia Buzzard to be revealed" – and in the article that followed the key paragraph ran:

For months the general public, both in Britain and overseas, has been speculating about the true authorship of *The Male Courtesan* and other writings produced under the name Amelia Buzzard, including *The de Vere Papers*, the new novel which is even now producing a sensation, barely a month after its release to the public. The *London Echo* is proud to announce that after weeks of careful detection by our intrepid reporters, the true authorship of these famous books is shortly to be revealed. The news will indeed produce a further sensation, but already we can indicate one part of the mystery. Amelia Buzzard is a man! Watch this paper in the next few days, and we shall reveal, first another amazing fact, this time about Emily Dove, the author whose work has so vigorously attacked the writings of Amelia Buzzard. Later, we shall reveal the actual identity of the author known as Amelia Buzzard. She, or rather he, will be unmasked! The news will surprise and shock and amaze. Watch for further revelations. They will only appear in the *London Echo*.

Simon immediately took a cab to his new home, trying during the journey to digest the implications of the article. He had known for some time that this or something like it was bound to be printed, but its actual appearance brought home the magnitude of what was involved. His life would never be the same again. From being a quiet Cambridge don and a pretty obscure person so far as the general public was concerned, he was shortly to be a celebrity. Both his secret life and his wealth were soon to be common knowledge. Fortunately, in the complexity of the city of London, and with his face relatively unknown there, he could, or so he hoped, continue to live in some quietness, but his life-style in Cambridge was soon to come to an end.

Two things, he realized, were now matters of urgency. First, he had to see Theresa and forewarn her of the coming revelations; second, he had to try and conclude his search for the Lolworth treasure before the final storm broke and, with it, the almost certain loss of his position as librarian, pro-tem, at De Vere College, along with the unique opportunities that gave him for investigating the old keep.

Simon found his house in good order. Mrs Peters had been in residence for two days and she had already, with his permission, hired one of the two maids. The butler had not yet been appointed, but Nogle, efficient as ever, had arranged for two likely candidates to be interviewed by Simon on Monday morning.

The furniture ordered from Jessop and Sons had arrived and between them Mrs Peters and the maid had already placed it around the house in provisional order. The wine he had asked to be delivered was also there, having been sent by rail from Bristol the day before, and then loaded onto a cart for the journey from the station. It was packed in wooden cases in the hallway, but Simon no longer felt in the mood to sort it. He simply carried the cases down to the cellar so that they would not be in the way of the furniture and books coming from Cambridge and left them to be opened and sorted another time. He accepted a dish of soup, his first meal in his new home, and then took a cab to Theresa's apartment on the second floor of a terraced house in Kensington.

He rang the bell but there was no response. Dispirited, he walked up and down the street for twenty minutes. The walk to his house would take about half an hour and he had just decided that this would be the best way to reduce his tension when Theresa came in sight, walking on the arm of a man in his mid twenties wearing a yellow waistcoat. Simon supposed this could be the Marcus Peabody whom Mrs Brown had referred to as a 'canary'. He was right.

Theresa looked at Simon without smiling, and with a steely stare unlike anything he had associated with her before. As he raised his hat, her eyes seemed to flash as she said, "Marcus, this is Dr Weatherspoon – Dr Weatherspoon, this is my old friend Mr Marcus Peabody."

At Theresa's front door Peabody waved his right arm and departed. Theresa began to open the door, making no suggestion about Simon coming in. Simon, his mind in turmoil, was desperately trying to think of something to say: something that might form the beginning of an elaborate apology if, as now seemed likely, Theresa had guessed the true identity of Amelia Buzzard and Emily Dove. Eventually, and rather lamely, he said.

"I just wanted to let you know that the house is beginning to get into some kind of order, and that I'm looking forward to seeing you for tea on Monday afternoon."

Theresa turned and continued her steely stare. "I don't think I'll be able to make it," she said, and then, after a pause she added, "I think you know why. After that report in the *London Echo* it didn't take me long to put two and two together, especially when I began to compare some of the writing styles in your *First Maccabees* and in the Buzzard books. Why the hell didn't you tell me? You know this is making me look a complete idiot – in the light of what I have written about women writers. You could at least have warned me so that I could write something that would begin to revise my earlier comments. Something like: 'further reflections on Amelia Buzzard'."

"But Theresa, don't you remember? I was trying to tell you when we last met, but you rushed off just as I was about to reveal my second secret."

"But you told me both secrets; the first was about the treasure and the second was about your plan to move into a house in London. You never suggested anything about your double life."

"Please, you've got it wrong. The London house wasn't what I meant by a secret – I was about to tell you the real second secret when you had to dash away."

"Frankly, I don't believe you, and I shall not feel sorry for you when the storm breaks in a few days time. I imagine you'll be under siege in your rooms at De Vere, with the nation's press struggling to get an interview. In fact you may find it hard to escape to London and go into hiding."

Simon stood speechless and Theresa's eyes softened, but only a little. "Don't worry, I can keep secrets. I won't tell about the treasure, or about your London house, but I advise you to forewarn your staff. If they start to gossip you'll have half the London reporters camped outside your quiet retreat."

Theresa seemed about to say something more when she turned, opened her door, and left him alone on the pavement.

Slowly he started to walk home. His thoughts were grim, and the

London life he had so much looked forward to now seemed much less inviting. As he got in sight of his house he remembered Theresa's words about his staff. In fact, he thought, despite her warning, he might be better off saying nothing to them. He had not explained to Theresa that Mrs Peters presently knew him simply as 'Mr Spoon'. This had been Nogle's suggestion, since this usage might well prevent the staff from finding out his connection with the upcoming scandal, while, on the other hand, it could well seem, if they or any of the tradesmen did discover the connection, that there was little if any deceit. His inner voice told him this was somewhat disingenuous, but, after all, it was not unknown for people to use a shortened version of their real names. All the staff knew was that Mr W. Spoon was moving from a house in Cambridgeshire to a new home in London, and the fact that the move would have occurred before the scandal broke – along with Dr Weatherspoon's flight from his college coming after Mr Spoon's move to London – would help to keep his true identity secret. At the same time, he realized, be must be careful not to have any post sent to his London home directly from De Vere College, for that name might well strike a chord. As soon as he returned to Cambridge he resolved to see Mr Roberts, his lawyer friend in the town. He could then arrange that, after he left Cambridge, all his post could be forwarded to his lawyer, who could then send it on to him in large brown packets addressed to Mr W. Spoon.

Chapter 22

London and Sudbury, Sunday,
5th April and Monday, 6th April.

Simon was glad of the activity that the arrival of his Cambridge furniture, and more particularly of his books, entailed. On Sunday he went to a morning service in the city at which Professor J. F. D. Maurice preached. Maurice had been a Professor of Divinity in London but had been forced to resign because of his liberal views, and in particular for his rejection of eternal hell fire for sinners, an event which had occasioned Tennyson, who was one of Maurice's friends, to write:

> *Should all our churchmen foam and spite*
> *At you, so careful of the right,*
> *Yet one lay-hearth would give you welcome*
> *(Take it and come) to the Isle of Wight.*

Maurice now held a chair in Cambridge and Simon had met him a few times, and very much admired him – especially for his seminal work in working-mens' education. The sermon was a welcome change from the nonsense he had heard on the last visit to London. It related both Old Testament prophecy and the New Testament to current problems of poverty, and was listened to with more than polite attention.

For a time the sermon lifted his spirits – but despite a well-cooked lunch at his home he soon began to feel lonely and dejected. Sorting out his books took the rest of the day, and helped to keep his mind off other things. Early on the Monday morning he saw the two potential butlers, sent round by Nogle, and hired one of them, an experienced man called Elijah Newton, who had recently been made available by the death of his former master. Newton continually called him either 'Sir' or 'Mr Spoon', and after hiring him Simon tried to give the impression, without actually telling lies this time, that he had moved (and Simon stressed the past tense) from the country to the urban life of London, so that he could have access to the great libraries there for his scholarly work.

Just before 10.00 he got a taxi to Bishopsgate station and boarded a train for Sudbury. He had not written to Mrs Pine, since a letter could not reach her in time, but he hoped fervently he would find her at the address she had given him during the visit to Hedingham.

On the journey Simon mused over one of the ironies in his situation. Fisher-White had encouraged his writings about amorous adventures for the sake of increased sales, and now the *London Echo* was deciding its policy on exactly the same principle. No-one seemed concerned with what was right, but with what would make money, a policy, he admitted to himself, that had to some extent taken hold of his own motives, although he had originally begun his writing of fiction more for fun than for money.

He was still absorbed in such thoughts, along with the idea that he might try to steer his next novel, perhaps even the one by Emily Dove, in a rather different direction – seeking to write something that Theresa would really approve of – when the train reached Sudbury. He found a cab at the station and immediately set off to find Mrs Pine, who lived in a village three miles from Sudbury, on the road to Castle Hedingham.

He was lucky. When he rang the door of the modest house that Mrs Pine lived in she came to the door herself. At first she looked blank.

"Mrs Pine, I'm so sorry to disturb you. I am Dr Weatherspoon, and you may remember that you very kindly showed Miss Theresa Brown and myself round Hedingham castle, just nine days ago."

Mrs Pine's face lit up. "Of course, yes, I remember you now, and the Colonel's niece. What can I do for you? I'm afraid I can't go out to Hedingham today, but I can easily arrange another visit. This time of year I'm normally there three days a week. Please come in."

As they sat in the small front parlour Simon explained the reason for his journey. "Thank-you, no, I am not planning another visit to the castle, at least not just now. The fact is that I am really interested in the architecture of Hedingham because it is so like our keep at De Vere College on which I am doing some research. This makes me very keen to find other people with a similar interest, and ever since you told me about the Dr Jones who visited the castle just before we did, I've been trying to work out which Dr Jones this could be, since it is such a common name."

Mrs Pine nodded, so Simon continued. "I have got a photograph here of some fellows, and I wondered if you would recognize your Dr Jones in it. I think one of them could be the man who came here."

Simon brought out the photograph lent to him by Talworthy. "That's him," said Mrs Pine. To Simon's surprise she pointed, not to Heatherington, but to the man who was standing immediately to the left of him and who had seemed vaguely familiar to Simon when he first saw the photograph! "I know him for sure: that is your Dr Jones."

With difficulty, Simon supressed a gasp of astonishment. Forcing himself to act naturally he thanked Mrs Pine, made a few polite comments on her house, and then rejoined the cab, which he had asked to wait for him.

On his return journey to London in the evening Simon suddenly remembered who the mystery fellow was. He was the guest Heatherington had brought with him to the dinner at which Lord FitzSimmons had tried to get the De Vere fellowship to rally round his cause, and at which – more significantly – Higgins had spoken of his discovery of the Courcey documents. He also remembered his name. It was a Mr John Lewis, a fellow of St John's College, and a Latinist. For his visit to Hedingham he had both invented his name and given himself a doctorate. Could he perhaps be capable of more serious crimes?

A number of possibilities now occurred to Simon. Heatherington's borrowing of the Latin verses had always puzzled him because although, like all the fellows, he had some knowledge of the classics, Latin poetry was certainly not a primary interest for him. But suppose he had borrowed the book for his friend, Lewis? That would make sense. Also it might explain why Heatherington showed some irritableness when Simon asked to see the book. If, without permission from the librarian, it had been lent to Lewis, this – as a rare book from the college library – would be against the rules and, not surprisingly, Heatherington might feel put out. Further, he would need a little time to retrieve the book. There was more. Talworthy had described the four fellows in the photograph as a group of friends. Perhaps Heatherington or Lewis, or both, had had some preview of the Courcey documents through their friendship with Higgins, and this had led Lewis to make a point of borrowing one of the books that had been starred. For a Latinist, a book of Latin poetry would seem like a natural choice.

In his mind, Simon went over the list of possible suspects. In order to complete this list one had, he now realized, to consider three ways in which one might be put onto the scent of either the Lolworth treasure or the manuscripts left by Edward de Vere. First, one might – as in his own case – simply have found the clue written in one of the ten books where William Courcey had left the Latin message. However, since he was probably the first person to find the clue in this way – over a period of nearly three hundred years – this was not how the other seekers were likely to have been put on the trail. Second, one might have access to the Courcey documents, and therein find clues, perhaps from the coded list of contents that Simon knew about from the notebook, or perhaps from some other indications that Simon didn't know about, not having seen the actual papers. Third, someone might have had just a glimpse of the Courcey documents, but found this sufficient to lead one to William Courcey's donation of books, and thence positively to look for the clue which Simon had come upon by chance. This would be made much easier if one had actually seen the list of starred books, and then decided to look at them carefully to see why they had been starred. He came into the first category – and it was just possible that there were others in this class – perhaps stimulated by the discussion of the Courcey documents in the Senior Combination Room; whoever had attacked the Master and stolen the papers came into the second category; Heatherington and Lewis – and just possibly Mr Bambridge, might, he suspected, come into the third.

Chapter 23

De Vere College and Jesus Green, Tuesday, 7ᵗʰ April to Wednesday, 8ᵗʰ April.

Simon returned to Cambridge on the Tuesday, and began to put his affairs in order. He had no lectures planned for the summer term, but he did have a number of students to supervise and one of his urgent tasks was to arrange alternative teachers, on the assumption that he would be absent. He started writing to other dons who could carry on the teaching, indicating that he might not be available in the summer, without saying why. One of the other matters preoccupying him was what to do, if anything, about the discovery that Mr Lewis of St John's College appeared to be on the same trail. All he could think of at the moment was to make some discreet inquiries among his friends.

On the Wednesday, immediately after breakfast in the Senior Combination Room, he set off for the library to see if he could find inspiration in his search for the secret room by going into every corner of the keep, bearing in mind all the clues he now had.

Crossing the old court he noticed two workmen coming out of the door to the chapel.

"Good morning," he said to the one who seemed senior, "Is there some work going on?"

"Yes Sir," he replied, "We've just opened up the crypt. The Master wants to check on some water he thinks may be getting in through the windows, just above the ground. He's there now, looking down below."

Simon checked his walk to the keep. Yet another coincidence – this time, once again, involving the Master! Perhaps he had been too hasty in classing him as an unlikely suspect following the attack in the Lodge. He walked to the chapel, opening and closing the door very quietly.

In the gloom of the unlit building he could see that the flagstone leading to the crypt had been pulled open and was held in position by a rope, attached at one end to the ring in the stone and at the other to the base of one of the wooden pews. He heard footsteps coming up from below and quickly ducked behind the tomb of the Tudor bishop, thinking as he did so how ridiculous he would look should the Master walk into the corner where he crouched. Fortunately he did not. Instead, Simon heard footsteps and then the opening and closing of the chapel door.

He emerged from his hiding place. The flagstone was still up. He walked to the opening and looked down at the stone steps that led to the crypt, about a dozen in all, which he had never seen before. He hesitated before going down himself. He could tell by the smell of candle wax that the Master had carried a light, and without his own candle it wasn't certain he could see much. Worse, he wondered what would happen if one of the workmen, not realizing where he was, closed the flagstone while he was down there; or, just possibly, whether the Master might trap him down there on purpose! Perhaps the flagstone could be pushed open from down below, but he didn't know, and if the more sinister possibility occurred, then something heavy might be put on top of it.

An idea flashed through his mind. He had been looking for more exciting and dangerous incidents to recount in the new novel by Emily Dove, and trapping his hero in an underground crypt, when the chief villain placed a heavy object on the flagstone that led to it, might provide just such an incident!

Despite the risk, he decided to take a quick look. It was fortunate that the body of Dr Higgins had been buried in the village where his sister lived and not placed in the crypt, for otherwise entering the chamber would have been a most unpleasant experience. He stepped into the gap and went down the stone steps.

At the bottom it was not as dark as he had feared, partly because his eyes had already adjusted to the gloom of the unlit chapel, and partly because the vents did let in a little light, even though this was much diminished by shrubs and grass that hid them from view on the outside.

The crypt, like the chapel, was made of narrow, red Tudor bricks of the kind used to build the old courts at Queens' and De Vere. It measured some fifty by twenty feet, with four small windows along each side, placed between the buttresses that helped to support the brick vaulting. There were no tombs, but about a dozen stone supports, on each of which stood one or more wooden coffins. All were dusty and old, and it seemed probable that no fellow or Master had been buried here for decades.

Walking quietly, by preventing his heel going down before the rest of his foot, he went from one end of the crypt to the other. The floor was dry, suggesting not only that there was no water coming in from the windows but, more significantly, that the Master needed some excuse to examine the crypt. However there was evidence of water entry in the past, for on the walls there were no fewer than three sets of what looked like tide-marks, probably the result of those rare occasions when the Cam rose so high that the water reached ground level in the old court. He hadn't heard of any rooms ever being flooded, no doubt because the original builders had raised the level of the whole building enough to prevent that, but it looked as if the crypt did flood occasionally. He knew that the wine cellar under the Great Hall sometimes did, and that on the last occasion most of the labels had come off the bottles and the only ones they could identify with certainty were those in bins exclusively given over to one wine.

This potential for flooding counted against anyone planning to hide manuscripts here but, on the other hand, it was probably dry enough most of the time and the intention might not have been to leave the documents here for hundreds of years.

The wall at one end held his attention. There seemed to be an ancient repair here, with a section standing out because of a change in the pattern of bricks. On the floor were drips of wax, and with a shiver Simon recalled the similar drips in the gallery of the College library. Was the Master, after all, behind these quiet visitations?

Footsteps rang above him. Suddenly fearful of being trapped, he went quickly to the steps, only to face an astonished Heatherington staring down on him as he climbed up.

"Good heavens!" said the Shakespearean scholar. "What on earth are you doing down there?"

Simon put on a rather forced grin. "I noticed the workmen coming out, and they told me the Master was carrying out a check on damp in the crypt. When I saw the entrance was open, curiosity got the better of me. I've never been down before."

"I've never been down either. I think I'll have a look too."

Much relieved, Simon led the way down again and they stood together in the semi-darkness.

"Well," said Heatherington, "I see no signs of damp, at least not recently. I wonder what gave the Master the idea – and come to that, why didn't he raise the matter at the last Governing Body meeting rather than just go ahead on his own? And in any case, I should have thought this was more the bursar's business."

Like Simon, Heatherington walked the length of the crypt, and he too stopped to look at the ancient repair in the brickwork, but made no comment. Was this merely curiosity, and the noting of something slightly out of kilter with the regularity of the brickwork, or had Heatherington a special reason for being interested in changes to the structure of the crypt?

Back in the chapel Heatherington seemed quite relaxed and friendly. "By the way," he said, "I've returned the Virgil to the library: I've finished with it now."

They left the chapel together and Simon continued his walk to the keep. The sun glinted off a pane of glass in one of the upper windows – and suddenly he had an idea.

Ever since Simon had noticed the telescope in Talworthy's rooms he had experienced a sort of hunch that it could be used to help him and yet he did not know how. It was like the situation when one half remembers a dream, enough to recall there was something interesting, but not enough to remember what it was. This was akin to the irritating situation he quite often experienced when working on an old text, trying to remember another that he was certain threw some light on the one before him, but not quite succeeding. But now – as when a half-forgotten memory suddenly comes to mind – he knew of a good use for Talworthy's telescope.

It was the word 'vented', found in the old clue, that lay at the basis of his idea: an idea that seemed to have been creeping around in the recesses of his mind ever since noting the same word in one of Courcey's books. The crypt was certainly 'vented' by the eight small windows, and indeed, it was this that made it a possible place to explore further. But if the secret place were in the keep, as he still thought likely, there was almost certainly some kind of small window that let onto the outside, and which made sense of the word 'vented' in the clue. It would also help to explain why it might be a suitable place for valuable manuscripts that could easily be ruined by damp in a hiding place with no current of air. In the case of the keep, any tiny window would very likely be high up. The thickness of the walls was partly designed to frustrate an enemy attacking the base with crowbars and partly to withstand rocks thrown at the walls by siege engines. For both reasons, the higher one went, the less important was the total thickness. This was why it was quite common to find small rooms within the thickness of walls in the upper storeys of castle towers. Furthermore, if the room were meant to be secret, a window would be much less obvious if it were far from the ground. In this case, it would also be an advantage if it were on the side of the keep that faced the river, since an attacker or a searcher would very likely be further away.

He changed direction, picked up the photograph from his own rooms and then went straight to Talworthy's. His friend was in and was happy to have the photograph returned, confirming as he put it away that one of the fellows it showed who was not from De Vere was indeed Mr John Lewis of St John's, while the other was a Mr Richard Hill from Trinity College, a specialist in Greek drama. Mentally, Simon added this Mr Hill to his list of suspects, and then he asked if he could borrow the telescope for the rest of the morning. It would be useful, he said – in a statement that did contain a small element of truth – to examine the fabric of the old keep. There was some question about whether the upper layers of stonework needed repointing, and as acting librarian this was now his responsibility.

The telescope had a three-inch aperture, and the terrestrial eyepiece gave a magnification of forty, which would be plenty for what he had in mind. He carried the telescope and its tripod outside the college and set it up on the open ground of Jesus Green, just across the river from the De Vere keep. Two walkers looked at him curiously and he told them that he wanted to get a close-up of the top of the keep, where a heron had recently perched.

He focussed on the battlements above the nearest wall of the keep at the spot where – in truth – a heron had recently been seen. In reality the stones were about two hundred feet away, but through the telescope they appeared to be only five. Slowly he scanned the wall, starting just below the place where the battlements rose from the wall-walk at the top of the keep. He moved the picture horizontally until he had made a complete sweep and then lowered it so that the top of the new image just overlapped the bottom of the previous sweep. On the third sweep he found – or believed he found – what he was looking for. About eight feet from the chapel window that faced the river there appeared to be a narrow vertical gap between two of the ashlar stones. Judging by the size of the stones, which averaged eighteen inches long and nine high, the gap comprised a narrow slit, exactly the height of two adjacent stones, and no more than an inch across. Near the bottom there seemed from time to time to be a small glint, as if a piece of glass were catching the sun and reflecting light

towards him. Simon continued the scan, spending more than an hour in a series of sweeps that ended just above the splay at the bottom of the keep. There were a few uneven bits of stone and a few cracks that could conceivably be tiny vents, but nothing that was as promising as the gap in the stonework near the chapel window.

Suddenly, the likely method of opening the door to the secret room struck him.

He returned the telescope to Talworthy and then went straight to the library to test his idea. If he were right he now knew exactly where the secret room was, and how the entrance worked, and the full significance of the clue given in the painting in the Master's lodge.

To his surprise, given that it was the Easter vacation, the library was open, indicating in all probability that the porter had opened it for someone to use. He was right. As he climbed the stair he thought he heard footsteps on a higher level of the same spiral staircase, and when he reached the Great Hall, there was someone sitting at one of the tables near the shelves, reading. It was Mr Lewis!

Simon nodded to him and then continued up to the rare books room. As a fellow of another Cambridge college there was no reason why Lewis could not use the De Vere library, provided he did not borrow any book without special permission, but taking recent events into account his presence was certainly unsettling. Simon sat down, wondering what to do. He wanted complete privacy for what he had in mind, and although he could lock the door he really did not want anyone else in the building while he carried out his exploration. In particular he did not want Lewis around, who, he now had good reason to believe, was on the trail but had not worked out – as he had – the probable place where the entrance to the secret room was to be found. If Lewis came upstairs to talk and found him locked in the rare books room, this in itself might give too much away. Reluctantly he went back to his rooms, noticing that Lewis still seemed absorbed in his book.

But what about those footsteps that he thought he had heard just as he came into the library? Perhaps, prior to pretending to be absorbed in reading, Lewis had been somewhere else in the keep and, when he heard Simon closing the outer door, or felt the draught of its opening, he had hurriedly gone to the Great Hall, where his presence would be less remarkable.

Chapter 24

De Vere College, evening, the same day.

During Easter week not only were almost all the students away, but several of the fellows were also absent from the college. Nevertheless, despite the reduced numbers, dinner in hall continued, followed by port and Madeira in the Senior Combination Room. However, immediately after the meal Simon excused himself and returned to the library. It was 9.00 when he unlocked the outer door and went in.

Before he tested his new theory about the location of the secret room he wanted to make sure that he was alone in the keep. With this in mind he made his way to the main floor, where he lit the two gas lamps near the entrance to the stairway. He walked round the different cases of books and looked into each of the eight window openings. There was no-one. Back in the centre of the room, right underneath the fine Norman arch, he looked up at the eight gallery openings, each of which ended in the windows that lit the upper storey of the Great Hall. His eyes concentrated on the one that interested him most, to the left of the fireplace – where the recent night-time visitor had left the candle wax. As with all the gallery openings there were two wooden rails placed, for reasons of safety, where the window opened onto the upper storey of the hall, and although it was difficult to see clearly in the dim light provided by the two lamps, there seemed to be something lying underneath the lower rail. It looked like an arm!

Simon ran up the main spiral stair and went round the gallery until he came to the place. There was a body, half wrapped in an M.A. gown, lying face down, with a large clot of blood on the back of its head, and one arm stretched out so that it just extended below the lower rail. He lit the gas lamp that was provided for that part of the gallery and went over to the body to feel the pulse: there was none. He turned the body over – it was that of Mr John Lewis!

Simon sat down on the window seat, shaking. Could the murderer still be around? He listened intently. He had noticed before that when the windows of the old keep were shut, as now, virtually no sound came into the building from outside, and the stillness seemed almost overpowering. There was, as always, the occasional creak from the wooden shelves as century by century they dried out, but apart from that he was aware only of the sound of his own breathing. If the murderer were still there he was certainly staying still, but more likely he had left before Simon's arrival, or had heard him come in and made his get-away, perhaps using the second staircase, as on the earlier occasion when someone had been surprised lurking in the library.

Simon began to stand up and, as he did so, one foot touched something underneath the stone seat. When he looked, there was a large wooden mallet and a wedge-shaped iron bar, a kind of heavy chisel – identical to some of the tools he had seen used by stonemasons. He examined the seat carefully. Where it ended by the window, right by the place where the bishop's ring was resting in the painting, there was a chip in the stonework.

Simon guessed the sequence of events. Lewis had been here before, and was quite likely the person he had surprised while he was examining the seat by candle-light some days ago. Lewis had returned to the place where he was sure the secret entrance had to be, following the same clues that Simon had found, and having discovered that Hedingham castle did not fit the clue. He had probably come to this place in the gallery that morning, carrying the mallet and chisel, very likely brought in under his gown. It was common for fellows to wear their gowns in Cambridge, partly as a way of disguising the often shabby nature of their clothes. He had retreated to the lower level of the hall when he heard Simon coming up from below – so as to appear to be merely reading. Later, while he was making a more brutal exploration of the place, using the mason's tools, he had been surprised by yet another person on the same trail: probably the same person who had murdered Higgins and attacked the Master.

But not everything added up. If this really did seem a likely place for the entrance to the secret room, the murderer would certainly not want to advertise the area by leaving a body in it – especially one furnished with mason's tools. Simon had now worked out that in fact this was very unlikely to be the right place for the entrance to the secret chamber, but it was clear that Lewis had not come to this conclusion, and it seemed improbable that the murderer had come to it either. It seemed more likely that the murderer was making the same mistake that Lewis had, whereas he himself had now realized the true meaning of the clues, and had strengthened his theory by the evidence provided by the telescope.

The more immediate problem, Simon realized, was to decide what he ought to do about the body. If he raised the alarm, the place would soon be swarming with constables, and that might make it extremely difficult for him to carry out his own search, albeit in another part of the keep. But, given the expected revelation by the *London Echo*, he probably had only a few days to carry out his own search, for shortly after that he might be banned from the college altogether. On the other hand, if he did nothing, and left the body for someone else to find, not only might there be awkward questions for him to answer, especially if anyone had seen him go into the keep: there would be the same problem of constables examining every nook and cranny.

His body was still shaking, if anything more than at the moment when he found Lewis' body, and he sat down again on the stone seat. There had been another murder, the second – or quite possibly the third – since the search for the treasure had begun. In ordinary circumstance it would be extraordinary not to report it and, come to that, probably illegal. But now that he was so close to finding the treasure he was loath to take any step that might jeopardize his search in what he realized had become a kind of obsession.

His thoughts turned to the immediate predicament, sitting in the near dark with a dead man at his feet. There was no sign of the murderer, but it was possible he was still there, quietly waiting in some other part of the building. In the circumstances it would be wise to get away quickly. As for reporting the death, surely a few hours would not make any great difference, either to Lewis's family or to the police? Tomorrow, either he, or perhaps someone else, would find the body and report it. Unless someone else knew about his search for the treasure there was no reason why he should be linked to the dead man.

He needed time to think, but meanwhile, consciously quashing feelings of guilt, he decided to leave everything as he had found it, so that if the murderer returned there was a chance he would not know that someone else had been there. He put the body back, as near as he could, in its original position and did the same with the tools. Then he turned out the lamps and went back to his rooms, hoping that no-one saw him leave the building.

Chapter 25

Despite the extraordinary events of the last few days, tiredness overcame Simon and he fell asleep shortly after his return. He awoke just in time to partake of the breakfast in the Combination Room. At the end of the meal Talworthy asked if he were about to go to the library. He needed to go there, and if Simon were also going – which Talworthy knew was his habit since becoming librarian pro-tem – this would save him the trouble of calling at the porter's lodge for the key, which would normally be necessary out of term.

Simon agreed. It was inevitable that the body of Lewis would be found, and he might as well use the present opportunity for the two of them to find it together. He would have to be careful, he reflected, to exhibit suitable surprise and shock.

They went together to the main floor where Talworthy wanted to consult a book, and Simon glanced up at the opening where he had found the body. Although the natural light was now quite good he could see no sign of the arm that had been in view the night before. Perhaps, he thought, he had not moved the body back to the exact position in which he had found it.

Excusing himself he went up to the gallery and followed it to the site of the murder. The body was gone! He looked under the stone seat – the mason's tools were gone as well. He looked again at the place where the body had lain. All signs of blood had been cleaned up!

For a moment he wondered whether he could have had one of those 'veridical' dreams that seem so real that one thinks the events in them have actually happened. He examined the area carefully. Where Lewis' head had lain there did seem to be some dampness, and the area was, perhaps, cleaner than the stone around it. He looked carefully at the window. There he saw what made him sure the events of last night were not a dream. On the window catch were threads of dark cloth – exactly matching the clothes worn by Lewis.

Simon was now certain of what had happened, although very uncertain about the exact motives behind the whole sequence of events. The murderer had returned to the scene of the crime, probably not guessing that anyone had observed the body, and had then opened the window and pushed Lewis through. At this point he would fall directly onto the stone plinth that surrounded the base of the keep, and then roll or bounce straight into the river Cam. At present the river was flowing quite fast, and the body might travel some way, possibly all the way to Ely, before it got caught up in something. It would probably be found, perhaps in a few days' time. The partly decayed body would then look as if it had been drowned, and any large bump on the head might be explained by an impact in the river as it tossed around in the water. Meanwhile the murderer had either thrown out the tools, along with the body, or taken them away and hidden them in some safe place.

Why, Simon wondered, had the murderer not pushed the victim through the window right after committing the murder instead of waiting till later that night? There were several possibilities. One was that he needed an assistant, since it would take a strong man to lift the body and push it right through the window – but it was most unlikely that the villain would let anyone else be privy to his actions. Another possibility was that Simon had disturbed the murderer, but there had certainly been no indication of this. The third, and most likely explanation, was that the murderer wanted to wait for complete darkness, since anyone walking on Jesus Green who saw a body being pushed through a window would be unlikely not to report the matter!

Simon had hoped for another opportunity to test his new theory about the entrance to the secret room, but once again, he sensed that the time was not right. He had no idea how long Talworthy would be

in the building, and it would be quite natural for him to come and chat with him in the librarian's office upstairs or in the rare books room, so that the absolute privacy Simon wanted would be lost. Also, the appearance and then disappearance of the body had left him in a nervous state: the kind of state that he habitually soothed by taking a walk.

He decided to take it – as he sometimes did – along the tow-path that led from the college in the direction of Ely. This way, in addition to the relaxation, he might hope to accomplish two further things. He could work out the details of the letter he had decided he must write to Theresa, and which he had already arranged to be carried on Saturday afternoon by one of his students who was journeying to London and who had offered to deliver the important missive personally. He might also be able to satisfy his curiosity about where Lewis' body had ended up, since Ely was downstream from De Vere College. There was one particular bend in the river, about three miles from Cambridge, where dead bodies tended to be found because of the way in which the current brought them into a thick mass of reeds.

It was a fine morning, and attired in suitable boots Simon set off along the path. In the heart of the town the tow-path ran in the middle of the river on a raised section of the river bed, so that horses pulling barges upstream could pass between the college buildings on either side. (In low water this meant that the horse could be led if the man did not mind walking in the filthy water, the river at this time being little better than a sewer after it entered the college area, but normally the horse would be ridden, or directed from the barge.) Going downstream, if there were a strong current the barge could simply be steered while the horse was led round another way, otherwise the same system could be used in reverse. However, after De Vere – which was the last college in the series that bordered the river – the path followed the western bank all the way to Ely. In the first half-mile of this path Simon passed a couple of horses pulling barges that were coming the opposite way: upstream. Then he reached the section where the students rowed and, although out of term, there were a number of eights training for the races in May and June.

For a time he pondered Lewis's death, and in particular the way in which it appeared that the body had been lifted through the window. Was more than one person involved in this act? If not, who would be strong enough to do it alone? Probably the Master, with his athletic walking and fencing; possibly Heatherington, who certainly used to be a good oar, and now in his mid forties and somewhat burly, still looked in good shape, especially when he bicycled along the tow-path while coaching the college's first eight. Or perhaps it was someone else altogether.

His ponderings turned to working out a strategy for making his search for the secret room in complete privacy. Following the discovery of Lewis's body, he had decided it would be wiser to make further attempts during daylight. One reason for this was that in proper light it would be much easier to ensure he really was alone in the keep. There was also the ancillary reason that wandering around the keep in the dark, all by himself, was obviously dangerous. He had hoped to make a daylight attempt that morning, but the presence of Talworthy had made it impossible. Tomorrow was Good Friday, and despite his present state of doubts about the Christian faith, he still had enough religious feeling to be unhappy about spending that day in a personal quest for a secular treasure. Perhaps Holy Saturday would provide a good opportunity.

He found his thoughts about the treasure giving way to thoughts about Theresa. Despite the extraordinary happenings of the past twenty-four hours his mind continued to return to her, and in particular to the painful memory of his last meeting, and – even more – to the look in her eyes. Had he destroyed, once and for all, the hopes he had been building up with respect to her? Was Marcus Peabody a serious rival for her affections? He did not know the answer to either question, but he was not going to give up. The next thing to do, and this must take precedence even over the search for the secret room, was to try and undo some of the damage his delay in confiding in Theresa had caused.

He watched some students row by, continuing to keep half an eye on the banks on either side of the river but at the same time mulling over the outline of the letter he had now virtually constructed in his mind.

Just before reaching the place he was specially looking for he rounded the bend and saw a small knot of people, on his side of the river, dragging something out of the water.

As he got close another walker explained the sight. The cox of one of the eights noticed a body snagged on some reeds and stopped the boat to investigate. Once it was confirmed that it was a corpse, one of the oarsmen ran for a constable while the others disentangled the body. As the current was strong, and the water deep right up to the reeds, this had taken some time and they were only now bringing it ashore.

Although normally squeamish, Simon needed to be sure that his suspicions were correct, so he walked up to the spot where the corpse was being landed.

He recognized the constable who had just arrived; it was the one who had been posted outside Higgins's door on the night of his murder. Simon kept back, anxious that his face should not be associated with another dead person. However, as the body came ashore he was able to see enough to know that it was indeed that of Lewis; and he also noticed that the river had washed the blood from his head. No doubt an expert surgeon could tell that his lungs did not contain enough water for drowning, but he doubted whether the constables would go to the trouble of checking this. Drowning would be assumed, and since Lewis was a fellow of a Cambridge college it would probably be thought to be another tragic accident, caused by too much drinking after a college feast or a private dinner party, followed by an unsteady walk along the river's edge. Simon knew of two such accidents in the eleven years he had been at Cambridge, though neither had involved his college. He fancied he could hear the coroner's caustic comments about the impropriety of such imbibing, especially in Holy Week.

He no longer felt like a long walk, and in any case he was not anxious to meet other constables on the river, who might wish to take names and to question people on the towpath in case they had information. He found a footpath that went at right angles to the river and which joined the road from Cambridge to Ely. He took this somewhat roundabout route back to his college and once in his rooms began to write to Theresa.

His first draft, although following the lines of the letter he had worked out on the towpath, just didn't seem right. He tore it up and began a second in the form of a rough outline – rather in the way he normally prepared a chapter in one of his novels. As he wrote he noticed the disengaged part of his mind reflecting on what he was about. The very fact that he was doing this, instead of deciding whether to say anything to the police, or to anyone else, about his discovery of Lewis' body in the library, indicated how his priorities had been re-arranged since his first meeting with Theresa.

An hour later he finished his third draft, and although not fully satisfied he wrote it out in fair hand and put it in the envelope. The student was expecting it just before dinner and, with luck, Theresa would have it in two days' time. But he still felt miserable, and writing the letter did not have the cathartic effect he had hoped for. He kept recalling Theresa's comments about trying to get an effect by naming it, which is exactly what he was now doing, yet again. But perhaps it was silly to apply her comments about writing skills to a letter – in which the evoking of emotional atmosphere by indirect means did not seem to be required. Nevertheless, in the light of her comments he found himself acutely uncomfortable with every way in which he tried to express his feelings.

He made a decision. Another concern that had been, as it were, roving around in the back of his mind during the walk by the river, and in his attempts to compose a letter, was the necessity to make a decision about the crisis in his life that was about to break. All things considered, it might be better to take the initiative, rather than just watch events unfold. There was still an hour before dinner, and he could make a surprise call on the Lodge. The dramatic effect of what he was about to tell the Master would also help to take his mind off the other problems that assailed him, and in a strange way might actually reduce the overall tension he felt. He would be at least partially in control of events.

Chapter 26

The Master's Lodge, De Vere College,
6.00 p.m., the same day.

Lovelock, the valet, opened the door, and Simon explained that he needed to see Dr James on a matter of urgency. This, he knew, would not please the Master, who disliked disturbance and rarely welcomed anyone to the Lodge. However, Lovelock returned and asked Simon to come upstairs to the study. As he entered the Master turned in his chair to look at him, but neither rose nor offered him a seat.

Irritated by the lack of welcome to a fellow of his own college, Simon made a sudden decision to change his plans. Instead of beginning with an announcement that there was soon to be a scandal and then following this up with an offer to resign his fellowship at the end of the academic year, he decided to approach the subject quite differently.

"The fact is," said Simon, "that I've come to you for advice."

The Master said nothing, but seemed to register mild surprise, for Weatherspoon had never approached him in this way before. He knew him as a quiet, but extremely able fellow, who just got on with his work and generally minded his own business – except that he was occasionally given to supporting some of the late librarian's Whiggish, and generally undesirable ideas with respect to both theology and politics.

Simon continued, "I am more than a little naive on the subject of financial affairs, whereas I know you as Master of the college have considerable expertise. What has happened quite recently – and this has involved a complete change of my personal circumstances – is that I find myself having a most unexpected amount of money."

With inner amusement Simon watched the transformation of the Master's face, from indications of offence at being disturbed, to mild surprise at being consulted, to what looked like a genuine interest. He decided to increase the drama.

"In fact," he added, "rather suddenly, I have so much that I don't know what to do with it."

The total change in the Master's demeanour was now there to behold. He stood up, waved Simon to a chair, and filled two glasses with sherry. (Unlike his late friend Higgins, the Master only kept one kind of sherry, and never inquired after the particular tastes of his guests.) When he spoke it was in a tone that reminded Simon of the voice he used when speaking to FitzSimmons.

"Well, yes, let me begin by congratulating you. I take it you have come into a considerable inheritance."

"No, the money has come as a surprise, but not as a result of inheritance."

A sudden cloud passed over the Master's face. "Have you – er – how shall I put it – made a discovery of some kind?"

Simon had no difficulty in interpreting the change in tone. The Master, he was now surer than ever, was one of the people on the trail of the treasure, and was therefore worried lest anyone else should get to it before he did. How far he was implicated in violence – that was quite another matter. There were still several people who might be involved in the hunt for one or other of the Courcey secrets, even though three of the original number were now dead. In addition to the Master and himself there could well be Heatherington and Mr Hill, and just possibly Talworthy. There could indeed be others, among either the fellows or the friends of Higgins. Then there was yet another possibility. Could it be that Lord FitzSimmons was some-how involved? He was present when Higgins first spoke about the papers, and he certainly had a motive for suppressing all connection between Shakespeare and Edward de Vere.

Simon replied. "No, it's not a case of discovery, except perhaps of a kind of talent I didn't know that I had. The unexpected source of money has come from writing."

The Master now looked both relieved and puzzled as he said: "Well, yes, I've heard that your *First Maccabees* is going into a second printing, but surely, there can't have been significant returns from that quarter?"

Now, Simon realized, was the time to explode his bomb. "No, it's a talent with fiction that I've found. Of course, I've been writing under an assumed name – but – and I'm sorry to break this news rather suddenly, the fact is that I am the author of the books penned under the name of Amelia Buzzard."

The Master almost dropped his glass. He stared at Simon, obviously unsure whether or not to believe him. Simon went on. "I don't know if you've been reading the *London Echo* in the past few days, but somehow they have found out that the author known as Amelia Buzzard is actually a man. They've also announced that in a very short time they're going to tell the world the actual name of this person and – well – I thought it would be a matter of courtesy to inform the college before the storm breaks."

The Master still seemed unable to digest the new information. For the first time in Simon's experience he appeared at a loss for words. He half stammered "Are you serious? This is an extraordinary admission for a fellow of De Vere College!"

Simon said nothing, watching the Master with fascination and trying to guess what was going on in his mind. There would certainly be horror at the association of such allegedly prurient material with the college; there would probably be envy for a fellow who had suddenly become rich; there would certainly be greed for an opportunity that might be bent to his benefit.

The Master now seemed to have recovered his self-control. He remarked, "So it wasn't really financial advice you wanted; you wanted to tell me about a storm that is about to engulf the college."

Simon realized that his opening gambit was running into trouble. Whatever one thought of the Master he was highly intelligent, and had immediately seen through a weakness in Simon's strategy. He did his best to repair the damage.

"No, I really came to see you because there are two important matters I wanted to bring up. One, as you say, is to warn you about some publicity that may affect the college; the other, quite genuinely, is to ask about financial planning. The two things are connected, because it's my role as an author that has led to the financial change."

The Master looked unconvinced on the subject of Simon's motives, but seemed now to believe the story of his authorship. However, it appeared that he had decided not to pursue an unfriendly line. Obviously, although Simon was about to become a source of embarrassment he was also, at least potentially, a source of profit, at this time when the college was trying to build a new wing in part of the fellows' garden. His tone returned to the gentler 'FitzSimmons' mode. "I don't actually read the *London Echo*, but others have passed on to me the substance of what it has claimed, and as you probably know, *The Times* picked up the story yesterday. When do you expect your name to become a matter of public knowledge?"

"Probably not for a week or so, but it could be at any time; and this is what makes the matter urgent."

Simon saw a way of regaining the initiative, and continued:

"I have a suggestion to make. I don't want to make trouble for the college, even though I don't think I've actually done anything wrong. I was going to suggest that I be given leave of absence for the Easter term, and simply, as it were, disappear from public view for a time, perhaps in France. If the college insist, then I could resign my fellowship at the end of the academic year and sever all my ties with De Vere's, but I would be sorry to do that, since I have a real affection for the college, and I may, in the future, be in a position to do some good for it."

Simon realized he had now gone much further than he intended when he first walked over to the Lodge. He did not, in principle, have any objection to giving some financial help to the college, but he had not intended to make such an offer at this time, and especially to the Master, in a way which might, indirectly, strengthen the latter's position in the college and the university as a person who could acquire financial support from the rich and powerful. He noted how careful one had to be in the language one used and the excuses one made, especially when talking in a charged atmosphere, and without careful forethought. He had now almost committed himself in a way he regretted. Nevertheless, he realized, this had probably helped him to recoup at least some of the initiative.

The Master finished his sherry, evidently having regained his composure. "Thank you for telling me about this," he said. "As you know, the Governing Body is not due to meet until just before the beginning of next term, but I shall discuss this matter with the Senior Fellow and between us we can probably arrange something that can later be ratified by the whole fellowship. I think perhaps your absence from Cambridge for a while might be a good idea. But if you leave Cambridge for a time I would like to know how we could be in contact, because, as you can guess, I would like to discuss with you the plans for the new wing. Are you – with your new-found wealth – planning to have your own home, in addition to some rooms you might retain in the college?"

While having no intention of giving away information about his new house, Simon decided that keeping the atmosphere friendly was strongly in his interests, especially since he wanted to retain access to the library for the time being.

"Yes, I am in the process of acquiring a property, situated some way from Cambridge, for the sake of privacy. But meanwhile I can give you the name of a London hotel I often use, and which already holds mail for me between visits. When the scandal has begun to die down we could meet together for lunch, perhaps in the same hotel."

Chapter 27

Good Friday, 10ᵗʰ April.

Coming to the Combination Room a little late, Simon found himself alone at the breakfast table. He had almost finished, and was gathering his strength for a serious effort to make progress with either *Second Maccabees* or the sequel by Emily Dove, when Talworthy came in. He was carrying a copy the *London Echo*.

"There's another piece about *The de Vere Papers*," he said, "and I thought you might be interested. This is yesterday's edition, and when the next one comes out on Tuesday after the Easter weekend, apparently there's going to be more."

Simon accepted the paper and found the article on the front page. It read:

The *London Echo* is now able to release the second part of the Amelia Buzzard mystery. Many readers will recall that the writer's second novel *The Errant Archdeacon* was followed by one that claimed to be written by a certain Emily Dove, called *The Upright Canon*, a book that was calculated to pour scorn on both the style and content of *The Errant Archdeacon*, and which succeeded to the extent of finding itself approved for reading among the more genteel classes. The literary battle has continued with Amelia Buzzard's withering attack on *The Upright Canon* in *The Coachman and the Countess* (although the attack is cleverly contrived so that it never actually mentions the object of its venom). Moreover, so the publishers of both authors (Fisher-White) inform us, Emily Dove's response to *The Coachman and the Countess* is due out later this year. Now we can reveal the amazing fact that not only is the author known as Amelia Buzzard a man, he is also the author of *The Upright Canon*. In other words, Amelia Buzzard and Emily Dove are one and the same!

In the light of this revelation readers may well feel more than a little annoyance. Surely, Fisher-White have, with the connivance of their author, produced a purely fictitious battle, solely for the sake of increasing sales. Contacted by the *London Echo,* the management of Fisher-White has responded as follows:

"It is a well known habit for many writers to use assumed names, and we cannot see why it is any more improper for a man to use the pseudonym of a woman than it is for a woman to use that of a man, which, of course, is common practice. As for the battle between the novels, this again is a perfectly acceptable literary device. If the books claimed to be history it would be another matter, but they are novels, that is to say, works of fantasy whose merit lies not in their correspondence with reality, but in their appeal as reading designed to provide amusement rather than instruction."

In the next few days the correspondence section of this paper will disclose how far this response by the publishers is convincing to the readers of the *London Echo*. Meanwhile, however, readers should watch for the most amazing revelation of all. On Tuesday more information will be forthcoming, and shortly after that, the name, profession and status of the unknown author will be revealed. These matters are likely to cause more than a little surprise.

Simon took the newspaper to his rooms. He re-read it, and then tried to get down to the new novel by Emily Dove but, once again, he felt too tense and too frustrated to concentrate. His most recent plan had been to make his first serious attempt to locate the secret room tomorrow but, to his intense irritation, two requests from fellows of other colleges to consult some of De Vere's rarer books on both Holy Saturday and Easter Sunday had just come in. It seemed that the end of term, and hence the end of lecturing, had prompted a sudden demand by those involved in research. As acting librarian the requests naturally came to him, and despite the annoyance this did mean that he had forewarning of who was likely to be in or near the top floor of the old keep during the Easter break. It now looked as if it would be Easter Monday, which everyone seemed to be treating as a holiday, before he could put his new theory to the test.

It being Good Friday, he was well aware that he ought to spend a quiet day in Bible reading and prayer, but now that working on the novel seemed impossible, he intended to spend it walking, resting, and – in all probability – in feeling generally depressed. The sense of excitement about the possibility of finding the treasure was more than counterbalanced by his dread of an irredeemable break with Theresa.

On his walk along the Backs he found himself reflecting on the Fisher-White response to the latest revelation in the *London Echo*. Novels, his own publishing house implied, were simply meant to amuse: they were not concerned with reality. This was, at best, he decided, a kind of half-truth. It might well be so in the case of his novels, but it was not fair in the case of what Theresa described as great novels. He had been captivated by George Eliot's *Silas Marner* not only because of the story but for at least two things that were not just matters of 'amusement'. The characters were drawn in a way that seemed to illuminate how one saw people in real life. There was a kind of truth here. Also, the situation, with its implicit commentary on aspects of social life, was, in a way, a reflection of the way things were. According to rumour in literary circles, George Eliot was in the process of writing a new novel that would be particularly relevant as a warning to him: a baleful picture of a scholarly but desiccated clergyman who was incapable of creating a happy marriage. Was he in danger of being just a 'dusty scholar', lacking real humanity?

His thoughts turned to Charles Kingsley's *Hypatia*, which Theresa had mentioned on the occasion when they first met – at that luncheon that would for ever remain engraved in his memory. At the very end of that novel Kingsley had expressly said that the story had a message for the present day, with parallels between the effects of fanatical religion in the fifth and the nineteenth centuries. But for him this ending was too patently didactic. He preferred the implications of good writing to be felt by the sensitive reader rather than actually spelled out. Otherwise it was rather like trying to get an effect by naming it, and as a result, much less effective in working on the human imagination, a consequence that Theresa's acute mind had helped him to see. Surely, better examples of writing that illuminated the reader were to be found in some of the novels of Charles Dickens, another of the writers he had begun to enjoy in recent years. His *Oliver Twist* was certainly more than a thing to amuse. Like the books by Eliot it described a kind of truth in the human condition, or at least in the condition of contemporary London, and moreover a truth that had implications for any meaningful form of Christianity. Professor Maurice, he remembered, had actually used allusions to *Oliver Twist* in the sermon he had heard only five days before.

Rather to his surprise, Simon's sense of anxiety began to settle, and he felt ready to turn his thoughts to Good Friday. There was, after all, a link between great novels and the gospel story, because in different ways they were both concerned with the human condition. He hadn't been sure for some time how much of the gospel stories he actually believed – that is, as history – but in a way perhaps that didn't matter because the stories, even if taken simply as stories, had immense power. There was, of course, a kernel of history in the gospels, for otherwise it was extraordinarily difficult to explain the emergence of the early church. Today's commemoration of the cross looked back to an historical event of some kind. But as with the rest of the New Testament story, in his present mood he was more interested in the symbolic meaning than in the history. The events said something profound about human suffering and the vulnerability of anyone who loved, a vulnerability that resonated with his present feelings.

He recalled vividly a long conversation with the only Muslim student he had ever had, a highly intelligent young man who had been sent to study in Cambridge by a wealthy Egyptian family and who, for the sake of form, had initially been sent with the implication that he was a Coptic Christian, so that the arcane rules of the university would more easily let him study there. However, with Simon he had been perfectly frank, and had argued for the Koranic claim that Jesus did not really die, but only seemed to. He had gone on to defend the popular Islamic belief that just before the crucifixion Jesus was spirited away, and his place taken by Judas. As a scholar, Simon had been able to explain to the young Egyptian the probable, fifteenth-century source of this non-Koranic legend. However, he was much more concerned with the basic historicity of the cross than with the legends about Judas. The death of Jesus was part of its symbolic importance: about the lengths to which love would go, and about what is likely to happen to those who really love. Some time after his student returned to Egypt he had been pleased to meet an Islamic scholar who interpreted the passage in the Koran to mean that Jesus was always alive in God, and not as a denial of the reality of the crucifixion. Here the link between love and being subject to pain was still affirmed.

Shortly after their talk, and perhaps stirred up by the conversation, the student, Khalid, had become more outspoken about his Muslim beliefs. The proctors had somehow got to hear about this, and when summoned before them he had – to his credit – refused to deny his allegiance to Islam. There had been a big row and, partly because of Simon's support, Khalid had eventually been allowed to remain as a student but, in accordance with university regulations, had not been allowed to take his B.A.

Simon started to muse on some of the Biblical stories that shone an extraordinarily strong light on the human condition, whether or not they were historical. It was the power of these stories, perhaps more than anything else, which had led him to feel that he could continue as a clergyman, despite his many doubts.

Take the story of the woman taken in adultery being dragged before Jesus, with the demand that she be stoned. Jesus had stayed silent, scratching something in the sand. His conviction was that Jesus was not so much writing some secret response as expressing his embarrassment, with a profound sense of sympathy and compassion for the woman brought before him, who was probably, all things considered, no worse a person than the hypocrites seeking her death. In any case, why should it be just her and not the man who was being dragged before him? Then came that brilliant response: "Let he who is without sin cast the first stone."

This classic pronouncement was a reminder that even single sentences, whether in the Bible or in great novels, could bring one up with a shock – a kind of revelatory shock – like Jesus's simple reply. In their own way good novels did deal with reality. Theresa was right, his own efforts were not first-rate because they failed this vital test. His thoughts returned to her.

Chapter 28

The Jolly Farmer, London, Holy Saturday, 11ᵗʰ April, noon.

Theresa Brown and Marcus Peabody met for lunch in the back parlour of the Jolly Farmer, a respectable public house where women, provided they were accompanied, could have a meal and a drink without sullying their reputations. They met here on most

Saturdays and surveyed the week that was past. For both of them this had become something of a ritual, and also a therapy. Peabody had brought along Thursday's edition of the *London Echo*. As they settled into their seats, he asked:

"Do you know what I did when I read the first report about Amelia Buzzard being a man – before you told me the author had to be Simon?"

"No, what was your first reaction?"

"I laughed! I was sitting in my club reading the *London Echo* as an antidote to *The Times*, which was more than usually pompous and boring. As I read the article I started to chuckle, and before I finished it I was almost rolling on the carpet. Fortunately this was the London Pantheon and not the Athenaeum, and a certain measure of ribaldry is quite acceptable there. When I showed the article to other members their reaction was much the same. You know I approve the aims of the women's movements, and certainly of their battle to be accepted in Cambridge, but I do think they sometimes take themselves too seriously."

Theresa looked neither mollified nor amused. Marcus was not known for his tact, but he decided that his friend needed time to see the funny side of the affair, especially since it was really her pride that was at stake. He could divert her for a while by setting her intellectual energy to work. "How did you work out the connection with Emily Dove?" he asked.

Theresa collected her thoughts, and then began:

"Once I realized that Simon had to be Amelia Buzzard I soon

worked out that he also had to be Emily Dove, long before this second article appeared."

After a brief pause she continued:

"I'll have to digress a bit to explain. Quite apart from the question of quality, people divide novels into three kinds. There are those written in the first person – as if the chief character were also the author. Secondly, there are those written in the second person. This is common in poetry, but in prose it is very rare, and I think I've only come across one in all my reading.* Thirdly, and most commonly, there are books like Simon's which are written in the third person – describing events from a kind of neutral space; 'he did this', 'James thought that', 'Mary loved the view' and so on. But I think the third person category needs to be divided up into sub-styles. By way of illustration, both Amelia Buzzard and Emily Dove use a particular variation of the third person narrative. There is a central character whose thoughts and reactions are revealed in almost all the scenes, while the inner thoughts of the other characters are never referred to directly, except in a few passages where the chief character is not present. It's quite a well known technique, and helps the reader to identify with the hero or heroine. It's as if the author – although writing with a kind of objectivity – is situated, not actually inside the main character, but in a sort of invisible cloud a few inches above their head. This is one feature of Simon's style, but in the case of both Amelia Buzzard and Emily Dove it's combined with another that is less common, and that, I suspect, has something to do with the way he actually thinks."

Marcus sipped his soup but did not interrupt the flow of thought.

"In both authors not only is there a central character from whose point of view almost all the action is seen: there is also a description of a kind of parallel train of words going on in the character's head, as it were analyzing what he is saying, and commenting on it, even as he says it. This certainly isn't unique, but it's not common in writing,

* Author's note. A relatively modern example of this rare kind of novel is Michel Butor's *La Modification*, Les Editions de Minuit, Paris, 1957.

although I cannot judge how common it is in real life. Moreover, Simon has a particular way of doing this, and a particular frequency in its occurrence that marks out the style. So, despite his attempt to be two different novelists, this is what gives him away."

"I see how this led you to identify Amelia Buzzard with Emily Dove, but how did you connect both to Simon? Did you find the same traits in his *First Maccabees* – in the volume you told me he'd given you?"

"Yes and no. I read that book before the first article in the *London Echo* came out, and quite enjoyed it; but the unusual internal dialogue of the novels does not stand out – and really you wouldn't expect it to, because it's not a work of fiction and is much more directly a third person narrative. But with hindsight, when Simon describes the character of Judas Maccabeus, there are occasional hints of the style, for example, when he imagines Judas's inner reflections on the occupation of his homeland. But no, I did not realize that Simon was the author when I read *First Maccabees*. But as soon as the *London Echo* gave the first indication that Amelia Buzzard was a man I felt a sudden weakening in the stomach. It was the kind of intuition that one can only partly explain after the event. I think it was connected with the discovery that Simon had money, and also something to do with the kind of explorative mind he has. Then, immediately I got home I went back to *First Maccabees*, and then I was convinced of his treble life as an author."

"Do you think the double – or treble act – was for the sake of sales, or was it just a bit of mischief?"

"I suspect it started as a piece of mischief, first to see if he could write a novel at all, and then to see if, besides the Amelia Buzzard style, he could write something altogether different. Then – in addition to the fun of making money – I think he began to enjoy the murder mystery of the Emily Dove style, partly because it was so different from that of the other novels. I suspect too that his academic side began to enjoy the controversy, and then, when Fisher-White pointed out how much the sales of both authors were being boosted by the row, he was fully committed. After all, who doesn't enjoy making piles of money?"

"Apparently the revelations in the *London Echo*, far from dampening the sales, have made them go wild. This is another comic twist. The *Echo* has put on a moral persona – total hypocrisy of course – and suggests that in the light of their revelations the books are somehow tainted, and the result has been more and more money – for the *London Echo* and Fisher-White and for Simon. I wonder what he will do with it all?"

It was Theresa's turn to laugh – and it was if a burden had fallen off her shoulders. As Marcus had suspected, the intellectual analysis of the situation had helped to soften the emotional annoyance.

"You know," she said, "I could almost believe that Fisher-White and the *London Echo* are in this together. As you say, everyone seems to be making money out of the affair. Anyway, now I know why Simon was so anxious to have a hide-away outside Cambridge, and why he's hinted at Continental trips and bought a great deal of expensive wine. He knew the secret couldn't be kept much longer, and perhaps he was trying to warn me the last time we had dinner together."

"What are you going to do? I think you know that if it weren't for – let us say – my preferences, I would be a very jealous man. But in the circumstances I think you will regret it if you don't make peace."

"I don't know. I'm a little frightened he might think I'm after his money; but when I've slept on it I think I had better do something fast, before the next revelation and his flight from view!"

Chapter 29

The keep was available to all students or college fellows who wanted to work in the Easter vacation, but today it was locked, because no-one had asked the porter for the key and this was not one of the days when it was opened in the expectation of general use. Simon fastened the entrance behind him, but did not leave his key in the lock since in the event of someone else coming to open the library he did not want to raise suspicion. On reaching the top floor he also locked the door to the old solar or reading room behind him. However, when he went into the rare books room he left the door ajar so that in the unlikely event of anyone coming to the top floor and unlocking the door to the reading room he would be more likely to hear them. He had worked out what to do in such an event if he were also in the midst of uncovering the treasure. He would rapidly return to the solar, and make an excuse about needing to keep the rare books room closed until he had finished some delicate piece of repair to an old binding. It might sound lame, but it would probably work.

Once in the rare books room he went to the window area immediately above the one in the gallery where the side-panel in the painting showed the bishop to be seated, and started to examine the wooden window-seat. If he were right, the bishop in the portrait was staring up towards the room immediately above him, namely the room in which Simon now stood, which was formerly the chapel, and indicating with his ring-finger exactly where the search had to begin.

Since there was no musicians' gallery on this floor, the wooden seat was much longer than the stone version on the floor below, in fact at least eight feet in length, running from the inside of the window all the way to the main part of the room. In the last few days Simon had come to realize that if one were to place a secret room within the thickness of the walls it would not make much sense to position the room at the gallery level, where the full eleven feet of thickness would not be available. Also, shortly before making use of Talworthy's telescope, he had come to see the implications of the fact that the solidity of the walls became less important as one went higher up, because enemy missiles were less likely to reach the higher floors. One further thing pointed to the likelihood of the secret room being on the top floor. The chapel was often held to be the most secure place in a castle, and one of the more obvious places to hold valuable items. This would make it appropriate for any secret chamber to be accessed from it.

Another element in the puzzle now occurred to him for the first time. What was now a secret room might not have been secret at all in the early days of the castle. The 'vented' room, referred to in the list of papers, might well have been a small vestry in which the altar silver and other valuable items were regularly kept, with a door that was hidden only after the wooden seats were added, almost certainly in early Tudor days. Courcey might not have needed to go to much trouble in making a secret room, only to a little trouble in hiding the entrance.

If he were right, the question was only how to move the seat, for behind it William Courcey, while he was Master, must have arranged for the upper part of the old door to be filled in with new stonework, while leaving the lower part of the door to be exposed when the bench was moved.

Simon put his hand on the end of the bench at exactly the point where the right hand of the bishop would have been if the portrait had been painted here. He pulled with all his strength, but there was no movement. He crouched on the ground and looked under the seat. Was it his imagination, or was there a very slight draught coming from between the bottom of the wooden board on which the seat was set and the stone floor immediately below it? He felt under the seat with his hand. There was something there that made him catch his breath. He crouched down, and with difficulty got his head right under the bench. It was almost dark here, but there seemed to be a wooden bar running under the seat in a kind of channel. He felt it again. It was substantial – about three inches square and two feet long – before it disappeared into the masonry near the window. It was, if he were right, a 'draw-bolt', preventing the seat from being accidentally pulled away from the wall. He took hold of the bar and tried to draw it to the right, away from the stonework. It was stiff, but gradually it moved, first with a little shudder, and then more freely. He drew six inches of wood from a slot in the stonework, and then the other end of the bar came up against a wooden stop, placed on the underside of the seat – but, with his hand, he could feel that the bolt was now clear of the stone. He got up, making an unclergymanly curse as he caught his head on the underside of the bench. He was breathing heavily as he pulled again on the end of the wooden seat, outwards and slightly upwards. It began to move!

He worked the eight-foot bench away from the wall, one inch at a time. The whole bench was slowly moving, that is, the actual seat along with the back and the wooden board on which the seat was mounted. When the end near the window had come six inches towards him he put his knees on the bench and looked behind. There was an opening, about eighteen inches across and thirty inches high! The walls to the side of the opening were neatly squared while the top seemed more roughly finished and ended in a wooden lintel, unlike the stone arches that topped all the other doors in the castle. This tallied with his idea that what he had exposed was the lower half of a door to a small room or cupboard. It was likely that the secret entrance was indeed an adaptation of a previous doorway, although the stone had been reworked above the wooden lintel so skilfully that the exposed area gave no hint of the earlier entrance.

Simon went back to his pulling until the end of the seat was nearly three feet away from its original setting. It was clear that he would have to crawl through the narrow opening he had exposed, and he suddenly realized, despite his earlier decision to leave the door to the rare books room unlocked, that once in the secret room he could not possibly hear anyone coming onto the top floor. He would have slightly to change his plan.

He went to the door that linked the rare books room to the solar and closed and locked it, returning the key to his pocket. He certainly did not like the idea of someone coming into the old chapel during the operation he was about to perform. He returned to the window and squeezed round the end of the bench, got on all fours, and crawled through the entrance. Six inches from the opening the passage regained its original height, just allowing him to stand, and then it ran smoothly through the stonework for about two feet. It opened into the secret room which was dimly lit by a tiny window on the left. He forced himself to breathe steadily as he looked around.

The chamber was barrel-vaulted, about eight feet long and five across – allowing three feet of stone between the room and the outside of the keep on the left, and another three feet of solid masonry between the room and the inside of the chapel on the right. The roof, at the centre of the vaulting, allowed him to stand comfortably. The narrow window on the left was indeed the slit he had detected as he had examined the stonework through Talworthy's telescope. It was less than an inch across and about nine inches in height, but it sufficed to give both a glimmer of light and some air. It was mostly filled with a thick piece of glazing – the evident source of the glint he had seen in the telescope – but the top inch was left clear, and through it Simon could feel the draught, now increased because the air could move through the open door behind him. The opening above the glass had been small enough to prevent the entry of birds, but not of flies, beetles and spiders – whose remains littered the floor and walls. The wall on his right, opposite the window, was lined with thick wooden shelves that rested on stone corbels, and under the dust and cobwebs he could see they were full of small and medium-sized wooden chests. The only other object in the room was a heavy black mace, propped up in the far corner below the lowest shelf.

Although Simon had forced himself to control his breathing, using a technique he had been taught by a school cricket coach when facing unpleasantly fast bowling, he had not succeeded in controlling the beating of his heart, which was still pounding. The dominant emotion, strangely enough, was not that different from fear: it was a strange mixture of elation and awe; elation at having solved the puzzle, awe at the magnitude of the discovery he had made. It was more than two hundred and fifty years since what he was about to examine had seen the light of day.

Simon decided to explore the contents systematically. He took the mace, which weighed at least fifteen pounds, and crawled with it through the opening. He cleared the two tables in the middle of the room, and laid down the mace on one of them, as 'item one'. In its journey from the secret room some of the centuries of dust and detritus had shaken off, and around the body of the mace and on its handle he could see the flashing of jewels. The main body, he realized, was made of solid silver, and had turned black with years of exposure to the air. This had to be 'Bishop Odo's mace', referred to in the treasure list.

He returned to the secret room. Altogether there were nine wooden chests of various sizes. One by one he pushed them through the narrow opening and then carried them to the floor-space just beside the tables. When they were all assembled he pulled back the lid of each one in turn. Four of them simply swung open on wire hinges that had not completely rusted through, while the remaining five had no intact hinges, and in these cases Simon simply lifted off the whole lid and laid it beside the chest.

The first chest he opened contained an enamel reliquary in the form of a metal box, about eighteen inches long and ten inches wide, with a blue background decorated with scenes from the Bible. He lifted it out, noticing as he did so that this reliquary was the only item in the chest, the four legs of the metal box having been laid directly on the wooden base. He placed it on the table. The lid swung open on hinges that seemed to be made of gold. Inside was a jawbone, and nothing else.

From his earlier reading Simon realized at once that, from the point of view of the monks of Lolworth Abbey, this was by far the most valuable item in the whole treasure. It was the famous 'jawbone of St Matthew' which had helped to make the abbey a centre of pilgrimage from its founding in the early twelfth century to its dissolution in the sixteenth. He lifted the bone out, thinking as he did so how a Protestant upbringing had given him his prejudices, and the ready assumption that this must be a fake. Probably it was a fake, but recent events in his own life had certainly been 'stranger than fiction', and their intrinsic improbability, however one measured the matter, no greater than the stories of ancient relics being carried from the Holy Land to early Christian centres at the time of St Helena, and then on to places like Lolworth. The jawbone still held five of its teeth, and he tried to imagine the whole skull from which it had come. He found the contemplation disagreeable, so he replaced the relic and put the reliquary back in the chest from which it came.

It soon became apparent that three other chests contained relics, each one with a number of small reliquaries rather than a single large one. At the top of the third there was a piece of rough wood about eight inches long – perhaps a part of the 'true cross'.

Rather than wading through the relics, he put these three chests, along with the one he had first examined, on the floor near the tables. Now came what was going to be, for him, the truly exciting part of the examination.

It took Simon more than an hour to place the contents of the five remaining chests on the tables, and before he had finished he had to move the mace, laying it on the floor near the door, in order to make room for all the other items. The whole display exactly tallied with the list he had found in the notebook. As with the reliquary, none of the items was labelled, and their general condition suggested they had been assembled in a hurry, in the case of the relics in the hope that it would not be long before pious hands could place them in a more dignified environment. One chest, the largest, contained a jumble

189

of chalices, patens, candlesticks and crosses, some in silver, some in ivory, along with one chalice in what looked – from its untarnished condition – like pure gold. There was also the top end of a crozier, worked in silver with enamel inlays. It reminded Simon of the magnificent crozier kept at New College in Oxford that had belonged to the college's fourteenth-century founder, William of Wickham. Several of the items were encrusted with jewels.

The remaining four chests were of still greater interest to Simon, although there could be no doubt that some of the jewelled items in the others were of immense monetary value. Two contained the eight illuminated manuscripts. Simon was no expert in this field, but a quick glance showed him that two of them were gospels, three were 'books of hours', designed to assist the prayers of a rich patron, one a copy of the Psalms and the other two theological texts in Latin, one of which he could identify on first sight as a copy of Aquinas's *Summa Contra Gentiles*. The Biblical manuscripts and books of hours were lavishly illuminated in what he suspected was the Flemish style, while the other two had fine coloured capitals and the occasional page of illumination in a geometric manner that reminded him of some of the Celtic work he had seen. These must be some of the items mentioned by John Leland after his trip to Lolworth Abbey and presumably the most precious books in the abbey's library, which had run to several hundred volumes.

Even more fascinating, in the light of their rarity, were the nine  sets of chessmen. All were complete, but it took Simon quite a long time to assemble them in their proper order, since within the chests they had been mixed together. One set was clearly French, made in silver and with enamel finishing in a way that paralleled the working on the crozier, and which might well have come from the same source. Each piece in this set, including the pawns, was a finely moulded statuette, and under the main figures tiny engravings

indicated that the portrayals were from life – or at least representations of real people. Two sets (and here he was grateful for the Master's brief lesson on chessmen) were made from walrus ivory, each piece having the coarse nerve clearly visible at its base. One of these was very similar to the famous Lewis chessmen which he had seen displayed in the British Museum, and which had been found in a cave in the Hebridean islands in 1831. The only difference was that here the pawns, instead of being merely carved shapes, were carefully figured foot-soldiers, in fact, very like small versions of the larger, mad-looking warriors that stood for rooks. The other walrus ivory set was similar, but the corner pieces looked like Norman keeps and the pawns like Norman or Saxon foot-soldiers. It looked as if it might represent the Battle of Hastings. He picked up the kings and saw the name 'Rex Willelm' scratched under one and 'Dux Harold' under the other. Could they, just possibly, have been cut from life or, in the case of Harold, from the carver's memory? Another set, carved in elephant ivory and Simon's favourite, was obviously Byzantine, very much in the style of the ivory reliquary boxes that he had seen from that country and made before its conquest by Muslim forces in 1453. It represented

crusaders on the one side (in white) and Saracens on the other (dyed black, although much of the colour had faded). It was ironic, Simon reflected, that the actual crusaders had been almost as brutal to the Greek Christians, who had almost certainly made this set, as to the Muslims. The pieces, perhaps, had been made for some wealthy patron in the West, who would be unlikely to be aware of such subtleties. The other five sets were of similar splendour, but Simon was unsure where they were made. One was in crystal, with silver and gilt ornamentations, one was in red and blue softstone and Simon suspected, from the style of the figures, might be Italian from the renaissance period, one was in amber (clear on one side and cloudy on the other), one in silver and the other (like the Byzantine set) in ivory. Except for the crystal set, which was turned or chiselled into patterns, all the major pieces were finely carved or modelled figures of men, women (for the queens), horses and castles.

Simon sat down on one of the Chippendale chairs that were provided for the fellows who used the rare books room, and surveyed the treasure. It was an incredible sight, and an incredible find. But now he had found it he was not quite sure what to do with it. He knew a little about the law of treasure trove, but he was unsure if it really applied in this case. If it did apply, then everything in precious metal and all the jewels would belong to the crown, while everything else would belong either to the finder or to the owner of the property – in this case, he presumed, De Vere College. He was not quite sure how things would work between these two parties. However, there was an obvious complication. Since, in 1539, the treasure had been hidden from the King's men, presumably, the whole hoard might be judged by the coroner to belong to the crown and not, in the strict sense of the term, to be treasure trove at all.

He was tempted to put everything back exactly where it came from until he had discreetly found out who would be deemed to own what, but that, he realized might be a grave mistake. Others were or had been on the hunt for this treasure. Almost certainly these included the Master, especially in view of his recent interest in the crypt; certainly Lewis, although he was hardly a current threat; and at least one other person – the one who had attacked the Master and, presumably, who had killed Higgins and Lewis. Heatherington was a possibility, so too was Talworthy, and although neither of them seemed to have the kind of character that would lend itself to extreme violence, recent events had proved how wrong one could be in one's assumptions. Then there was Mr Hill, whom he hadn't had time to inquire after. Whoever it was must have unearthed at least some of the clues and it followed that, if he put everything back, the treasure might simply be spirited away in the next few days. The person who had committed the murders and struck the Master would surely not scruple at a little burglary – or rather – at a large burglary. It wasn't even certain that these were the only persons in the hunt, among other reasons because it was possible that the person who committed the murders was not the person who had struck the Master while he sat at his desk. Further, it was possible, though unlikely, that Higgins and Lewis were not murdered by the same person.

There were also some moral and legal considerations that he had been vaguely aware of, but had not really confronted until a decision had to be made. If some or all of the treasure did belong to the crown, either outrightly or because it was treasure trove, then moving any of it now might be deemed to be tantamount to theft. So he faced a real dilemma. If he simply put everything back in the secret room, the Master, or someone else on the trail, might find it and then, he was pretty sure, it would quickly disappear! However, it he moved the treasure, say to his rooms, and if it were found there, how could he prove that he intended to hand it over to the proper authorities? Some of his deceptions had certainly stretched the ordinary standards that most people would expect from a clergyman, but any suggestion of theft, especially on such a grand scale, would be something far more serious.

Suppose he moved the treasure to his rooms with a view to reporting the find to the proper authorities, then other problems arose. First, the move would involve considerable time and effort, especially if it were not to be observed. In fact, in case anyone came into the rare books room, he would have to make the move tonight, under cover of darkness. But more importantly, the question of who constituted the proper authority was part of the problem. In ordinary circumstances he would be expected to go straight to the Master and report the find, but now that was the last thing he wanted to do. Perhaps he should move the treasure and then go straight to the police – but then he would have to explain why he had felt it necessary to move it, and this would be impossible if he didn't explain about the finding of Lewis's body – as well as a whole series of other episodes. He could well be in deep trouble for not having gone to the police before. All in all, he realized that he had been foolish not to think about these things before. So perhaps, after all, he should put everything back until he had made more inquiries about the law, and just risk the possibility that someone else would find the treasure.

Simon sat with his back to the door that led from the chapel to the old solar. He didn't hear the door open, but he heard a gentle click and then felt a sudden current of air.

Chapter 30

The rare books room, De Vere College,
the same day, 3.30 p.m.

Simon looked round quickly. The Master was standing twelve feet away, framed by the doorway. In his right hand he held his bunch of library keys; one for the entrance, one for the reading room and one for the rare books room. As he placed the keys in his pocket he drew aside his long Master of Arts gown, revealing a scabbard containing a narrow rapier, hung at his belt. With a practised hand he drew the blade, aiming the point straight at Simon. At the same time he stared at the objects on the tables, and Simon could see a kind of light in his eyes as they settled, riveted, on the chess pieces.

After a long silence the Master spoke in a hushed, almost reverential voice. "Thank you for finding these things for me. Once I eliminated the crypt I knew they had to be somewhere in the keep, but I was having trouble finding the exact location. When I observed you come to the library this afternoon I had a hunch you might be using your last days at the college to find the treasure, so I came prepared. Now, please get up and stand by the wall, right in the corner."

Reluctantly, Simon obeyed, while the Master stood by the tables, his eyes still fixed on the chess pieces, and, Simon now noticed, with a slight dribble of saliva running down the side of his mouth. He had wondered if the collector's instinct could be enough to account for murder, and now, at least in this case, he was sure.

"Yes, yes, – unbelievable," the Master whispered, "and exactly in accord with Henry Courcey's letter. One set from Norway, or perhaps Sweden or Denmark; two from France, one in enamel work and one in quartz; two from England, one in silver and one in walrus ivory; two from Germany, one in amber and one in ivory; one from Italy, in glorious lapis lazuli and coral; and one from Constantinople: the only pieces I've ever seen from there."

"So it was you who killed Lionel Higgins and John Lewis – and I suppose, Nathan Bambridge?"

"It was necessary. When Higgins told me the letters from Henry Courcey indicated what was in the Lolworth treasure I suggested a little quiet investigation on our own – but he would have none of it. 'This is something of national importance and national interest', he said. But it was a Master of De Vere that had charge of these wonderful things, and it shall be another Master of De Vere that reclaims them for safekeeping – in private, of course, until after my death, when a generous bequest to the nation might be in order. The deaths are regrettable, but in the great scheme of life what do such things really amount to? And in your case it will at least bring an end to your obscene scribblings."

Simon's heart was beating fast, but he felt surprisingly calm. His inner voice seemed to be saying two things at the same time; first, that he ought to be preparing for death, and second that it was odd he didn't seem to be in a panic. Meanwhile, he found himself ready to argue with the Master, almost as if he were in a high table conversation. Was it, perhaps, that all his reflections in the area of the Gothic novel had somehow prepared him for events of this kind? Whatever the reason, one part of his mind observed himself framing a sentence that might help to get him out of the present crisis.

"But you have a problem. One body was enough to bring the police here, three (if you count Bambridge and Lewis) must have raised further suspicions, and four will have the police positively swarming over the place."

"Ah yes, but they won't find your body. Your corpse can simply be put back into the secret room along with all those silly relics. With all the scandal surrounding your name it will be assumed you've gone on a tour of the Continent – or something like that – and it's not unknown for people to disappear on such travels. As for these splendid things, I've already worked out how to explain their arrival on the public scene, bit by bit. I shall purchase an old chateau in France, complete with all its furniture and as I gradually search through the contents they will turn out to be truly spectacular! Of course, I'll have to be careful with the religious items, and perhaps I'll put most of those back, along with the relics. But with the manuscripts for selling, and the chessmen for putting in my collection, there will be quite enough."

"But you're not the only person besides myself to be on the trail of the secret room. There's someone else who has been following the clues, and when he finishes decoding them my body will be found, and then there will be a lot of explaining to do."

"Yes, yes, but I'm afraid you're just not clever enough. In the first place, I realised some time ago that Lord FitzSimmons is on the trail. When we were together in Higgins's rooms I was indeed surprised, but not by the body – it was the set of skeleton keys that caused me to feel faint. It took some time to see how they got there, but after I was hit on the head I began to work things out. FitzSimmons was showing a huge interest in the possibility of there being papers from de Vere, and it had to be he, or more likely one of his men who robbed me; and the same person had clearly tried to steal the papers from Higgins, only to find they were already gone. Secondly, if you were alive to read the papers in the next few days you would find that there has been another murder! FitzSimmons is presently staying in the college guest room. He's come for a kind of Easter holiday and is expecting to meet me in his rooms in an hour or so. He knows our discussion is to be very private, so he will have told no-one that I am about to see him. In the morning he will be found with his head crushed, in the same manner as that of Higgins. So there won't be any risk of him finding your body. Thirdly, now I come to think of it, your disappearance will fit in very well with his death. The police will put two and two together – and, as they often do – will make five. Your body, of course will never be found so it will be assumed that the unhinged person who wrote *The de Vere Papers* had dealt with both Higgins and FitzSimmons, and is now hiding away, probably abroad.

In fact, your disappearance from the scene might also lead the police to ascribe the deaths of Bambridge and Lewis to you – that is, if they decide they were murdered."

Simon was sweating but also thinking quickly. Perhaps his recent experiences of mixing reality and fantasy could be used now to good effect, by a judicious combination of the truth and a lie. The truth was that although his first clue had come independently of the Courcey documents, through the Latin message underlined in the book, this might not have been enough without the information in the old papers that referred to a vented room – fortunately copied by Higgins into the notebook he had stolen.

"But you've got it wrong," he said. "Yes, I understood that FitzSimmons was probably close to discovering the treasure, because he or one of his men was the most likely person to have stolen the clues from your desk. I agree that he isn't after the treasure, or at least that's not his primary concern. He's terrified there might really be de Vere manuscripts here that would threaten his grand scheme. But there have been at least two other people on the trail; people who found a clue in the same way that I did, without any use of the Courcey documents you stole from Higgins. Lewis was one; and if he ever saw the papers, he didn't see enough of them to find the clue you found – and there's at least one other."

"And how did you and these other people get a clue without those papers?"

"You don't really think I'm foolish enough to tell you? If you knew that, then you might work out who the other person is who is on the trail and then deal with him as you intend to deal with me."

The Master stared at Simon malevolently. For a moment he seemed unsettled, but then a look of relief came over his face. "You're lying," he said, "just as you have for so long about your revolting scribblings. I know about your private dinner parties with your friend Higgins, and I'm certain he let you see the Courcey documents, just as I'm sure he let Lewis see them. That's how you both got onto the scent. Yes, yes, there's no other way you could have worked things out, and there's no other person Higgins would trust to see them, except, of course, Mr Bambridge, and you know what happened to him. Lewis and you both had a good look at the letters from Henry Courcey – the ones I've now got hidden away under the floor-boards in the Lodge. It's in the old papers you found your clue. I hadn't worked out exactly where the hiding place was, but you've done that work for me. Unfortunately, just before I was attacked I'd taken the de Vere letters out of their concealment to have a closer look at them, but now that doesn't really matter. I expect Lord FitzSimmons has hidden them safely somewhere."

"You're wrong. Mr Bambridge was anxious to see the papers, but I happen to know he never did. Killing him was not only a horrible crime, it was quite unnecessary."

Although the situation was dangerous Simon was angry, and he couldn't resist adding something that, given the Master's pride, would infuriate him. "There are other clues which you've just been too stupid to see."

The Master's face went white. "You lie! You just don't like to admit that I have a finer brain than you and that I worked out a way of finding the treasure and covering all my tracks. You're the stupid one!"

He advanced, sword in hand, and as he did so Simon caught sight of a movement behind him. He forced himself not to look, lest his eye-movement might alert the Master to the possibility that there was someone else in the room. It could be an accomplice, or it could be someone else entirely. The sword was now level with his heart.

"There's something else you should consider very carefully," said Simon, trying to keep his voice steady.

"And what might that be?"

"Like me you are a priest in the Church of England. Do you not think that there will be some kind of judgment for acts of murder?"

"That is more evidence that you have an inferior brain. You've read your Darwin. What I used to believe, and what perhaps you still believe, is false – quite simply false. We have to go along with the outward form, at least if we are to keep our positions in Cambridge, but no intelligent person still believes in a creator-God, not in their honest and private thoughts."

"But now you're being stupid again. Don't you remember what Higgins was saying in the Combination Room? Why does creation have to be sudden? Darwin doesn't answer the ancient questions, only demand that they be seen in a new context, just as Frederick Temple and others are saying. You know perfectly well that theology has to be re-thought in every age."

"That's rubbish. Either there is the one faith, once delivered, or it's all myth, there is no third option. But I'm not going to argue theology with you now. This is where our conversation ends."

The Master drew back the sword, ready to plunge it with full force into Simon's heart. But the thrust never came. There was a thud and the Master fell at Simon's feet. There stood Viscount FitzSimmons, staring into his eyes. In his right hand he held Bishop Odo's mace – which was dripping with blood!

Chapter 31

The rare books room, De Vere College,
the same day, 3.45 p.m.

FitzSimmons's stare turned to the body on the floor. He grimaced and laid down the mace .

"So you're not going to use that thing on me!" said Simon.

"My dear Weatherspoon, I may be a thief, and perhaps a scoundrel, but I am not a murderer, or rather" – and here he surveyed again the body at his feet – "I will only kill in defence of myself or of some innocent person. Perhaps I should rephrase that to say that I will only kill to defend myself or some relatively innocent person! In fact we are much alike: both of us with things to hide. In any case, I don't think I have anything to fear from you. We're both into the business of purloining ancient things, and I think we may find that everything can be arranged to our mutual benefit."

"But what about the Master? It looks as if you have a dead body to deal with."

The Viscount knelt by the body of the Master and examined his head. Where the heavy mace had struck there was a crumpled mass of bone and brain. Death had been virtually instantaneous.

"Well, well," said FitzSimmons, with amazing calm. "I didn't intend to do so much damage, but I underestimated the power of the old mace. However, Dr James's death certainly simplifies our problems, because he does not have to be party to what we plan to do. And in any case," he added, "after hearing what he was going to do to me I can't say that I'm really sorry."

He stood up again, and continued. "I heard his plans for your body: that is, before he went off to deal with me. We can apply his solution to our problem. After we've divided the spoils the secret room will make a very convenient tomb for his body – unless there really is someone else on the trail who might find their way in there."

Simon hesitated. He was almost certain that in fact no-one else was close to unlocking the secret of the chamber. Talworthy's use of the book belonging to William Courcey had probably been pure chance, while Lewis, of course, was no longer a threat. However, he was not absolutely sure where, if anywhere, Heatherington fitted in, except for his lending of the book of Virgil's works to Lewis. His guess was that Lewis had indeed seen the Courcey documents and, intrigued by suggestions in them, had examined the catalogue of rare books and compared it with the list of starred items. This would explain how Lewis got onto the trail. He had found the same Latin clue and somehow he had got into the Lodge to see the portrait, which had led to his trip to Hedingham. The question was, had he let on to Heatherington about any of this – or indeed, had he and Heatherington been making plans together? Faced with this possibility, the story of the additional searcher was not a total fabrication. It was made up primarily to scare the Master, but it was possible that Lewis, or just possibly Mr Hill, was in collaboration with Heatherington. On balance, however, this was unlikely, since Lewis had been alone at Hedingham and also seemed to have been exploring the library on his own, and surely, if Heatherington had scented the treasure, or been desperate to look at the de Vere letters, he would have been there with him. Also, when the news came through of Lewis's death, allegedly by drowning, Heatherington had been upset but not, it would appear, suspicious, as he certainly would have been if they were into a treasure hunt together. However, there was still a problem. If FitzSimmons were told that there really was no-one else on the trail, then the Viscount would have nothing to fear from killing him, and putting both his body and that of the Master within the secret room.

Simon stared again at FitzSimmons, and a conviction gripped him – although it was more a matter of feeling, he sensed, than of rational deduction. FitzSimmons was right. He was a scoundrel, but he was not a murderer.

Simon found himself relaxing. He was thinking fast. If the police were not to be involved, along with – at the least – all the explanations there would have to be about the death of the Master and of Lewis, he had to make some kind of deal with FitzSimmons.

"You're right," he said. "I was trying to scare off the Master by letting him think there was someone else on the trail – that is, in addition to you; and yes, I think we might be able to arrange things to our mutual advantage. But there is a problem for you. I've opened all the chests, and there's no sign of the de Vere papers, as we might call them, and unless I've got things quite wrong, that is what you're most interested in."

FitzSimmons moved to the tables and sat down on the chair that Simon had been using when he had been surprised by the Master. "There must be some mistake," he said, "the letters from de Vere clearly indicate that some manuscripts had been given to William Courcey to be hidden away. One of them actually says that he had planned to give them to his cousin, Horatio, but that he is away fighting in Holland and that he doesn't want to risk them being found in his house if he dies and perhaps being destroyed – as he puts it 'by those who would have an interest in their destruction'. In his final letter he asks for an assurance that Courcey has received the manuscripts and has put them in the safe place within his lodgings he had told him about. This is how I knew there was a hiding place somewhere in the keep, and probably on the top floor, and this, I am sure, is how Dr James knew it, for he had seen all the letters before I was able to get them. Edward de Vere doesn't actually say what the manuscripts are, but I have a strong suspicion – and whatever they are, they are likely to be here."

"But I've been through all the chests, and there's no sign of manuscripts – except for the illuminated ones in this pile over here."

"What about those chests on the floor?"

"They're full of relics."

FitzSimmons sat down and brushed back his hair with his hands, a characteristic gesture when he was thinking hard.

"In point of fact," he said, "I came over to the library to try and see you. I had been unable to work everything out, and when I realized that Dr James was looking for the secret room I decided that caution must give way to urgency, so I thought of levelling with you and trying to get your help. As acting librarian you had access to the whole keep, and knew it better than anyone. When you weren't in your rooms I guessed you would be here. I found the keep unlocked, but before I got to the top of the stairs I heard voices. I was in time to hear the reference to your secret life as a novelist – which I had already discovered – and what Dr James intended to do to both of us!"

"He must have left the main door unlocked when he came here to find me – but I'm as puzzled as you are about where the de Vere manuscripts can be. I had better have another look inside the secret room."

Simon crawled back and looked carefully in every corner. There was nothing. When he was back in his chair he thought hard. "Now I come to think of it," he said, "I haven't actually emptied out the reliquary chests, except for one which seems to hold the so-called jawbone of St Matthew."

They both started to empty the three chests containing the smaller reliquaries, and the ancient piece of wood. At first they found nothing, but in the second chest they examined, below a layer of religious items, they found a pile of papers. Simon looked at the piece of paper on top of the pile and read the opening words.

"I thought the king had more affected the Duke of Albany than Cornwall."

"Good God!" FitzSimmons sat down again, looking pale. "So it's true, as I feared it might be once I found the letters in Dr James's desk. You recognize the lines?"

"No, I'm not a Shakespeare scholar; although I am familiar with some of the plays."

"Those are the opening lines of *King Lear*. What's more, that play is traditionally dated to 1605, or perhaps later, and the first performance was thought to have been in December 1606. But this manuscript has to be before de Vere's death in 1604. I've made it my business to know this sort of thing. Let me have a look at it."

Simon handed over the paper along with the rest of the bundle from which it came. FitzSimmons started to look at it carefully.

"This is the original. Look, there are words crossed out and some corrections. Also, I recognize the hand: it's the same as that in de Vere's letters to William Courcey. If ever this manuscript sees the light of day the scholars will have to look again at Ben Jonson's claim that Shakespeare 'never blotted a line' – unless, perhaps, the corrections are in another hand, possibly that of John Fletcher. I'd often wondered about Jonson's assertion because of the many differences in the early editions of the plays."

"Perhaps the corrections are in the hand of Shakespeare – if he and de Vere were in some kind of collaboration," volunteered Simon.

The Viscount scowled. "That would certainly put a whole new twist on what people call the de Vere hypothesis."

Simon's recent interest in plots and conspiracies, as required by his entry into the world of fiction, led him to hazard yet another possibility. "Perhaps Shakespeare, as part of his arrangement with de Vere, copied out the whole plays, after all the corrections had been made, so that he could present them to the players in his own hand. People tend to assume the players knew who the real author was, but if de Vere were to keep his secret safe I think it's likely they didn't – or at least, most of them didn't. If that is the case, it would look as if the author 'never a blotted line'. In fact the young Ben Jonson might actually have seen some of the copies in Shakespeare's hand."

He drew out the bundle that lay immediately below the manuscript of *King Lear* and handed it to FitzSimmons. As the Viscount scanned it he pulled out the next bundle and opened it at random. He recognized the words instantly: "Get thee to a nunnery." This, he realized, must be the actual holograph of *Hamlet*! He made no comment as FitzSimmons announced that he was now scanning an early draft of *Julius Caesar*.

After a careful search Simon extracted a total of seven Shakespeare manuscripts, four in one chest and three in another. Why William Courcey had hidden them underneath the reliquaries they could not understand, though FitzSimmons hazarded a series of guesses. In his letter indicating the intention to send the manuscripts to Courcey, de Vere specifically asked that they be well hidden because he did not want there to be any chance of their discovery until the time was right. When the time came, de Vere said, Courcey would receive a message from his cousin, Sir Horatio Vere. Meanwhile, William Courcey already had the ideal hiding place, although this was not specified in the letters. Back in the late 1530s, on the urgent request of his brother Henry, the last Abbot of Lolworth, he had carefully prepared the chamber. The secrecy of this room was all that was really required but, perhaps, as FitzSimmons suggested, by hiding the plays under the reliquaries he felt he was carrying out his friend's last plea to the letter. In any case, it was evident that no request for their release came, or if it did come, then William Courcey was already dead, and the new Master of De Vere College probably had no idea of the existence of the secret room. FitzSimmons concluded, "Ever since reading the letters I've wondered about Sir Horatio. My suspicion is that when he returned from campaigning he did try to carry out his cousin's request – but by then, since all the original manuscripts were either hidden here, or destroyed, he found himself thwarted."

Simon suggested the final part of the puzzle. "Before he died," he said, "William Courcey left some clues. I think he was anxious that eventually the treasure, and with it the true genius of his friend, would be discovered. He placed the clues in such a way that only those with similar interests to himself would be likely to find them. I suspect, he never thought this would take more than two hundred and fifty years."

While Simon was speaking FitzSimmons stood up and began to replace the holographs underneath the reliquaries. "You're not going to put them back?" Simon protested.

"That's exactly what I'm going to do. After all, what is the harm? The plays are great, and who actually wrote them doesn't really matter, except to me and others who have a stake in – let us call it, 'the Shakespeare hypothesis'. I must admit that I'm having second thoughts about the new buildings at Stratford-upon-Avon, and I might decide not to go ahead with them. It's one thing to let the Warwickshire hero continue to receive glory: it's another thing to add to the glory when I know it's undeserved. I may be a businessman, but believe me, I do have a respect for the plays, and for the person I now know to be their true creator. So I'm not sure what I shall do – but I certainly don't propose to release these manuscripts – especially in the light of the way we came by them."

After a pause he continued, "What I propose is very simple. I'm sure you don't want any of these horrible relics, although I admit that some of the containers are very fine. We shall simply put the four relic chests back where they came from, along with Dr James's body and, of course, the rapier and the mace. The mace is covered with blood and we really have no time to clean it properly. I think we should also put back all those religious trinkets. It would be hard to explain how we came by them. As for the rest, I suggest that I have the de Vere plays and the illuminated manuscripts and you can keep all the fancy chess pieces. All in all that's about fair. As for the plays, as part of my share, I choose to leave them here. As for explaining how we got hold of the precious objects we keep, I think you would do well to make use of Dr James's idea about emptying out an old French chateau. With your money from royalties you should have no trouble arranging that: in fact you might enjoy actually owning a French chateau. As for my illuminated manuscripts, I have contacts through whom I can dispose of them."

In the name of scholarship Simon protested at the hiding away of the de Vere manuscripts, but even as he did so he realized that he was 'not protesting too much', to invert a Shakespearean expression. After all, his position was not strong. Unless they made an agreement he would have to explain his actions, including what might look like an act of theft and, more seriously still, not reporting the finding of Lewis's body. But FitzSimmons' position was also vulnerable. If he did not make an agreement with him, then he would have to explain both his killing of the Master and (with much more difficulty, since striking the Master with the mace had saved Simon's life) – the attack on the Master in the Lodge by his henchman. Also, he did not seem anxious that the true authorship of the Shakespearean canon should emerge, even though it looked as if he proposed to abandon his new plans for Stratford. After all, he had already linked his reputation with that of the bard from Warwickshire.

Sitting by the treasure, they bargained. Yet Simon's internal dialogue was going on side by side with the outward discussion. The stifling of important scholarly material was obnoxious and contrary to all his instincts, but he was in no position to insist that the truth come out. In a way, he thought, he was in a similar position to that of Edward de Vere who longed for the truth to be known but who was caught in a situation in which he could not let it emerge, at least while he was alive. Perhaps, like both de Vere and Courcey, all that he could do was to find a way of leaving clues, so that eventually, when personal considerations no longer applied, an equivalent to Horatio could divulge all. What made the whole situation bizarre was that his own book, *The de Vere Papers* had in fact, and without his knowledge, pointed to a version of the truth. Surely, if ever there were a case of truth being stranger than fiction, this was it! Finally, he realized that what was probably the moral thing to do, namely to return everything back to its hiding place until the legal situation was made clear, was no longer a real possibility. FitzSimmons would never agree, and furthermore, if the legal authorities were ever involved, their handling of the Master's body would require more than a little explanation!

FitzSimmons repeated what they had agreed. Simon was to have the chess sets and – the result of some hard bargaining – one of the illuminated Gospels and the book of Psalms; the rest was to be his. He concluded: "As the only two people who know about these treasures, we agree to divide them in the way I have just suggested."

"But what about the third person who knows?"

The new voice rang out from just beyond the door to the rare books room, and both men looked round in alarm.

Chapter 32

The rare books room, De Vere College,
the same day, 4.30 p.m.

A slender figure stood in the doorway, exactly in the spot where Simon had seen the Master. At first, recognition was difficult, since by late afternoon the light was already poor, coming as it did from the two deeply set windows in the former chapel. The figure discarded a gown and mortar-board, and Simon recognized Theresa! He almost uttered a gasp of recognition, but a flash of the newcomer's eyes warned him of the need to say nothing.

It was the Viscount who broke the silence.

"Who, in God's name, are you?"

Theresa spoke with a slightly strained accent, as if she were trying to disguise her voice which, Simon thought, was very likely the case. There was really no need for this, but in the excitement of the moment it might seem a fair thing to do.

"My name, I think, had best be left unknown. But this I can tell you. I am a reporter for the *London Echo*."

Lord FitzSimmons continued to stare at the totally unexpected apparition. "Don't tell me you've been following clues to this treasure-trove."

"No, nothing so dramatic. What I see spread before me comes as a total surprise. I've simply been on the trail of the author of some recent sensational dramas, and after working out who it probably was I came to flush him out. I calculated that as acting librarian he might be here so, as I passed the porter's lodge, I made myself look as like a man as possible and came to the library. By luck I found the place unlocked, and I arrived upstairs just in time to overhear part of a very interesting conversation!"

Theresa walked across to the body of the Master and, Simon thought, with amazing calm, poked at it with her foot and then added.

"Who, may I be so bold as to ask, is this? Or perhaps I should phrase the question, who was this?"

Simon replied. "It's the man who tried to murder me as I was assembling the treasure. My friend here came just in time to save my life. As you can see, he had to take sudden and rather drastic action."

Theresa glanced from one to the other. "It didn't sound as if you were exactly friends – not from the way I heard you arguing." She looked at Simon, "You, I presume, are Dr Weatherspoon and, unless I'm very much mistaken, you are the one my paper is going to unmask in the next few days. I would very much like an exclusive interview with you, and in return for that I might – I stress might – agree not to mention some other aspects of this extraordinary case!"

She turned to Lord FitzSimmons. "May I ask the name of the person who so valiantly saved our controversial author by wielding what looks like an ancient mace?"

FitzSimmons lied with an ease that amazed even Simon. "My name is Charles Thorncliffe. I'm an antiquarian who has been on the hunt for this treasure for some time, and it so happened that it was only today that the two of us finally worked out where it was. I left my friend, or perhaps I should say my colleague, while he began to sort through what we had found. As you can see, I came back just in time. This villain – who had managed to obtain some of the clues – was ready to commit murder to get his hands on the whole treasure."

Theresa sat down, surveyed the scene and then said:

"I heard the last part of your discussion, and the agreement you reached. I suggest that we continue the discussion, but this time with a three-way split. After all, there is a considerable advantage to you if I take some of the treasure because then I too will be party to any illegal activity, so you will have little to fear from me. My only other condition for silence is that Dr Weatherspoon gives me the exclusive interview I have asked for, and which I can then print after the disclosure of his name."

"Do you know when this disclosure is to be made?" asked Simon.

"Yes, indeed: on Wednesday. The editors wanted to wait till the Easter holiday was over. Tomorrow there will be some more information and an indication that the whole extraordinary story will be given by the paper the next day. This way," she added with a cynical smile, "they can guarantee a huge sale of the paper and, with luck, one that can continue for some time as further details are released. Our interview can provide material for the continuing saga."

All three sat round the tables covered with the treasure. Simon was at an extraordinary height of elation, though tinged with a certain nervousness. The most obvious reason was his escape, only a few minutes ago, from almost certain death, but in fact the greater cause was the appearance of Theresa, along with what that probably implied. She had almost certainly received his letter and, quite obviously, was playing a game which suggested that she was fully on his side. But did this mean love, or did it mean just a measure of forgiveness, plus an extraordinary opportunity to share in the riches displayed before them? He would have to wait till they were alone before he could find out.

"I shall be happy to grant you an exclusive interview," he said, "on two conditions. First, we three must come to a thorough understanding of what to do with all this" (and here he waved at the objects lying around them) "and second, nothing from the interview shall be published before Thursday, by which time I shall hope to have escaped to a place where other reporters are unlikely to find me."

FitzSimmons, whose composure was now fully restored, added. "That sounds a very fair arrangement to me. We shall make our division, then we shall return all the things we're not going to keep to the secret chamber we have uncovered, along with the body of this murderous person. Then I suggest that this good lady wait in Weatherspoon's set of rooms for her interview while we two clean up this place, and leave it as if nothing had happened." He turned to Theresa and then added. "When everything is set back in order, Dr Weatherspoon can order a carriage for you at the porter's lodge. I suggest you leave the chest in his rooms, and carry your trophies in some more ordinary box."

The proposal received general agreement, and was followed by another round of bargaining. This time, however, in addition to the fact that three were to share in the bounty, FitzSimmons no longer seemed content to put the de Vere papers back in the secret room. Now that there was another person who knew about the holographs, he wanted to take them with him, along with his medieval manuscripts, and Simon had a distinct and uneasy sense that he proposed to destroy the de Vere holographs. The scholarly part of his nature recoiled in horror at the idea, and he devised a way of at least partially thwarting the Viscount.

As details of the proposed agreement began to take shape, he started to make three piles of treasure, one for each party. The Viscount's share was now to be the de Vere holographs and just two of the medieval manuscripts but, fortunately, Simon had not actually shown the *Hamlet* to FitzSimmons, nor had they remarked on the fact that there were seven bundles of de Vere papers. As a result, and with luck, the Viscount would think that the six de Vere holographs he carried away represented the whole. With this in mind, while FitzSimmons was distracted by looking again at the *King Lear*, Simon managed to place the *Hamlet* underneath the six medieval manuscripts, which were to be the lady reporter's share. As he did this he noticed Theresa looking in his direction, and gave her a wink. Her face remained impassive. Was she continuing to act out her part with professional skill, or was she really cold towards him?

Meanwhile, Simon's share was to be the nine sets of chessmen and a few of the religious items that he said he could put to secular use, including a lovely pair of silver candlesticks which he had previously examined with admiration. The candlesticks carried hallmarks on the bases; the crowned leopard's head of the London assay office, a maker's mark in the form of a crossbow, and a date letter – 'D'. On the upper part they also carried an inscribed coat of arms, which Simon did not recognize, and the date '1481'. They were probably a gift to the abbey from some noble family. He had said nothing to FitzSimmons about the marks, but reflected that the candlesticks might be among the earliest examples of hallmarked English silver and there could be considerable speculation about how this silver from the London of Edward IV ended up in a French chateau!

The agreement finalized, all three piles were put inside chests: two for Simon's hoard and one each for those of FitzSimmons and Theresa, while everything else was piled back, somewhat unceremoniously given the nature of the contents, into the other five chests.

Already the light was fading and Theresa indicated that she wished to be out of the place quickly. Leaving FitzSimmons to begin the process of tidying, Simon escorted Theresa to his rooms, helping her to carry the chest that contained her part of the treasure – along with the priceless *Hamlet* – the chest being wrapped in part of an old curtain taken from his office in the next room.

Chapter 33

De Vere College, the same evening.

Back in his rooms, as soon as the oak shut, and before the gas could be lit, Theresa burst into laughter and threw herself into Simon's arms.

"We did it!" she cried.

Simon began to wrap his arms around her, but she untangled them. "I see that I am going to be the practical one in this relationship. There will be plenty of time for kissing, but now you must get back to FitzSimmons – I assume that is his real name – with the soap and water you promised to bring. If you delay he may think that all is not what it seems."

Theresa almost pushed Simon out of the door. With soap, bucket and towels in hand he went back to the rare books room. There the Viscount had placed all the items that were not to be carried away close to the secret entrance but had not gone farther. He was both older and fatter than Simon, and, moreover, it was evident that crawling on his hands and knees did not accord with his sense of dignity. Neither, needless to say, did washing the blood-stained part of the floor, but reluctantly he agreed to start this while Simon pushed the chests, one by one, ahead of him into the secret room.

When all the chests they did not need for their own use were safely back there along with the rapier, and the blood-stained mace was back in its original corner, they turned to deal with the Master's body. Simon was about to start the task of dragging it towards the narrow entrance to the chamber when FitzSimmons knelt down and started to go through the dead man's pockets. From one he extracted a silk purse that was found to contain banknotes and a few gold coins. He offered half of these to Simon, who simply shook his head. Somehow, although there seemed no point in leaving these things with the body, the pillage of them was something he just couldn't bring himself to take part in. He had a vision of FitzSimmons as a gentleman buccaneer of Elizabethan times, happy to combine the lofty life of court with the pillaging and rape of Spanish merchant ships. In another pocket there was a watch, made not of gold but of pinchbeck, but a nice object nevertheless. FitzSimmons calmly put this in one his own pockets, alongside the banknotes and the gold coins. From another pocket he drew out a beautifully turned piece of black hardstone, of the shape and size of a swan's egg. He handed it to Simon, saying "Can you guess why he carried this?"

Simon felt the heavy smooth stone in his hands. "Yes, indeed. I'm sure this is what he used to strike Higgins – and Mr Lewis too, when he found him in the library. He probably had it with him when he went to deal with Bambridge, but found he didn't need to use it because, following a request to see the view from the chapel roof, a simple push was enough. I had imagined something much bigger, but it's hard and heavy enough to do the work and still fit into a pocket. I think it was his preferred weapon when he could come up on someone from behind, but in my case it would be too risky, so he carried his rapier as well in case he had to approach me from the front."

Simon handed it back, and to his surprise FitzSimmons put this also into one of his own pockets. It was a good thing, he thought, that the Viscount had no special interest in the chess pieces, or he would have tried to get his hands on as many of those as possible.

They turned to the task of disposing of the Master's body, the noble lord pushing from one end and Simon pulling from the other, twisting it round the end of the wooden bench and through the narrow entrance to the secret room.

When the corpse was fully inside Simon had a sudden vision of FitzSimmons pushing the entrance shut, drawing the bolt, and leaving him to starve to death beside the decaying body of the Master. FitzSimmons would still have to deal with Theresa, but if he were capable of Simon's murder he might be just as capable of hers. However, as Simon climbed out, he was greeted by the sight of the noble lord's ample rear end as he crouched on all fours in the middle of the room, vigorously rubbing one of the floor boards with a wet cloth. He wished he had one of Talworthy's cameras with him.

As they worked together on the bloodstains, FitzSimmons waxed surprisingly talkative. Despite the indignity of his posture he was clearly in a good mood and the presence nearby of the dead body did not seem to worry him, or if it did, the realization of his successes more than compensated for it.

"That bolt underneath the seat explains quite a lot," FitzSimmons said. "When I started to puzzle out where the treasure could be hidden I spoke to a mason about making secret doors in stonework. He told me that although fairy tales were full of sliding stone doors, in practice it is virtually impossible to make them without giving away clues: by lines in the stonework or by draughts of air. This is what led me to think the entrance might be made of wood, although I had not thought of the benches. I puzzled about how a wooden door that led into a stone room could be both secure and secret, but now I understand. However, I don't think this entrance can remain secret for ever. Eventually someone will want to restore the whole keep, or perhaps the wood will get dry rot. In any case, one day some carpenter will probably come across this entrance; but I don't think it will be in our lifetimes."

Simon said nothing, only remarking inwardly that the Viscount was now talking almost as if they were old friends. Partners in crime made for strange companions.

Before they parted, the Viscount made another observation. "I

215

overheard Dr James's remark about hiding the other documents under the floor boards in the Lodge. I don't like the idea of these being found, and perhaps leading someone else to follow our search. I think it will be some time before a new Master gets elected, and while the Lodge is empty it shouldn't be too difficult for a certain Mr Tumbler to find them. We can both rest better if I look after them."

Chapter 34

De Vere College, later, the same evening.

They carried their respective chests to their rooms, discreetly covered in more of the old curtains purloined from the librarian's office, and then met in the rare books room for a final inspection. Simon had to wait several minutes for this meeting and was beginning to be anxious – wondering whether FitzSimmons had decided on some variation on their arrangement. However, it transpired that the Viscount, not being used to being dressed other than immaculately, had taken the opportunity to clean himself and change his clothes. Everything appeared in order. Just before parting, at the entrance to the old keep, they agreed to put on a show, acting as if nothing had happened. This would include going to chapel, which was about to take place, and then taking dinner in hall.

Simon changed from his dusty clothes into something more respectable and then, after a quick and quiet conversation with Theresa (for they did not want anyone to hear voices in his set of rooms), he went to Evensong. He was a little late, but in time for the General

Confession; which he found himself saying with unusual earnestness. Then he went directly to the Senior Combination Room. The seven fellows present processed into hall, led by Townend, who asked Lord FitzSimmons to follow him, apologizing for the fact that the Master – his host – had not shown up.

Only a scattering of students were still in residence and, despite the Easter season, dinner was quiet. Several comments were made about the Master's absence, and a general concern was expressed concerning his health. "In my view," said Heatherington, "he hasn't been taking things easily enough since his nasty accident. He still insists on going to that fencing club and competing with much younger men."

FitzSimmons added a comment that was clearly meant to be passed on in the days to come when the Master's absence was bound to cause alarm. "When I saw him briefly this morning he said he would meet me at the chapel service. He also said he intended to spend the afternoon taking a long walk along the tow-path, walking perhaps half way to Ely, because he needed to clear his head. Perhaps he went farther than he intended and stopped at one of the public houses near the path. I certainly hope he didn't fall into the river."

After dinner, the eight at high table retired to the Senior Combination Room where, notwithstanding it being Monday, the port was good because Dr James had pre-arranged it for his guest. FitzSimmons was still in the genial spirits that had characterized their final conversations in the library. Perhaps he was a good actor, but more likely he was pleased, not only to have acquired two extremely valuable manuscripts, but also – so he believed – the de Vere papers that might embarrass him.

Simon tried to be polite to Talworthy, but as soon as the Junior Fellow got into conversation with Heatherington he slipped into an inner reverie. Theresa, at his suggestion, would now be munching some bread and a couple of apples that were in his kitchen, downed with a little sherry. Before he left her, they had just had time to begin the careful wrapping of the more fragile treasures to prevent damage in the move to London, using various pieces of his personal clothing

217

for the purpose, a task that was left for Theresa to complete while he was at Evensong and dinner. As they wrapped the first item, he had – though rather diffidently – mentioned his qualms about taking all these precious things away to their homes, even though he had already indicated to her that he intended to make sure they ended up in one of the national museums. Her reply had been somewhat brusque: perhaps another indication that not everything was going to be plain sailing in their future relationship. "Don't be absurd!" was her response to the possibility of returning their booty to the secret room, after FitzSimmons had departed. She did not seem to share his unease about what they were doing, and given all the complex circumstances he had decided not to pursue the topic any further, at least not at this time. However, he wondered whether she too would be anxious to see that her share of the spoils ended up as national treasures, and he realized, with a slight sense of foreboding, that her decision might not be along quite the same lines as his. The story of a discovery in a French chateau could provide an explanation for both of them about the origins of the works of art, but what Theresa would decide to do with her share was another matter.

When he left her she had seemed in high spirits, even though she had only the prospect of a meagre meal. Throughout their hurried discussion her organizing skills were again in evidence and, despite his eager anticipations of the evening and of beyond, he again felt a twinge of concern. How much of his freedom was he going to lose?

Just before his exit for chapel she had outlined their plan – or was it her plan? – in a few hurried sentences.

Although FitzSimmons would assume she was in London, she would in fact spend the night there, and in making this clear she glanced at the single bed that could be seen through the open door that led to the bedroom. After Simon had breakfasted in the Senior Combination Room, perhaps hiding a few pieces of bread in his pockets for Theresa, he would carry the three chests and his bags to the porter's lodge and order a carriage to take him to the station. The chests would be wrapped in his sheets, thus both disguising what they really were, and bringing some more of his belongings to London.

She would slip out before the carriage came, and a few hundred yards away would wait for Simon to pick her up on the way to Cambridge Junction. The driver might seem a little surprised, but that really didn't matter.

Despite these plans, most of the details for the future were left more than a little vague, and Simon wondered what Mrs Peters would say if Theresa came to stay in his London house. He also wondered what he would do with his part of the treasure. The Master's idea about the French chateau might well be pursued and when the extraordinary sets of chessmen turned up there, he might even start to add to the collection by other means, perhaps by buying the late Master's pieces if they came on the market. But what about the *Hamlet*?

A mischievous idea came to him. Perhaps, when all the dust had settled he could arrange for a real Jane Bartholomew to find the holograph, and then alert the scholarly world to the truth about Shakespeare. This really would be a case of fiction paving the way for truth, and would make *The de Vere Papers* still more famous. Viscount FitzSimmons would certainly be annoyed and might well suspect that he had not really played fair, but there would be nothing to be done about it after the event. Also, since he hadn't actually seen the *Hamlet*, he might be genuinely unsure of exactly what lay behind the discovery. Simon would enjoy making plots of this kind with Theresa.

His roving thoughts centred, yet again, on the woman waiting for him in his rooms. Theresa's last words, before speeding him off, were that she was looking forward to the night, and that she thought she'd be able to teach Simon quite a lot. His meditations in chapel, like his present feelings, were not exactly what the others present would have expected. Ah well, let those without sin be the first to cast stones.

Chapter 35

15 Elm Place, Overfield, Surrey,
Friday, 30th September 2008, 5.00 p.m.

J ane Bartholomew sat down in the armchair but did not feel like turning on the TV to watch the news. Her sixth form class in English Literature that afternoon had gone quite well, but she felt exhausted and just wanted to rest. She eyed the morning mail that she had picked up on her way into the house and noted one piece that didn't seem to fit the usual pattern. The envelope indicated it was from Booth and Tendril, a firm of London solicitors of whom she had never heard. Perhaps they were advertising for business or, perhaps, as in some of her wilder fancies, one of her Australian cousins had died and left her a fortune? She would certainly be glad of the latter, having found it harder to keep up with the mortgage payments than she had expected. She tore the solicitors' letter open and read the contents – with an increasing level of astonishment. The letter was dated the previous day, and ran as follows:

29th September 2008

Dear Miss Bartholomew,

We are acting on instructions from the executors of the late Doreen Theresa Weatherspoon who passed away on March the 18th of this year at the age of ninety-seven. According to the will of the deceased, we, as executors, are charged with finding a schoolteacher named 'Jane Bartholomew', who is to become the beneficiary of an unusual but, (we are led to believe) valuable, bequest. The remainder of the estate has gone to members of the family. In the event of more than one person being found who fits this description, then the executors are given absolute discretion to choose one of these persons. In fact, you are the first person found to fit this description, and whether or not there are others, the determination has been made that the bequest shall be yours absolutely, unless you should choose to decline it.

By way of further explanation the following information may be of interest: Doreen Theresa Weatherspoon, whose estate we represent, was one of the grand-children of the Biblical scholar and novelist the Revd Dr Simon Edward Weatherspoon (1839–1915) and the literary critic Theresa Anne Weatherspoon, née Brown (1844–1933). The former is known not only for his novels, some of which are still in print, but also for the 'Weatherspoon collection' of chessmen in the Victoria and Albert Museum, while the latter is known for an important bequest of illuminated medieval manuscripts to the British Museum, which are now part of the British Library. It would appear that the unusual nature of the present bequest, including the identity of the beneficiary, reflects the wishes of Theresa Anne Weatherspoon as expressed in a conversation with her grand-daughter shortly before her death in 1933. For a variety of reasons Doreen Theresa Weatherspoon felt unable to fulfil the full terms of this request during her life, in part because of long periods spent abroad. However, she left explicit instructions in her will that the request should now be fulfilled as soon as possible.

The bequest comprises (1) an old English chest, made in oak and dated 1604 – acquired, we understand, by the aforementioned Theresa Anne Weatherspoon in the 1890s, after a considerable search to find a chest with that exact date; and (2) a manuscript (within the said chest), the details of which are unknown to us, but which is to be yours, along with the chest.

With the bequest of these two items the will contains a request to the beneficiary: a request that, we should add, is not legally binding. It is to the effect that the manuscript be shown to an expert in the field of Tudor and Stuart literature. Subsequently – according to this request – you should feel free to keep or dispose of either item as you see fit, as the absolute owner of both items.

We look forward to hearing from you at your earliest convenience.

Yours sincerely,

Henrietta Booth

Henrietta Booth
(partner)

Epilogue

The plausibility of 'The de Vere hypothesis'.

Serious doubts concerning the true authorship of the Shakespearean canon have been around for a long time. The first alternative hypothesis to be given substantial support concerned Francis Bacon, for example in Delia Bacon's *The Philosophy of the Plays of Shakspere Unfolded* [*sic*] (London, 1857) – although this writer was not the first to put forward the claim. With respect to the 'de Vere hypothesis', as it is called in this novel, although there were earlier intimations, the first full-length defence was made by a man with the somewhat unfortunate (and some have claimed appropriate) name of J. Thomas Looney (pronounced 'Loney') in his *Shakespeare Identified in Edward de Vere, the Seventeenth Earl of Oxford* (Cecil Palmer, London, 1920). For what it is worth, Sigmund Freud read this book twice and declared himself convinced by it. (See Peter Gay's *Freud – A Life for Our Time*, Dent, London, 1988.) Most of the evidence can also be found in Andrew Field's invented autobiography, *The Lost Chronicle of Edward de Vere* (Viking, London, 1990; Penguin 1991).

With respect to the de Vere hypothesis, while personally I remain 'agnostic' (in the strict sense of that term), I think that many academics dismiss its plausibility too quickly and without due awareness of the case that can be presented for it. At the same time, the case against it must also be admitted. (One reason for my interest in this topic is that in my search for an adequate balance between competing theories there is an analogy between literary and criminal detection.)

The starting point for the de Vere hypothesis is the well supported claim that during his life-time Edward de Vere did write plays in which he used a false name in order to protect his position at court. The case against the de Vere hypothesis can be summarized under five headings:

First, as soon as one espouses a complex theory for which proof is virtually impossible to find, and then begins to look for evidence, it is notorious that all kinds of things turn up that seem to fit the theory. The problem is that one is looking at the data through the 'lens' of a certain perspective, and in doing so one tends not to be aware that someone else, using a different lens, may come up with an equally strong case for an alternative theory. This is a very important point to explore in the history of scientific theory, which is one reason why – in the case of science – an adequate theory nearly always requires confirmation through some kind of predictive test. Outside the realm of science, a good example of finding evidence to fit one's theory is provided by defenders of Nostrodamus. Many writers who defend the accuracy of his predictions claim to have found a complex code in terms of which (so the theory goes) it can be shown that he truly predicted all kinds of important events. This is a theory I have examined in some detail, and have concluded that the lens of the true believer has systematically skewed the reading of the prophesies (most of which are expressed in ambiguous and metaphorical language) so that massive evidence appears to be provided within historical events, when in fact no such evidence exists. Among the grounds for this negative view is the fact that whenever believers in the theory have been bold enough to apply their reading of the code to the future, they have failed to make a significant number of precise forecasts. In other words, a predictive test has been attempted and failed.

In a corresponding way – with the lens of the de Vere hypothesis – an amazing number of connections can be made, especially perhaps in the reading of *Hamlet*. (Among many other examples, in addition to the point made in the text concerning the historical Horatio Vere, there is a conjectured link between Edward de Vere's ill-fated investment in the search for a northwest passage to Asia, in which he lost heavily, and Hamlet's line "I am mad, north by northwest". There are also some striking similarities between his father-in-law, Lord Burghley, and the character of Polonius.) However, one has to offset against these apparent coincidences the way in which, say, a Marlowe or a Bacon or a Mary Sidney lens can also amass an extraordinary number of 'coincidences'. This is not a disproof of the de Vere hypothesis, but a warning about how easy it is to be lured into belief by reading one commentator's reflections on a detailed text. For example, those who are attracted to the de Vere hypothesis might do well to read the ingenious defence of the Bacon hypothesis in *The Great Cryptogram* (London, 1888), written under the pseudonym of Ignatius Donnelly, in which – through a heroic manipulation of numbers – the alleged certainty of a Baconian authorship is demonstrated.

Nevertheless, despite these sceptical comments, I still find it amazing how many references in the plays can be seen as oblique references to an Oxford authorship.

Second, many supporters of the de Vere, and of other radical hypotheses, argue that William Shakespeare, given what we know of his education and social background, could not have written the canon. I agree with those who dispute the de Vere hypothesis that this is not a powerful argument. Despite the implicit criticism of A. L. Rowse within the novel, this scholar was right to point out that genius does not demand an 'explanation', in the ordinary sense of the word. (It should also be pointed out that we actually know very little about Shakespeare's education and early life.) In various fields of human endeavour, geniuses arise whose originality defies all attempts to say exactly how and why they were so creative. The phenomenon of Shakespeare, is, in a sense, exceedingly improbable – but the same could be said for all other geniuses. The fact is – and this is incontrovertible – that human nature is such that extraordinary genius does crop up now and again, often in the most unforeseeable circumstances. Nevertheless, it needs to be made clear that the de Vere hypothesis does not need to rely on this problematical argument.

The second point highlights the weakness of one ground that has been used to support the de Vere hypothesis, but does not attack the hypothesis directly, as does the third. This argues that if it is the case that *Macbeth* was written after the gunpowder plot of 1605, since Edward de Vere died in 1604, then there are obvious difficulties. In reply, some supporters of the de Vere hypothesis think the apparent references to the plot of 1605 can be explained in other ways and others (more plausibly) argue that some of de Vere's manuscripts were reworked, after his death, in order to make them more appropriate to the time of production. [On this matter one could read Jonathan Bate, *The Genius of Shakespeare*, Picador, London, 1997, p. 65 and following.]

Fourth, if it is true that the Shakespearean canon includes a significant number of Warwickshire allusions and idioms, as is sometimes claimed, this is strong evidence against the de Vere hypothesis. I put this argument cautiously, since in order to have force it is not enough to support the positive claim that terms arise in the canon that were popular in the Warwickshire of Tudor times, one has also to support the negative claim that these terms are not found, or are only very rarely found, elsewhere.

Fifth, there is the claim that a technical analysis of the language in the known poems by Edward de Vere does not match the language of the Shakespearean canon. Again, this is a difficult argument to assess, especially since the poems that are known to have been written by de Vere date from early in his life.

Needless to say, there are counter arguments to all of these points, one of which has been suggested, namely that some of the plays may have been reworked after de Vere's death in order to make them more topical.

The only other counter argument I shall explore here concerns the fifth point, where an interesting analogy helps to reduce all or most of its force. For centuries scholars were extremely doubtful about the authenticity of Plato's letters, and one of the principal reasons for doubt concerned the alleged difference in both style and content between the letters and the dialogues that were accepted as authentic. However, more recent scholarship has stressed the major changes in Plato's writings between the early and the later ones (such as the

Laws), in terms of both literary style and of philosophical content, and has strongly supported the authenticity of many, and possibly all, of the letters. Both the style and content of the seventh letter (the longest and most important) actually match the later dialogues very well. [For an insight into this topic see Glenn R. Morrow's introductory essay to Plato's *Epistles*, Bobbs-Merrill, Indianapolis, 1962.] Of course, this does not prove the case for de Vere, but it disarms the final and some consider most important argument.

Also on the positive side, in *Alias Shakespeare* (The Free Press, New York, 1997) Joseph Sobran discusses close and frequent parallels in the choice of imagery used by de Vere and the Shakespearean canon, especially in appendices 2 and 3, which examine de Vere's poetry and letters. He revisits this theme in his chapter, 'Shakespeare Revealed in Oxford's Poetry' (in *Great Oxford*, ed. Richard Malin, Tunbridge Wells, 2004), where he argues for "the working of a single mind".

All things considered, the case for the de Vere hypothesis merits more consideration than the establishment tends to give it. The character of FitzSimmons is made up, but his prejudices are not uncommon.

Notes and Acknowledgements

Apart from Edward de Vere and the other historical figures, the characters in this story are fictitious, and bear no resemblance to living persons. Although this is a work of fiction I have attempted to be accurate in a number of ways. For example, although De Vere College and Lolworth Abbey are products of imagination, Castle Hill exists and there appears to have been a stone tower on its motte at one time. (Those familiar with Cambridge will realize that the putative existence of De Vere College would mean a re-routing of Chesterton Lane and the disappearance of parts of Hertford Street and Alpha Road. I apologize to those whose properties have been made to vanish.) Harriet Buckley has made appropriate changes on the maps which she has drawn.

Other accurate details include the fact, already mentioned, that during his lifetime de Vere was known to be a playwright who, because of his position at court, used another's name; the date of his withdrawal from public life; and the (somewhat puzzling) grant of a substantial pension by Queen Elizabeth in 1586. Also, I have used contemporary sources including *The Times*, the *Cambridge Chronicle and University Journal* and Bradshaw's railway timetable to give accurate times of trains, correct details of London concerts on the days concerned, and many other matters of detail such as the ownership of Hedingham castle in 1868.

Most of the pictures in the text are made from a variety of mid-nineteenth century engravings. The chessmen illustrated are from the author's collection, with the exception of the medieval pieces, which are original line drawings by Rob Howard based on actual pieces in various museums. Permission to use the picture on p.104 has been sought.

My thanks to Jenny Uglow, Amanda Helm and Elizabeth Imlay for their helpful suggestions, and to Jeremy Crick for his kind permission to use his photographs of Hedingham Castle in the text and on the cover.